M000046826

Black

A NOVEL

Book Two of The Firebrand Trilogy

David Kettlehake

BROTHER MOCKINGBIRD

Copyright ©2021 by David Kettlehake
All rights reserved

This is a work of fiction. Names, characters, businesses, places, events, locales, and incidents are either the products of the author's imagination or used in a fictitious manner. Any resemblance to actual persons, living or dead, or actual events is purely coincidental.
Library of Congress Control Number: 2021947573

Cover Design by: Alexios Saskalidis
www.facebook.com/187designz

No part of this book may be reproduced or transmitted in any form or by any means without written permission from the publisher.

For information please contact:
Brother Mockingbird, LLC
www.brothermockingbird.org
ISBN: 978-1-7378411-1-1
ISBN: 978-1-7378411-2-8 Ebook

To my mom,
who always made sure I had a book in my hands.

CHAPTER
ONE

My name is Scout, and I'm a killer.

Over the past twelve months, I've killed two hundred and thirty eight times. Not two hundred and thirty seven. Not two hundred and thirty nine. I know the exact number, and when I lie down at night and close my eyes, I can recount the horrible details of every single one. Remembering in such clarity amazes me, because before the Storm I had to be reminded to complete even the most mundane tasks. You know, simple stuff, like packing my lunch for school, or not flushing the toilet when someone was taking a shower. Perhaps the difference is killing is such a primal, basic thing. Maybe because the taking of life, even the life of something as monstrous as a Gray, is fundamentally against my nature and so contrary to the person I thought I was. Whatever the reason, I've become a killer. And it gives me no pride in saying so, but I'm very good at it.

Take right now, for instance. Three Grays are rushing at me through the muddy grocery store parking lot. A toddler has more sense than they do when it comes to fighting, strategy, or even the basics of personal hygiene. Grays only know one thing – hunger. And a hungry Gray is an aggressive, murderous creature that will rip you apart and eat you to survive. And to them, I'm looking like a tasty morsel, a meek, helpless little girl in a black poncho, standing all by herself in the rain.

Before the first one reaches me, I feel a familiar tingle in the back of my head, almost like several bees have taken up shop at the base of my neck, and suddenly the world goes into slo-mo. That's what I call it, anyways. The charging Grays seem to freeze in place, moving no faster than the minute hand on a clock. I've got all the time in the world to reach beneath my poncho and pull out a very large hunting knife. I've named it Chuck. Chuck's leather-wrapped handle is stained and worn smooth from use, and the blade is nicked up and scratched. Battle scars. Chuck and I have seen a lot of action together. He's been with me for all two hundred and thirty-eight kills. But unlike me, he doesn't seem the least bit bothered by it. I take a heavy, deliberate step forward, gradually shifting my weight to my front foot. Any movement in slo-mo is hard, like pushing your way through wet cement, the sloppy kind fresh out of the truck. To me my actions may seem sluggish, but to someone watching from outside my reality, I just darted forward hummingbird fast. It's bizarre, but I've gotten used to it.

And to be honest, without slo-mo, I would've been dead a long time ago.

Now that the gap has closed between me and the first attacker, I can tell this one's been around for a while, at least a month, which is pretty much the max lifespan for these things. Its face is an origami skull of sharp creases and angles, with its ashen skin stretched over its cheekbones as tight as a snare drum. Its eyes are so sunken they're nearly invisible, and even this close they're little more than two dark smears beneath its brow. Its long, filthy hair is fanned out behind it and gently moving in my slo-mo vision. It reminds me of white seaweed swaying in an ocean. The creature's basically naked, with only a few scraps of a shirt around its bony neck and shoulders. I can see it was a male before it changed. Not that it matters now.

Straining with the effort of fighting through the wet cement, I bring Chuck up and toward the lead Gray in a smooth, practiced motion. Did I mention I'm also extremely strong? Freakishly strong? The long blade connects just under the creature's chin and slices clean through its neck. My arm barely registers the connection. Why decapitation? It's one of the few ways to be certain a live Gray doesn't stay that way. This particular one is dead and doesn't even know it yet. I force myself to the side while the torso continues its forward progress, the freshly detached head just starting a slow, backwards tumble. Yeah, it's pretty gross. Black blood begins a glacial, pulsating eruption from its neck, but I'm already stepping past it and targeting the next one. In my head I hear myself say, "*Two hundred and thirty nine.*"

Everything is happening so fast in real-time that the second Gray hasn't had a chance to notice the death of its buddy. I've found for some reason these things usually travel in packs of three or four, even though I can't tell if they care or realize when one of them dies. But really, who knows what these monsters think? Before the Storm we had a Golden Retriever, a big, happy guy with dark brown fur and an eternally sad face. His name was Jerry, but I couldn't pronounce my Js very well, so I ended up calling him Larry. Larry knew three tricks: sit, shake, and leg humping. I'm convinced Larry was smarter than a Gray.

The second one is almost on me now, so I surgically separate its head from its body but with a wicked backhand cut this time. *Two hundred and forty*. Due to momentum, its decapitated body is still on its feet and headed my way, so I give it a slight shove to one side and take a step to my left. I'm already searching for the third one, with Chuck at the ready. Where the hell is it? Then from behind me a powerful hand grabs my throat and squeezes. The grip is scalding hot. Body parts that aren't designed to make noise begin to crackle in my neck. Muted grinding sounds travel up and into my inner ear.

Shit. Shit. Shit. This last Gray is a fast one.

Grays come in all shapes and sizes, which

makes sense because before they changed they were normal everyday people, just like you and me. Teachers, ministers, lawyers, students, baristas. Brothers. You can also break them down into two general categories, regular and fast. All Grays are super strong like me and are hard as hell to kill, but a fast Gray is just as quick as I am and probably shares my ability to see and operate in slo-mo. Fast Grays are pretty rare and just about as deadly as anything left on this flooded Earth. Well, maybe deadlier than anything but me, of course.

The Gray steps to face me and draws me in close until our noses are nearly touching, and I'm staring into its eyes, the whites now the color of frozen meat. God these things are ugly. Its breath is heavy and steamy hot and reeks of food long forgotten in a broken refrigerator. Effortlessly it lifts me off the ground. I raise the knife to start slashing, but its free hand snatches my wrist out of the air and tries to crush it. I should be able to toss this nightmare a dozen feet or more, but its strength is equal to mine, and I've got no leverage. All it has to do is hold Chuck at bay with one hand while it strangles the life out of me with the other. I try to pry its scalding fingers from my throat, but they won't budge. White fireworks dance and flash around my outer vision, and I can feel my consciousness waning. My grip on Chuck is weakening, the bloody blade twitching in my hand.

Before the light fades from my eyes forever, I

manage to place my feet on its scrawny thighs and slowly walk them up its torso. When both feet are firmly planted on its chest, I thrust backwards with everything I've got. As strong as this thing is, there's no way it can't hold me, and I perform a slow-motion backflip, landing ten feet away before ingloriously falling on my ass in a mud puddle, my poncho twisted around me. Chuck bounces away as gently as a butterfly lighting from flower to flower, eventually ending up under a car, out of action. The stupid Gray hasn't realized what just happened as it stares in confusion at its empty hands. Then it lifts those dead eyes and comes at me again. Besides their heavy breathing or the slap of their feet on the ground, these things don't make a sound. But if it could, I'm pretty sure it would be howling in frustration and rage.

I move as quickly as I can and leap onto the roof of a car. I've learned the hard way this past year that defending yourself from a position of strength is key, and shy of running away, gaining the high ground is the strongest position out there. Arms outstretched, the Gray launches itself at me from ten feet away. I've got all the time in the world to set my feet and prepare. When it's almost on me, I grab its wrist and yank like I'm jerking the cord on a stubborn lawn mower. The Gray soars past me in a smooth arc and smashes into the side of an SUV parked a few spots behind us. The SUV's windows shatter on impact, and a million glittering shards of glass blow outward in a donut shape, like an exploding star. The big vehicle rocks so far sideways I can't believe it doesn't topple over. Sounds in slo-mo are different, with the higher tones all clipped and flattened out, the low ones muffled and thick. The window's implosion sounds just like a huge wave crashing on a beach.

If I get out of this, Chuck and I are going to have words about ditching me, but there's no way I can retrieve him just yet. The Gray is already crawling out through the broken windows. It's covered in broken glass and has suffered a thousand cuts, which don't seem to bother it one bit. I quickly search for another weapon. The only thing nearby is a rusted shopping cart that's toppled over on its side. That will do just fine. I leap down slower than Neil Armstrong jumping from the lowest step of the lunar lander and grab the cart's handle. I swing it at the rushing Gray. The cart smashes into the thing's side, and the creature goes cartwheeling across the parking lot. Dark red blood starts slowly oozing from its head and arm, but it doesn't care. They never do. It comes at me a second time, and again I send it soaring when I smash it with the shopping cart.

The creature's in bad shape. Its arm is shattered and its jaw is hanging loose, flopping limply back and forth on a hinge of flesh and tendon. The side of its face is fresh hamburger, so pulverized I can no longer make out distinct features. But like all Grays, the thing is too dumb to understand it's been terribly, maybe mortally, wounded. It lunges at me again. I've got the upper hand now, and this thing has royally pissed me off.

I go medieval on it. I connect with the monster so hard that the cart nearly shatters in my hands. Angry vibrations course up and down my arms. The Gray is sent spinning once more, and this time when it tries to get up, it can't. Dragging the remains of the ruined cart behind me, I walk up and start beating it over the head. Again. And again. After ten or fifteen times I stop when I realize it's really and truly dead.

Two hundred and forty-one.

And then, just like that, the tingle in the back of my head stops, and the world snaps back to normal. Had anyone been watching at regular speed, the entire fight would have taken no more than fifteen or twenty seconds and would've been an eye-blurring haze of spraying blood and utter mayhem. To me, in slo-mo, it took a few minutes, although to be honest it felt a lot longer.

I gather up Chuck from beneath the car, quietly scolding him under my breath for ditching me like that. I wipe the dark blood off his blade and slide him into his sheath underneath my poncho. The parking lot is deathly quiet now, the only sound being the steady rain dappling the puddles and slicking my poncho. With a sigh, I drag each dead Gray over near the SUV, so they're lying next to one another. I carefully cross their arms over their chests. After that, I gather up their heads and place them with the right corpses, trying my best to make them look as natural as I can. I shut their eyes.

I'm not a religious person. Even if I had been before the Storm, there's no way in hell I would be now. Not after what I've seen. Not after what I've done.

Then I sit down in the rain and cry.

CHAPTER
TWO

Later that evening I paddle my kayak through the soupy, poisonous brown water that surrounds me. A few months ago I found a nice compass in a tumbled down house, a snazzy gold one with a closable lid, and I follow the ornate needle in a southerly direction. An omnipresent cloud of mosquitoes buzzes around my head. It's dark out, and it's raining so hard I can only see a few dozen feet in any direction. The sounds of my rowing are masked by the steady hiss of the rain. Of all the boats I've tried out, a kayak is far and away the best. It's maneuverable, light, and easy to portage when needed. You can't haul much with it, but that's a tradeoff I'm okay with. I've had to manhandle plenty of aluminum Jon boats around in the past, and I pray I never have to use one of those horrible, awkward things again.

I'm in southwest Ohio. For the last year I've been scouring the western half of the state for Lord. Finding my brother is all I think about every day, from the time I wake up to the time I lay my head down each night. I know that together we could learn how

to stop this horrible sickness from turning more innocent people into monsters, saving not just ourselves,
but the people we love, too. I need his strength, his
courage, and his intelligence. I have to find my brother, because he's so much more than I am. I don't think
I can do this by myself.

I keep paddling. A little while ago during
a break in the gloom, I could make out the top few
floors of a black glass skyscraper just peeking above
the waterline, a dozen antennae jutting up from its
roof like a forest of dead trees. It's the final remnant
of downtown Dayton. Farther south is Cincinnati,
nestled along the Ohio River. I'm guessing Cincinnati
is completely submerged, too. In fact, I'm pretty sure
the entire bottom half of the state is now one massive
lake that stretches hundreds of miles in all directions.
There used to be five Great Lakes. Now there are six.
Maybe more. The geography we studied in school has
become outdated and worthless.

But downtown is not my destination. I'm head-
ed a few miles south of there. I can tell I'm getting close
when the stench hits me, and I have to convince the
meager contents of my stomach to chill out and stay
put. The reek is different each time I'm here. Today
it's a combination of scorched motor oil, singed hair,
and eggs that have been left all day on a hot skillet. I
breathe through my mouth and keep paddling until
a massive form starts taking shape directly in front of
me. As my kayak glides closer, the shape solidifies into

the peak of a massive flat-topped mountain. Scattered around the flanks of the mountain are a dozen orange flares that knife through the gloom, their searing yellows and reds such a contrast to the rest of this almost monochrome landscape. Small, sad structures, tents and tin shacks that are blurred by distance and rain, crowd each other on the plateau that's bigger than a city block. As I draw closer, the orange flares morph into geysers of flame spewing from pipes as thick as phone poles. I feel a kinship for the fire; not only do Grays hate it, but it reminds me of my time with my brother, back when I was the Firebrand of our group. I subtly adjust my course to come up on the mountain's eastern flank where I know the road should be. The road itself is constructed of mud and packed gravel and is wide enough to handle those huge garbage trucks, the ones loaded down with an entire city's trash. I paddle my kayak up to where the brown water laps on the edge of the road, surface trash like plastic bottles and grocery bags thick on the surface.

"Hey, BamBam!" I yell into the dark.

From behind a mound, a tall, scrawny figure steps out. He's dressed like me in a black rain poncho that hangs loosely on him. I can't see his face in the gloom. At his side, he's carrying a baseball bat. I know for a fact there are other weapons behind the mound. He nods in my direction.

"That you, Scout?" he calls out warily.

"Yeah. Here, catch." I toss him a rope, which

he deftly snatches out of the air.

He pulls me in until the kayak's bottom scrapes gravel. I jump out and reach into my backpack and withdraw a clear cellophane packet. It crinkles. Inside is a pair of Twinkies, those awful yellow sponge cakes filled with white frosting. Mom used to pack them in my lunch until I begged her not to. As hungry as I always am, I just can't bring myself to eat one of those.

"Is that for me?" BamBam asks.

I toss it to him. His face is still shrouded in shadow, but he's so excited his hands are shaking and he's bouncing on his toes like a little kid. This is as close to BamBam getting ruffled as I've ever seen. He rips open the wrapper and stuffs an entire Twinkie into his mouth and starts chewing faster than a dog going after a dropped steak. I can't hear any moans of pleasure, but I'm betting they're there.

"I found them while scrounging in a grocery store north of here. Enjoy. Is Google in?"

BamBam nods. "You know it," he mumbles around yellow cake and white cream. "Where else would he be? Go on up. You know the way."

I toss him another package of Twinkies. "Watch my stuff, okay?"

He's already jammed the second snack cake into his mouth, so he can't readily reply. But he nods at me, and I know he will. BamBam can be trusted. He drags my kayak over to where other boats are moored and ties it up.

I start the long hike up the road. I pass close enough to one of the flaming pipes that I can feel the heat caressing the side of my face, and I linger there for a few moments. The noise it makes isn't quite jet engine loud but more like the low roar of a giant's blowtorch. Google told me they're powered by methane from the heart of this trash mountain, and I have no reason to doubt that. They never go out, no matter what the weather. I love having them around. Free fire is a blessing and a thing of beauty.

When I finally reach the summit, I navigate around the tents and other flimsy structures scattered randomly on the plateau. There's been no city planning going on, that's for sure. A few tents are inhabited by people my age and younger, sleeping or fitfully resting; it's tough to really and truly sleep when you're always hungry. But most of the tents are empty, their owners working the mountain or out scrounging. As worried as they are about themselves, no one pays any attention to me. My final destination is a large, permanent building near the northern edge of the plateau. It's constructed of cinder blocks and has a sloping metal roof. Above the door is a nicely printed sign that reads Welcome to Mount Rumpke. I walk up and knock.

"Google? It's me. Scout. Can I come in?"

I wait for a moment, then hear a buzz and an electronic click. I open the door and walk inside. The building is one large room partitioned off into this small area, while the rest of the space is a much larger storage section behind it. This front section feels small because every inch of the place is stacked floor to ceiling with electronic gear on metal shelves. TVs, microwaves, sound equipment, radios, and more cell phones that I can count. Google collects them. He insists they'll be worth a fortune when the world gets back to normal. I gave up trying to convince him that what he considers normal is likely gone forever. And besides, he's so serious and hopeful about the whole thing I just can't break his heart like that. It smells hot and electrical in here, an aroma reminiscent of my mom's curling iron left on too long in her bathroom. I can't see the storage section due to all the crap in my way, but I've been back there before. I know it's stacked floor to ceiling with food and supplies.

It's also so damn hot in here it would make a Finnish sauna feel chilly. Google's always got the fire cranked up because he swears it will dry out the equipment. I don't know about that, but I do know I'm already sweating to the point I have to rip off my poncho, revealing my flimsy T-shirt and shorts. I'd like to lay the poncho down somewhere, but I can't because he'll yell at me for getting his precious equipment wet. Google's a little intense like that. I drape it over my arm and start winding my way through the stacks of dead electronics, careful not to brush up against anything.

Against the partition wall there's a long, white

counter buried under bits of wire, opened equipment cases, and hundreds of gizmos that mean nothing to me. There's also a desk light on a spring arm and bent over that light is Google. He's tiny, smaller than me, and quite a bit younger. He's smart as hell, scary smart, actually, but comes up a little short in the personality department. No, I take that back — he has plenty of personality; he just seems empty of empathy. Quirky is a word that always comes to mind. When he turns to me, his eyes border on comical behind thick, Coke-bottle glasses. He's such a nerdy guy he should have black electrical tape holding his glasses together. His long brown hair is greasy. He's so pale and thin, I could probably see right through him if I held him up to a strong light. He blinks once, studying me.

"Did you lock the door behind you?" he asks.

"Oh. No, I didn't. Sorry."

He compresses his thin lips in disapproval, then flicks a switch on the counter. I hear the door click behind me. He goes back to tinkering with something on the counter. I don't come any closer or say a word. I just wait. I've learned.

Finally, still concentrating on his work, he asks, "Did you find anything?"

"Yeah. A big grocery store a few hours away. Lots of stuff inside. In pretty good shape."

"Hmmm. Grays?"

"Yeah. Three."

"Problems?"

I rub my neck, which doesn't hurt at all even after that fast Gray tried to pop my head off. Thankfully, I have an amazing ability to heal myself since I started my own remarkable change a year ago.

"One was fast. He got me around the neck before I could do anything."

He glances up from his work. I can't say there's concern in those huge eyes, more like clinical disappointment. He stares at me for a few seconds, and I can track his gaze as he looks me up and down. I'm sure he's inspecting my salt and pepper hair, seeing if it's become even more salt than pepper. My hair used to be a dark brown, but since my weird transformation it's slowly turning white. I can't tell day to day if it's getting worse or not, but someone that hasn't seen me for a while might be shocked at the difference.

"Hmmm. Sloppy on your part," he admonishes. "And it went for your neck? Typical." He stares at me with those cool, magnified eyes for what feels like ages. "Any sign of your brother?"

I compress my own lips and stare down at my muddy boots. I've been searching hundreds of miles around for Lord since I left Church Island a year ago. I've encountered so many Grays, met other survivors, and looked long and hard, but I haven't found a trace of him. I won't give up, but my constant lack of success is wearing on me. I worry more every single day, because even though our changes are different from everyone else's, I'm afraid he might be too far gone now, if he's even alive. I finally look down into his cool, magnified eyes.

"No. Nothing."

"Hmm. Too bad. What else?"

I briefly fill him in on what happened, skipping over the gory details and what I did with the corpses afterwards. That was for me, and he doesn't need to know about it. I slide off the backpack and toss him a few packages of Twinkies. He calmly uses a small pair of scissors and surgically slices open one end. He extracts the first and takes a measured bite.

"Ah, Twinkies. They're supposed to outlive cockroaches, you know," he mumbles around the gross yellow cake.

I make a face. "Anything new here?"

He carefully chews his treat while I stand there waiting. Finally, he connects a wire to a car battery on the desk and flips a switch on a rectangular piece of equipment. The face of it sports a bunch of dials and lights like an old stereo receiver. I hear a low hum from the speaker next to it. He fiddles with several large knobs, and I nearly jump when a woman's steady voice starts talking.

"...nineteen, four...nine, one...eleven, four..."

I take a step forward, unable to help myself. Words tumble out of my mouth. "Holy crap, who is that? Can you talk to her? What's with all the numbers?"

Google calmly turns the volume down, but I

can still hear her talking in a steady monotone. Her passionless voice holds all the emotion of a bored deli worker at Kroger's calling out the next customer's number.

"Yes, I've tried to answer, but nothing happens; she keeps going on without a break. I think it's a recording. And before you ask, I have no idea what the numbers mean, at least not yet. But I'm working on that." He taps on the black box. "This is a shortwave radio. Shortwave radios can send and receive from great distances, although they receive signals better at night due to optimum atmospheric conditions. That means the broadcast source could be as close as the next town or as far away as Australia. I have no way of knowing."

My shoulders slump. I've seen so few remnants of civilization in my travels I was irrationally hoping for something more, someplace that had survived the flood. Maybe a secret government base full of scientists close to perfecting a cure to going Gray, or a fortified town or city. I promised myself I would find a way to stop these horrible changes from happening before they claim more people I love, but I haven't made a damn bit of progress so far. And time is running out for all of us.

"So this is nothing then? Just some weird recording of a lady spewing out random numbers?"

He holds up a finger. "Oh no, not random. It's a sequence of numbers that begins to repeat itself after a few minutes. I simply don't know what it all means yet."

"But it means something?"

"That remains to be seen. If it does, I haven't figured it out. Yet."

Disappointed, I unzip my backpack and dump the contents onto his workbench. "Okay. Whatever. Here's a sample of what I found. Some canned dog food, pouches of Ramen Noodles, and powdered fruit punch. The store has a ton more, but I didn't explore much because I was…interrupted. We need to check it out."

Google pulls the tab and opens a can of dog food, sniffing it cautiously. His nose twitches like a rabbit. Convinced it hasn't gone bad, he plucks a fork from his pile of tools and stabs a piece. He smells it again, then puts it in his mouth and chews.

"That's not bad at all. You say there's more of this? Yes, let's get a scrounging raid set up for tomorrow. You want to lead it?"

I nod and put the other can of dog food back in my pack for later. Yes, I'll go, but after that I need to move on. I've become too comfortable here, and I need to find my brother or a cure. Or both. One more scrounging raid, then I'm gone. I'll need the supplies. I tell him that.

"Pity. You and your pseudo Gray abilities have been very handy so far. I'll hate to see you go, but I understand. One more raid."

Sure. One more raid. What can it hurt?

CHAPTER
THREE

When I leave Google, I strike out toward a tent he's letting me rent while I'm here. I'd say he's letting me "borrow" it, but that's not in his nature. I earn my keep around here with scrounging missions like the one earlier today. The tent's not much, but it's been home to me the last few months. I skirt around a pit that's about twenty feet across and half as deep. I hear wet thuds and clunks coming from the bottom. The stench oozing from the pit is so strong my gut clenches, and I have to fight the real threat of vomiting what little I have in my stomach. I peek over the lip, careful not to edge too close and slide in. Two young boys are digging in the near dark, their words indistinct as they whisper in low tones to each other. They're so filthy dirty I can't tell what's skin and what's slop. They smell horrible, but they don't seem to mind, or they're so nose-numb they don't notice. I spy what might be a shock of muddy blond hair on one of them.

"Simon, is that you?"

The muted chatter stops. "Scout? Yeah, it's me."

"Any luck?" I ask.

He holds up something I can't see very well, a long shape with a handle on one end and a dark blob on the other. He brushes slime and gunk from it. "Not much. I found a few bottles of detergent that still have some in it. And an old jar of peanut butter with a little in the bottom. And this. I think it's an electric weed whacker or something. Can you tell?" He holds it up higher, out of the heavy gloom. The words Black & Decker run up and down the shaft in white.

"Yeah, you're right. I'm sure Google will give you something for that. Even if it doesn't work, he might want the parts. Good job. Anything else?"

He kicks at some objects around his feet. "The normal nasty stuff, and about a zillion of those flimsy plastic bags. How could people use so many plastic bags? Oh, and we almost sliced our hands up on a broken mirror we found. Otherwise, not much, I'm afraid. Pretty crappy day."

"Have you two eaten anything lately?"

Simon murmurs something to the other kid, a question. "Just a few mushrooms we found on the north side of the mountain," he answers.

I feel so sorry for him. They're kids, older than my little Carly but much younger than I am, probably less than 120 months old. Their only chance for survival is digging for junk and trading it for food and supplies, and going on scrounging runs. This is no living for them. They should be playing little league baseball and heading out on fun vacations with their families, not digging in a literal mountain of garbage. I remember a saying I heard once, One man's trash is another man's treasure. This entire mountain is nothing but trash buried in layer after layer of dirt and mud. I pull a can of dog food and the last two packages of Twinkies from my backpack and toss them down. I was going to eat the dog food and barter with the Twinkies later on, but these two need it more.

"Here. And clean your hands off first, okay? You don't want to get sick."

I walk away as the two of them devour what is, for them, a feast. I wish I could do more, but I've got little to spare. I try to ignore the rumbling in my stomach. Going into slo-mo burns an amazing number of calories, or I guess it does, because I'm always famished afterwards. Instead, I drink water from a plastic bottle clipped to my side and hope it fools my stomach into thinking it's actually food. It's not that easily duped, I'm afraid. I've got one last can of dog food stashed in my pack, but that's for breakfast tomorrow.

On the way to my tent, I dodge around five more rancid, smelly pits like Simon's, the slow, moist sounds of digging coming from all of them. An older boy with crazy eyes stalks cautiously by, clutching some bulging and dented red and white cans. The cans don't look good, but I'm sure he'll devour what's in them. It's amazing what you'll eat when you have to. He gives me a wide, wary berth before scampering away. The rules here on Rumpke Mountain are clear: you can eat whatever you manage to unearth, but all electronic and mechanical gizmos go to Google. He'll pay you in food for what you find, depending on what it is. He pays people from the stockpiles in the back of his building, stuff that comes from raids. Yeah, it's not much of a system, but it works.

When I get to my tent, I hang the poncho outside and crawl in, slapping at a few pesky mosquitos that somehow snuck in with me. The annoying things are everywhere. It's almost as hot inside as Google's building was, but I'm so tired I barely notice. I retrieve my toothbrush from a zippered pocket in my backpack and gently brush my teeth. I ran out of toothpaste a few months ago, but this is better than nothing. The brush still carries the faintest hint of peppermint, more of a memory than an actual scent. Then I carefully withdraw a heavy book from a Ziploc bag, and for the next few minutes I try to read. But I'm exhausted, and Hamlet is too depressing on a good day, much less after the one I've had. I wish Singer were here to read it to me. I desperately miss his soft voice, the way he would hold me quietly when I was cold and scared. But he's not, so I cover myself with my thin blanket and instantly fall asleep with Chuck clutched to my chest.

The next morning I'm awakened by a voice from outside. I rub sleep from my eyes and poke my head from the tent. One of Google's men, I think his name's Brian, is standing in the dim light. Google has a lot of strong, silent types like him and BamBam around to help keep order and enforce his rules.

"Let's go. He says it's time to scrounge."

I wave at Brian, and he lumbers away. I'm pretty sure I heard the beginnings of a crack in his voice when he talked, and there was definitely a faint Fred Flintstone shadow of a beard under all the grime. The poor bastard can't be far from the change, not now. I watch as he turns a corner, then I seal up Hamlet and crawl outside to stretch. I pop open the dog food and gobble it all down, licking my fingers and the inside of the can when I'm done. Google was right: it's not bad, although it's a little bland and could use some salt. There's no rain today, just a light mist covering everything like a fine, glistening powder lending the roof of the tents a ghostly silver glow. I slip into my poncho and trudge toward Google's building. My feet make gross sucking noises as I kick my way through muck, loose trash, and debris, the mud constantly trying to yank my boots off. I don't like to think about what I'm stepping in.

There are a dozen people waiting outside of his place, a mix of guys and girls, most older, a few very young. Several of them are Google's goons. To a person, they all suffer from sunken cheeks and hollow, bruised eyes. They stare at me and spread out as I get close, giving me plenty of space; they all know who and what I am, and it makes most of them nervous. How can I blame them? I'd be nervous around me, too. I walk past them into Google's open doorway.

"We're ready!" I yell.

I hear him rummaging around in the back room. "Yes. I'll be right there."

I consider waiting for him inside and out of the mist, but it's too damn hot in there. I step back outside and almost bump into Simon. He's one of the few friends I have on this mountain of garbage. I'm okay with that. He smiles when he sees me.

"Oh, hey, Scout. You going? Awesome."

He's dressed like most of us in a rain poncho, backpack, and tall rubber boots. I can't see his weapon of choice, but I'm assuming it's a pistol. The one important survival item that doesn't go bad is ammunition. We don't ever seem to be short of it, although that won't last forever, of course. Lucky for us so many pre-Storm people were gun-happy.

"You going out scrounging, Simon? You sure? You know it's dangerous as hell out there."

He nods at me without hesitation. People on Rumpke Mountain can't survive simply by digging in the filth. Everyone knows that. Balance that against Google's rules dictating you get to keep half of whatever you find on organized raids like this, and a good score can keep you fed for weeks. Like I said, Google keeps the other half and doles it out for those mechanical and electrical finds. It's a rather simple and elegant barter system, in its own way.

"Yeah," he says. "I'm starving here. I gotta go."

I purse my lips. "Just stay near me, okay? I don't want you to get hurt."

He nods at me again, a little fast and nervous. He's short for his age, but I'm small, so we're almost the same size. His young face is hidden under layers of grime. Any grandmother worth her salt would be mortified at our filthy condition, and wouldn't stop attacking our faces with spit and a white hanky until we were clean. The only two clear spots on Simon are his eyes, and they're the dazzling blue of the ocean on a sunny day, that Caribbean blue that's so beautiful. It's ironic that with so much water everywhere we don't have an easy way to clean ourselves short of standing in the rain. But how surprising is it that personal hygiene takes a back seat to everything else, when every waking second is spent scrounging enough to eat? Not very.

Google steps out, and I have to stifle a laugh at his choice of foul weather gear. He's wearing a yellow rain slicker that's too big for him, bright red rubber boots adorned with ducks, and a dark green bike helmet. Clear ski goggles protect his eyes. The last thing anyone cares about these days is how you dress or look, but even so, this is a little extreme. He reminds me of a cartoon character, like Paddington the Bear. Simon coughs under his breath, and like me, he's struggling to hold back a laugh.

"You pick that out yourself?" I ask, forcing the giggle from my voice.

He looks himself up and down, befuddled, and is honestly clueless what I'm talking about. That's just the way he is. Function over style. Oh, Google.

"What's wrong with it?"

I shake my head. "Nothing, really. So you're going with us?"

"Yes, I'd like to see this store you found and have a look around."

I shrug. It's not everyday Google leaves his cinder block lair, but he does once in a while. He'll have several of his hired muscle with him, and I'll be there, too. We'll keep him safe. I mean, Rumpke Mountain isn't much, but it's a bastion of order and sanity in these dark times. We need people like Google, there's not many of them left.

We head off down the gravel road, past the flaming methane torch, and end up at the boats. Bam-Bam is there, bat in hand. It says Louisville Slugger on the barrel in black ink. He unties all the boats and pushes us off, one by one. Google's bass boat is last, and as BamBam gives it a mighty shove, he hops in, too. I raise an eyebrow at this as well — I don't think I've ever seen him leave his post.

My kayak is a sleek Lamborghini compared to the wallowing, Winnebago-like aluminum row boats. Time and again I'm forced to stop and wait while they catch up. Each time I pause, it gives me a chance to consider what's below me, and what's hidden underneath two hundred or more feet of deadly brown sludge. Up ahead and to the right is the top of the black glass skyscraper I saw before, the late morning light barely reflected in its dirty windows. That means I'm close to what used to be downtown Dayton again. I shudder to think of how many corpses are trapped in all those buildings down there, never again to see the dim light of day. When the world flooded, millions of people went Gray, and just as many were killed by them. Even so, an untold number eventually drowned as the waters rose and higher ground vanished. The nightmare vision never ceases to clutch at my chest, and I imagine I can hear their muffled screams reaching up through the floodwaters below. Thankfully, the rest of the boats soon catch up. At the stoic urging of Google I paddle on again, grateful for the diversion. Everyone follows me, their oars clunking and splashing as they try to keep up.

Without watches or the sun, we have no way of knowing how long we row, but every few minutes I refer to my compass and keep us on a course heading generally north. If I had to guess, it's pushing early afternoon when we finally see a bump on the otherwise flat horizon. It's the hill where the grocery store sits, along with a smattering of other stores and a neighborhood of small frame houses behind that. When I was there before, I never had an opportunity to investigate the rest of the area, but I'm hoping we'll get a chance to do that today.

We near the water's edge. I cruise past a partially submerged BP gas station, its muddy green roof just above the waterline. Telephone poles march like obedient soldiers into the water and eventually disappear behind me. I paddle on until my kayak runs aground, then turn to the assembly of boats a few dozen yards to my stern.

"You guys stay here. Let me check it out first, okay?"

There's no argument, not that I thought there would be. They're quite happy to let me go ahead alone. They know I've been in this situation more times than I can count, and I'm probably the only person capable of coming out alive. I'm calm as I hop out of the kayak and trudge through the smelly muck at the shore's edge, knocking mud off my boots. My hand gently caresses the sheath at my thigh where Chuck is securely housed. I walk up the hill toward the grocery store parking lot, my scuffing footfalls as loud as firecrackers in the eerie silence. I spot a dozen or more turkey vultures circling high in the sky a few blocks distant. Besides mosquitoes, vultures are the one species that have had a field day and full bellies since the Flood began. Google once told me a group of vultures in flight is called a kettle. He's full of fun facts like that.

I pass by the SUV from my fight yesterday, the one with the shattered windows. I resist looking in their direction, but I can't help myself and catch a glimpse of the three supine Grays in my peripheral vision. Their bodies are untouched. Here's my own fun fact: vultures won't bother with a dead Gray. They're simply left to slowly rot. Smart vultures.

I keep going. I'm a little more cautious now but still amazingly at ease considering the circumstances. Stepping up to the broken glass doors of the store, I stop and peek inside, listening. There's not a sound except for my breathing, and the patter of the rain that chose this moment to come down harder. I put one foot inside, then the other. Shards of glass crunch under my boots. My left hand rests on the cool metal of the door, while my right hovers near Chuck. I go in farther. Drops of water fall from the hood of my poncho and onto my face. I ease the hood back and wipe rain from my eyes.

Past the cash registers and self checkout lanes, the darkness starts to deepen to the point where the receding shelves converge into nothingness. I ease up to the first endcap where I found the Twinkies yesterday. Just around the side are the cans of dog food. The Ramen noodles and powdered fruit punch are just beyond that. This is as far as I made it before I suspected Grays were inside, and I retreated to the parking lot. I quietly make my way deeper into the store, checking down all the aisles as I go. I think I'm alone this time. More relaxed now, I go back the way I came and exit the store. In the distance, the boats still float where I left them, their passengers anxious for an all-clear sign from me. I don't give it. Not yet. I trot through the heavy downpour to one side of the store, and then back to the other, checking to make sure we're safe. Once that's done, I give them the thumbs up, still keeping a wary eye out for any danger. In no time all twelve of them are gathered around me. Google in his colorful gear is flanked by BamBam on his right and another goon on his left. They're both jittery out here in the open, away from the safety of Rumpke Mountain. They should be.

"Everything okay?" Google asks, his voice low. Grays don't have super hearing, we don't think, but the obvious sounds of people will always draw them in if they're in the neighborhood.

I nod. "Seems to be. But let's not take any chances. Everybody keep quiet and head inside. Each of you take an aisle and gather as much as you can. When your bags are full go back to the boats, unload, then come back for another round."

"What are you going to do?"

"I'll stay out here and stand guard. If you hear me yell, run like hell for the boats. Got it?"

They all nod in unison and scurry inside, quickly spreading out. As Simon passes me, I grab his sleeve.

"No, not you," I whisper. "You stay up near the front where I can keep an eye on you."

He doesn't say anything, but his huge blue eyes blink once, and he nods. I direct him to the dog food. From under his poncho, he pulls out several large canvas bags and starts filling them up. I'm glad to see he's focused on the protein, not the Twinkies that are tantalizingly close by. Good for him.

Soon a few of them emerge from the darkness, their backpacks bulging. I wave them on, and they hustle to the boats to unload. I hear some commotion from deep inside the store, two or more people arguing, voices escalating, followed by a crash that sets my teeth on edge. I sprint toward the sounds and find a pair of kids I don't know in a tug-of-war over a box of beef jerky. Their bags are dumped on the floor and by the way they're going at it, I can tell it's going to get ugly soon. I step up and grab their wrists.

"Stop it!" I hiss.

They both try to yank away, but they'd be just as likely to jerk their arms free from a crocodile's jaws. I could squeeze harder and shatter the bones in their arms if I wanted to. Ever the diplomat, I pull them in close.

"What's the problem?"

"I found it first!"

"No, you didn't. And your bag's full, anyways!"

I keep my voice low, but firm. My teeth aren't gritted, but I bet it sounds like they are. "Listen, if you keep making noise, you'll attract a Gray, and I might not be inclined to save either of you. Got it? Now you," I stare at the kid on my right. "You take the box, and we'll split it up when we get back. Understand?"

A compromise pleases nobody, but they know

they've got zero choice in the matter. They follow my orders and get back to filling their sacks with supplies. Leaving them to it, I navigate through scattered debris to the front of the store. Simon's bags are filled to overflowing with cans of dog food. They're so heavy I'm not even sure he can carry them.

"You sure can manage that load?" I ask, motioning to the bulging canvas bags.

He grunts as he swings first one, then the other, over his small shoulders. He smiles at me to prove his point, and, although he wobbles like a toddler a little under the load, his grin never slips.

I pat him on the back and point to the boats. "Fine. Head over and unload, then hurry back for another round. I don't like being here any longer than we have to. Go."

He waddles away under the weight. When he reaches the safety of the water's edge, I turn back to the store. More people have filled their bags and start heading out. I make my way to the parking lot, so I can keep a better eye on everything. Google and two of his goons come and stand with me. His two guys have bags, but they haven't gathered any loot yet.

"Not scrounging today?" I ask him. "This place is a gold mine."

His big eyes behind the goggles look up at me. He blinks. "We will. We're simply making sure everyone else has their share first. You?"

"Same here. I'll take care of myself when everyone's done."

We watch together as the rest of the crew go back and forth several more times, until the boats are so full I'm not sure where everyone will sit. These guys are going to eat very well tonight. I'm glad. They deserve it.

Google takes note and motions to his guys. "Go load up."

They take off into the store at a jog, and it's just the two of us. Rain patters against my poncho and against Google's ridiculous outfit. The guys behind us in the boats are still keeping their voices down, but a soft peal of laughter makes its way to me once in a while. Now that the worst is over and they're safe in the boats, they know as well as I do that Grays can't swim, so being on the water is one of the best places possible.

We continue to stand in silence. Google's not much for small talk, but I give it a shot. "Any updates on the shortwave recording of the lady?"

He keeps staring at the front of the store when he answers. "Not really. My hunch is it's a holdover from before the Storm. It's likely a coded message of some sort. A location, maybe. Or directions. Without a key, it will be very challenging to decipher. Having an actual reference library would be extremely helpful."

I nod. "I miss libraries, too. Not for the same reason you do, of course."

"Ah, yes, you prefer fiction, don't you? Didn't you find an actual library some time ago?"

"Yeah, I did. Last year, up north. But almost all the books were ruined. The rain and humidity, you know. And bugs. Paper doesn't like those kinds of conditions. But I'm not sure what you'd hope to find. It's not like there's a special book out there brimming with secret codes or anything."

For a few moments, he doesn't say anything. Then he stares up at me with those big, magnified eyes in that unnerving way he has, like he's peering through me and into another world. I wonder what strange gears are meshing in that intense brain of his. Finally, he looks away, back to the store. Nothing in his demeanor changed, but I get the feeling something important just happened.

"What is it?" I ask. "Did you just figure something out?"

"No. Maybe. I'll know more later, after I've had a chance to think."

I press him some more, but he's gone silent and won't discuss whatever revelation he may have had. I'm starting to get aggravated with him when his guys come out dragging overstuffed bags. He motions to them.

"Get those supplies to the boats and hurry back."

I continue to pester him for more answers, but it's no use. He's clammed up and won't say a word now. I'm tempted to shake it out of him, but I know it won't do any good. Well, it might make me feel better, which wouldn't be all bad. I'm still simmering when BamBam and the two other goons join us.

"You ready?" he asks the three of them. They nod. "Good. Proceed."

The three of them walk away towards the parking lot, leaving the two of us alone again. Bam-Bam steps up to a car, lifts his bat, and smashes the windshield. It shatters with a sharp crash, pea-sized bits of glass flying everywhere. The other two aren't carrying any weapons that I can see, but they start slamming doors and yelling. One picks up a derelict shopping cart and starts going to town on a minivan. After trying so hard to be quiet, the sudden din is more jarring than a NASCAR pileup.

"What are you doing?" I shout at him over the racket, my voice bumping up against the falsetto register. "Are you crazy? You're going to attract Grays!"

"Exactly," he replies calmly, watching his guys go berserk on more cars. They're laughing and whooping it up, enjoying the mayhem they're causing. A sliver of my mind not occupied with potentially awful outcomes wonders why idiot boys always love breaking stuff so much.

I bolt away from him and grab BamBam's arm as he's getting ready to take out another window. He grunts as he struggles to bring his bat down, genuinely surprised such a little girl like me is able to hold him back. But there's only one of me, and I can't do anything about the other two. They continue making a racket, slamming doors and yelling at the top of their lungs. I easily wrench the bat away from BamBam and fling it aside. It bounces away before rolling in a graceful arc and coming to rest in the middle of the parking lot. No matter what I do I can't stop all three of them from whatever they're up to.

"Are you insane?" I scream at Google, stalking back toward him. "We've got to get back to the boats. Now!"

But he doesn't answer me, just points to the far end of the store about a hundred yards away. I follow his finger. Three Grays have rounded the corner and are running straight at us.

Shit. They'll be on us in seconds.

CHAPTER
FOUR

I can't relate just how pissed I am right now. If I had Superman's heat vision, Google would be sliced in half when I swing my fierce stare back at him. Startled at my intensity, he stumbles backwards half a step and pulls his head so far back his chin almost disappears into his neck, like a turtle. Those huge eyes remain locked on mine.

"What are you waiting for?" I snap at him. "Get back to the boats!"

As pissed as I am at this moment, I'm still sensible enough to know we need him alive and well. I don't know what game he's playing, but protecting the crazy little genius has just become my number one priority. I take a deep breath and turn to face the oncoming Grays, and I wait. I'm relaxed and at ease considering what's about to happen., but I've done this so many times before that it's becoming commonplace. I wait for the tingle in the back of my head that lets me know that my slo-mo is about to kick in.

Only it doesn't. It's not happening. There are no bees buzzing back there.

The charging Grays don't slow or hesitate. In the past, my slo-mo would have taken over by now and dispatching this trio would be an easy task, just like yesterday. But something's not right. It's not working.

Google glances my way. "Scout. I want one of them alive."

I do a double-take from him to the Grays. "You want what?"

"When you go into your slo-mo, take out two of them but be sure to leave one alive. I want to capture and study it."

His three goons have pulled netting out of their canvas bags, and two of them are now brandishing huge pistols. With all the junk Google has saved up in the storeroom, I'm not surprised he has nets. Bam-Bam has retrieved his bat. The three of them have closed ranks around us in a protective wedge.

"Anytime you want to go into slo-mo now, go ahead," Google says, his voice no longer quite as confident and calm as it was. "Just leave me one."

"Nothing's happening! I can't just turn it on and off! It doesn't work that way."

A sudden look of desperation clouds what little I can see of his face. "Oh. Well, that's not good. Nuts. BamBam, take them out."

The two with guns open fire, but the targets are moving fast. His men are not nearly the marksman my one-time companion Hunter is. Two of the creatures stumble as they're hit, but the wounds aren't critical, especially not where a Gray is concerned. Only a direct shot to the head or maybe a close-range shotgun blast will stop one. I've seen one have its entire arm blown off, and the stupid thing was still eager to come after me. I slip Chuck out of his sheath and hold him in front of me at the ready. Even under the overcast sky his blade gleams.

I'm wondering where my damn slo-mo is, but I don't have any more time to think, because they're on us.

I shove Google back as the first one leaps at me. I slice at it with Chuck, opening a huge gash across the creature's chest. It tumbles past me but is back on its feet almost before I can react, its gaping wound barely bleeding. I spare a glance at the other two. One has BamBam around the neck already. He's swinging his bat, but he's not able to connect with any kind of force. The few hits he manages are no more damaging than a bird slamming into a window. Several more rapid gunshots ring out as the two goons start panic-firing. A Gray knocks one of them to the pavement and pounces on him. It slashes downward with a clawed hand and shreds his throat. Blood splatters the wet blacktop. Any scream he was about to utter dies with him.

I yell something incoherent and throw myself at it, Google temporarily forgotten in my rage. The Gray is straddling the dead kid, leaning over to start feasting. It sees me coming and raises a hand, maybe in defense. On a run, I grab its wrist and heave as hard as I can, like a sidearm pitcher putting everything he's got into a fastball. I launch it into the air, and the monster skips across the parking lot and comes to rest in a heap of twisted arms and legs. It's dazed but not out of the fight.

Hearing a strangled scream behind me, I turn. The monster I sliced across the chest has Google hoisted up by the neck. I run up and plunge Chuck deep into its back with a two-handed thrust. I yank the blade out and stab it again, Chuck's stained steel sinking deep between its shoulder blades. The creature spins and with an outstretched fist connects with the side of my face. The force of the blow sends me crashing to the blacktop, my head ringing. Before I can gather my wits, the thing bends over and picks me up, its scalding hand around my throat. My feet are dangling off the ground. My vision is blurry. I can't seem to control my arms or legs. To my left, I hear a gurgling sound. That must be BamBam. I can't help him. I can't even help myself.

Then I hear a click, and a thunderous boom. Suddenly my face is covered in something hot, wet, and sticky. The Gray holding me spasms and its hand jerks open, allowing me to tumble to the ground. Standing behind the dead Gray is Simon, holding a pistol with both hands, his blue eyes huge and terrified. Smoke leaks from the end of the barrel as it shakes in his grip. I stagger to my feet, wobbling, the bells in my head still ringing.

"Simon, get back to the boats!" I scream at him.

But he doesn't, or can't, move. He drops the gun and stares with his mouth open at the Gray on the ground, half of its head missing and brains splattered everywhere, including all over me. I grab my diminutive savior around his waist and stuff him in a nearby SUV, slamming the door behind me. Hiding someone in a car is no long-term solution, but at least he should be out of immediate danger. Out of sight, out of mind, at least where Grays are concerned. That's what I'm hoping for, anyway.

The Gray holding BamBam pulls him close, almost as if it's performing an inspection to see if he's dead or not. BamBam has dropped his precious bat. His face is turning sickly shades of blue and white. His feet are barely twitching. So no, he's not dead yet, but I'm afraid he's very close. I sprint toward the two of them, my head clearing with every step, my enhanced healing ability kicking into overdrive. I reach for Chuck, but he's not on my thigh where he belongs. I realize he must still be in the back of that dead Gray. Instead, I scoop up the Louisville Slugger and swing it at the Gray's head with all my might.

I don't know what I expected. Honestly, I don't. But when the bat connects, the Gray's head explodes like a rotting pumpkin. Brains and bone explode in a red and white mist. *Two hundred forty-two.* BamBam's bat shatters in my hands, and the splintered barrel goes spinning across the parking lot. Both the Gray and BamBam collapse to the ground, neither one of them moving. I quickly roll the dead Gray off of him, so his skin won't be singed from the heat. I'm reaching down to check for a pulse when I hear a muffled cry. I turn and see the remaining Gray, a large female, beating on the SUV where I hid Simon. It shatters the window with its fists and reaches inside. My heart skips a beat.

"No!" I scream, so loud the Gray pauses and turns to me. And just then, finally, I feel the familiar tingle at the base of my head, the sound of the bees congregating. The world stops.

The SUV is fifteen or twenty feet away. I take slow, deliberate steps towards it, forcing my way through the thickness. The Gray hasn't changed position yet, hasn't had a chance. It's in mid-blink, probably wondering in its own dim-witted way what the hell is going on. After what feels like a minute or more to me, but probably only a second to it, I'm by its side. Out of habit, I start to reach for Chuck again, but dammit he's still AWOL. In my hand, I have the splintered stub of BamBam's bat. My true desire is to smash the horrible creature to pulp against the side of the SUV, but a sliver of sense prods me, and I hold back. Google wants one of these things alive for some reason, and as much as I want to kill it, I figure I owe him that much for all he's done for me and everyone on Rumpke Mountain.

So instead of adding to my gruesome tally, I take the knob on the end of the bat and crack it on the top of the Gray's head. I hit it again. Under my breath I'm muttering, "This is for Dog." Crack! "This is for Tommy." Crack! I keep smacking its skull, and each time I do I invoke another friend or relative's name lost to these horrible creatures. Outside of my slo-mo, I can't imagine what this high-speed hammering must look like. But in no time the Gray's scalp is a mass of blood and ravaged tissue, and its white hair is shot through with pink and red. I put my hand to its face and shove down hard. At that moment my slo-mo turns off. The Gray slams down to the pavement and is still.

Not waiting to see what might happen next, I scramble around and gather up the nets. I quickly truss up the Gray in all three of them, to the point where I'm surprised it can even breath, much less move. I slowly turn to Google, who is cowering next to a car.

"Here's your damn Gray." I toss the bloody stump of a bat to the ground, then turn to retrieve Chuck. "I hope it was worth it."

CHAPTER
FIVE

The trip back to Rumpke Mountain takes forever. Google, Simon, and BamBam are in no shape to row, so the rest of the group has to pick up their slack. BamBam is in terrible pain. His neck is crushed so badly he can't even talk. He just lays in the bottom of the boat and suffers in silence, an arm thrown over his face, his breath whistling through his crushed throat. I hope he'll be okay, but I'm no doctor. Hopefully time and the healing power of youth will be enough to get him through this.

Before we left, I wrapped our one casualty in a blanket and put him in the trunk of a car, like we did with Dog. No one knew this kid's real name, not even Google. He just went by Mad Max. I said a silent prayer for Max before we shoved off. It's not much of a funeral, but sadly that's the way it is these days. At least the vultures won't be able to get to him. I didn't have time or the inclination to take care of the bodies of the Grays this time. I was too pissed.

It's nearly dark when we spot Rumpke Mountain's flames in the distance, and we hurry towards them with the single-minded urgency of moths. There's no one there to pull the boats to shore, so I hop out and take care of them myself. Each healthy person dutifully grabs whatever they can carry and trudges in silence up the wide road to the plateau. When we get to the top, everything is dropped at Google's door, and everyone heads back for another load, their footfalls slow and heavy.

When the entire take is piled at the threshold, they look to Google to divvy up their shares. But he's a train wreck, his hands shaky, his voice barely able to exceed a whisper. The front of his pants are wet, and I'm guessing he peed himself at some point. He starts to ask BamBam to oversee this, but realizes his right-hand guy is in no shape to help out. In fact, four boys had to help BamBam to his tent. Google is uncharacteristically indecisive, then notices me and nods in my direction instead.

"Scout? Would you?"

I give him a tight-lipped smile. "Sure. No problem."

"Thanks." He turns and enters his cinder block home, leaving the door open. I watch him shuffle inside, his shoulders slumped, his colorful outfit still a ridiculous sight even in the darkness that has settled around us. I turn and survey the rest of the group.

"Okay," I say loudly, startling a few of them, "line up, and let's get this done. Youngest to oldest. Let's go. We'll do five at a time for now."

After some muted discussion and a disagreement or two, they're all lined up. Simon is second in line, behind one of the boys who was arguing about the beef jerky in the store. He steps up.

"Pick five," I tell him. With only a little hesitation, he chooses four cans of Dinty Moore beef stew and a package of red Twizzlers. For every item he picks, I choose the same thing, or a close equivalent, and pile it up behind me for Google. Like I said, the system is simple and straightforward: you get to keep half of what you take on these raids and the other half goes to Google. When this first boy is done, he stuffs his share in a bag and goes back to the end of the line to await another turn. Simon steps up next.

"Take whatever you like, Simon," I assure him. "You deserve it."

But he's having a hard time talking, much less making any decisions. I grab five more cans of beef stew from the pile (good protein, plus some veggies), a half dozen packages of beef jerky, and bags of dried pineapple. From the back of the line, I hear someone mutter a complaint, and I lift my head and deliver my best icy stare.

"Hey, he saved my life. Without him, a bunch of you would be dead now. Any more complaints?"

There aren't, at least none I can hear. Simon puts his stuff in a sack and heads to the end of the line. The next kid steps up, and we go through the process again, and again, until they've had multiple turns, the pile is gone, and everyone has their cut. When they've gone, I rummage through Google's portion and pull out my own share, stuffing it all into two sacks. Google's pile is still quite impressive, and I take the next ten minutes and shuttle it into his building, just inside the door. I cart the sacks to my tent and toss them inside. I stand there and sigh. It's been a long, hard day, but I'm not done yet. I have one more chore to complete.

I make my way back down to the boats. Standing beside them, I stare at the Gray that's trussed up tight in the bow of a rowboat. It's awake now, struggling in silence to free itself from the nets. I think I'd rather go naked down a slide of razor blades than touch the disgusting thing, but I grab hold of the netting and fling the creature over my shoulder. It's amazingly light, but the heat coming off of its skin is still hot enough to be uncomfortable as I lug it up the road.

When I reach the summit, I take the creature to Google's place. The door is still open, so I go inside. The temperature in there is as oppressive as always, and that, coupled with the Gray over my shoulder, is enough to make me break out in a full body sweat. Google is nowhere to be seen, so I go deeper inside towards the lighted workbench area. Once there, I flop the Gray down and, using some wire that's laying around, I tie it up to the workbench itself. Certain that it can't get loose or go anywhere, I finally allow myself to relax a little. I slide to the floor a dozen feet away from the trussed-up Gray and lean against the wall, exhaling noisily. I'm certain I won't be able to sleep, and I'm right for about five minutes. Then I feel my head bobbing around as I drift off, and I'm out.

I'm awakened by the sound of thrashing close by. I sit up straight and look around in a moment of panic, ready to leap to my feet. It's the Gray, crashing and banging into everything around it as it tries to escape its mesh prison. Fortunately, it can't, but it has managed to gnaw a hole into the netting around its mouth. It stops when it sees me move, its predatory eyes tracking me as I stand. Some of its front teeth are broken, and there's blood around its mouth where the netting shredded its lips. I've seen hundreds of these monsters up close before, and damn if they don't still creep me out.

We stare at each other, but only for a moment, because then it starts thrashing again, trying to get at me. The stupid thing probably doesn't understand why it can't move. My grandmother once told me turkeys are so dumb they'll drown by staring up at the rain, and I'm convinced this Gray is only marginally smarter than that. I'm still looking down at it in disgust when I hear a slight noise behind me and turn. Google is standing there, munching on another Twinkie.

"Oh, you're awake. Good," he says.

He seems to have recovered and is back to his

normal self again. I narrow my eyes at him and take a step in his direction. The vision of his goon having his throat ripped out and BamBam nearly killed is front and center in my memory. He senses my anger and backs away, nearly tripping over his feet.

"What?" he asks.

"You, that's what!" I yell, barely controlling myself. I jab a finger at him. "You almost got us all killed. What the hell were you thinking? How could you plan something like that without even telling me? What is wrong with you?"

He pats the air in front of him with one hand. "Scout, please. Let's be civil. Trust me on this. We can't defeat an enemy without knowing more about them, and I knew you wouldn't go along with capturing one of these things. But I need to study one before we have any hope of winning. And I thought you could handle them. Although your slow motion ability not working was certainly a problem during the fight. Has that ever happened before?"

I stare at him, fully aware he changed the subject on me. "No. Never. It's never let me down before."

"Have you figured out why?"

I shake my head. I haven't had much time to think about it yet. But losing my slo-mo ability is serious business. I've never been able to control it, but it's never failed before. Not until yesterday.

"No. I haven't. I don't know what happened."

He taps his finger on the counter top, thinking. "That's unfortunate. Let's hope it doesn't become a recurring thing. Regardless, in hindsight, perhaps I should have told you what I planned on doing."

"Ya' think? Even with me you lost a man. Max is dead, Google. He's dead. His body is in the trunk of a car in a parking lot because of you."

Google sighs, and whether it's real or contrived, he does appear upset, although someone who didn't know him probably wouldn't be able to pick up on that. "Believe me, I know. But Max was over 220 months old and would have gone Gray soon anyway. He knew that. We all did. And he was fully aware he could be killed in that raid, and he went along anyway. He wanted to help."

"That's bullshit," I bark with a coarse laugh. "He went because you told him to."

"No. He went because he knew he needed to."

I glare at him for a few moments, fuming. I have told myself a zillion times we need Google, and people like him, to help us survive in this insane world. Now, I'm wondering if it's somehow because of people like him we're in this predicament in the first place.

"Whatever," I say. "I'm done here. I'm heading out in the morning. I need to find my brother."

"Are you sure?" he asks innocently. "Wouldn't you like to know what the lady in the shortwave radio is talking about first?"

I freeze. I've got to give him credit. He knows

how to play people, including me.

"You know what all those numbers mean?"

He finishes chewing and sits at his counter. Above all the random electronic equipment is a shelf full of books. Because they're books, I've looked them over before, but there's nothing in those dusty things that interests me. It's all science texts, reference stuff, and warranty manuals people have found for him, full of subjects that thrill him but bore me to tears. He reaches up and withdraws an old red leather bound volume with a faded gold cross on its cover. There's a green ribbon looping from the spine that acts as a bookmark.

"I've had this Bible since we got here," he explains as he opens it to the marked page. "It was here already. Whoever ran this place kept it in a drawer. Honestly, I never thought I would need it. I don't have much need for religion."

Neither do I. A Bible holds zero interest to me. I knew it was there, but if there's one book I never cared about, it's a Bible.

"After the events of yesterday, I couldn't sleep last night and was up thinking and listening as that woman reads off numbers," he continues. "I knew she had to be speaking in some sort of code. Nothing else seemed to make sense. I plotted the sequences, ran them against everything from phone numbers to addresses to social security numbers to calendar dates. Everything I could think of. In the end, nothing made sense, not immediately, that is. But I was still convinced she was speaking in a code of some sort."

"Why would she be speaking in code? What good is that now?" I ask, interested despite myself. I step up and peek at the open page, but the print is tiny on the flimsy pages. I can't make anything out. "Code for what? There's nothing around anymore. There's no government, no cities, nothing. If this stuff is a code, then for what? And why would we care?"

"That is the question, isn't it? But I recalled reading once about something called a Number Station. Does that ring any bells to you?"

"Number Station? No. I've never heard of that before. What is it?"

"Back around World War II, there were reports of strange shortwave transmissions originating from different parts of the world. No one knew what they were or what they meant. These transmissions were rarely more than numbers being read over and over, usually in English, sometimes with a British accent. They seemed to make no sense. Sometimes it was a man's voice, sometimes not. Sometimes it was a synthesized voice. People became convinced the messages were ciphers, transmissions meant for American spies in Europe during the war. They were also used in the Cold War. Remember — many times these spies were deep in enemy territory, and there was no way to send them updates, information, new mission objectives, and so on. There were no cell phones, no internet, no way to get in touch with them. Their handlers had to have a way to contact them, and it was thought that Number Stations using shortwave radios were that way. Remember what I told you yesterday? Shortwave radio can be broadcasting from right down the street or from thousands, even tens of thousands of miles away."

I point to the Bible. "And this? What does this have to do with it?"

"Ah, this. Well, if this broadcast we're hearing was indeed a Number Station coded message, then a spy would have to have a relatively simple way of deciphering the message, right?"

I nod slowly, still not catching on. He's enjoying the fact I haven't figured it out yet, which does nothing to lessen my simmering annoyance with him.

"Think of it," he says, warming to the subject, his eyes sparkling behind the huge glasses. "You're a spy in enemy territory. Deep in enemy territory, perhaps. You may have a radio of some sort that could hear the message, but you would need a simple and everyday way of decoding it, right? You couldn't keep a deciphering key on you in case you were captured, so you would need something ordinary, something you could pick up anywhere, to help you do it. My question to you is, what's the most popular book of all time?"

"The Bible?" I say, half guessing.

He slaps his hand on the counter. The Gray,

which we've almost completely forgotten about, starts thrashing around again. After a quick glimpse to make sure it's still secure, I turn back to him. Google peeks over my shoulder at it. I think his already pale complexion dials one notch closer to pure white. I'm sure he's replaying yesterday in his mind.

"Exactly. You said it yourself yesterday, when we were outside the grocery store. What was it you said? 'It's not like there's a book out there brimming with secret codes or anything.' Right?"

I think back, and I remember our conversation. I also remember thinking he had come up with something he wasn't ready to talk about yet.

"You could get a Bible anywhere," I continue. "You wouldn't even need a library."

"Exactly! Any church, chapel, library, or almost any bookstore. They were everywhere. And except for a change from the King James version to the more modern Revised Standard version in the late 1950s, the majority of the text is similar enough that what you might need shouldn't be an issue."

I take a step back and stare at him. "Oh my god. King James? Revised Standard version? How do you know all this stuff?"

He blinks once, apparently confused at the question. "I went to Sunday school. Didn't you?"

"Well, yeah. But I don't remember any of that."

He gives me a shrug, his head tilted a few degrees to the side. It's impossible for him to be embarrassed for me, since that's not in his nature, but I may detect just a whiff of pity at my ignorance.

"Anyway," I continue, barely able to keep the irritation out of my voice. "From your smug attitude I'm guessing you already decoded the message?"

"Of course. It took a little time, but I was up all night anyway. Look at this," he says, sliding the book towards me. It's open to the book of Revelations, and he's got red sharpie marks dotting sections all over the first pages. "I thought about looking through the Old Testament first, but realized some modern Bibles don't even carry that, oddly enough, so that wouldn't always work. Then because of their popularity, I focused on the Gospels of Matthew, Mark, Luke, and John, but nothing in those sections seemed to fit the puzzle."

"But Revelations did? It was your magic decoder ring?"

He taps the Bible, smiling. There are little bits of Twinkie cake still stuck between his teeth. I want to tell him they're there, but I'm not good at that sort of thing. Probably my Midwestern upbringing. "Exactly. Revelations is the story of the End of Days, the apocalypse, the end of man's time on Earth. And it made sense if whoever was running this spy network was, in their mind, working to stop what could have been World War III, or something even worse, what better book of the Bible to use? Revelations would have been the perfect reference manual. And that's where I found it."

Okay, damnit, he's got me hooked. I feel my heart rate increasing. "Found what?"

"Locational coordinates, of course. Each number she reads adds up to a single number, and the next few sets of numbers add up to different ones. The first set pointed to a specific chapter in Revelations, and the others to individual verses within those chapters. In each of the verses there is a number or set of numbers. For example, right here." He flips the page and points at one of his red dots. "At one point she says the number two, followed by twelve. Chapter six, verse five, 'When he opened the third seal, I heard the third living creature say Come!' Third. Three is the key. He turns the page and points at another red dot. "And here. She says thirteen, followed by one. Chapter thirteen, verse one. 'And I saw a beast rising out of the sea, with ten horns and seven heads.' Ten is the key here. And it goes on like that. Once I had the sequencing down, it was a simple matter to determine the exact latitude and longitude the entire sequence was pointing me to."

I cross my arms and stare at him. "Okay, I have to admit, if you're right, that's an impressive bit of detective work, Sherlock. But I don't understand what that has to do with us. Why would we care about coordinates to some far off land? It's not like I can hop a plane to Europe or anything. If what you say is true, these Number Stations were a big deal during World

War II and the Cold War. To me, that means overseas and out of reach."

He smiles again. "Of course, and while that's a good assumption, you would be wrong. The coordinates aren't pointing to anyplace like that. They are directing us to somewhere much closer."

"Closer? How close?"

Instead of answering, he grabs a folded piece of paper from the bookshelf. Impatiently shoving electronic bits and wire out of the way until he's got an open space, he unfolds the paper until I can see that it's a map. Across the top in bold cursive, it says "Welcome to Dayton. The Gem City & Montgomery County." He grabs a red pen and circles a squiggly area near the center.

"This is us. Rumpke Mountain," he says. "And according to the decoded coordinates, she is talking about a spot in Ohio. In fact, it's not far from Dayton, and where we are right now." He carefully draws a dotted line southwest of Rumpke Mountain, but not very far. Not far at all. He makes another circle near a town called Miamisburg. "It's pointing us here. To this place right here."

Trembling a little now, I move closer to the map, nudging him out of the way with my hip. His second circle is just outside of Miamisburg, around a series of concentric ovals on the map that must signify height. Like a huge hill. The text simply reads "The Mound."

"The Mound?" I ask, my voice shaking with excitement. "What's that?"

He steps back and shrugs. "I don't know, but I think you need to find out."

CHAPTER
SIX

I'm packing up my meager belongings from my tent and stuffing them in my backpack. The food takes up a lot of room, but I'm taking every last calorie with me except for a can of beef stew I pop open and inhale on the spot. Strangely enough, it tastes remarkably like the dog food from the day before, which I find funnier than I should. Hamlet is wrapped up snug as a bug and crammed into one of the big pockets. Every time I hold that heavy book it reminds me of Singer, and a sense of sadness and great distance always clenches at my heart. I sigh and finish up, then go out in the rain to search for Simon. He's not at the pit from the other day, so I trudge through the disgusting muck and heavy drizzle to the small tent he shares with several other boys.

"Simon?" I call out. "You in there?"

I hear some rustling inside, and after a few seconds his blond head pops out from between the flaps. He crawls the rest of the way out and stands next to me. He looks better than last night, which is what happens when your stomach is full and hasn't kept you awake all night with hunger pangs. But he's quiet, and I can tell the events at the grocery store are weighing on him. He notices my backpack.

"You leaving?" he says quietly, his hands knotting up in front of him.

"Yes. Google found something I need to check out. I don't know how long I'll be gone. But I wanted to thank you for saving me yesterday. What you did was very brave. Stupid, but brave."

A wisp of a grin comes and goes in a flash. He's a good kid, and I'm going to miss him.

"I want you to take care of yourself," I continue. "You have enough food for a while, right? I don't want you to go on any raids until I come back. Deal?"

He nods, his eyes momentarily widening at the thought of having to participate in another raid when the events from the last one haven't had the decency to be blanked from his mind yet. That terrified deer in the headlights look on his face tells me he never wants to go out again, which we both know is impossible. No one can survive on Rumpke Mountain without going on raids.

"How long will you be gone?"

I sigh, looking over his head into the hazy distance in what I think is the direction of the Mound, whatever that is. "I don't know. But I'll come back for you as soon as I can. And when I do, we'll leave together, okay? We'll leave and won't come back. We'll go to that place I told you about, Church Island. You'll be safe there."

He nods again, then lunges forward and hugs me. He's shorter than I am, but not by much. He grasps me in his thin arms and squeezes me tight, not wanting to let me go. I squeeze him back, carefully, so I don't hurt him. His scrawny body shakes once or twice as he sobs soundlessly. I hesitate, then kiss him on top of his blond head before we separate in silence. His face tries to work into the shape of another smile again, but we're both smart enough to know it's man-ufactured. I'm once again forcefully reminded how much I hate this world.

"Okay. Bye, Scout. Be careful."

My eyes are welling with tears, tears masked by the rain, and I give him one more hug. Then I turn and clump away through the mud towards Google's place.

Once there, I bang on the door. After a few moments I hear a click and it opens. Google is standing there with a red and white can of Campbell's chicken noodle soup in his hand, some of the spoils from the raid. He looks me up and down as he takes a big slurp from the can.

"You're leaving now."

"Yes. Can I have the map, please?"

He pulls the paper from his back pocket and hands it to me. I fold it in half and stuff it in the side pocket of my backpack.

"You're going to the Mound?" he asks around a mouthful of noodles.

"Yes. I'm going to find out what's there, in case it's something important. I'd never forgive myself if I found out later it was a secret government hideout and they had a cure, and I hadn't gone. Then I'm coming back to get Simon. Keep him safe while I'm gone. No raids. No dangerous jobs. Take care of him."

His forehead creases ever so slightly, and he stops chewing. "I make the rules here, Scout. Rumpke Mountain is mine. Don't forget that."

Pent up irritation flares in my mind, and I grab him by the front of the shirt. I'm still fuming at his actions that got Max killed and put so many of us in danger. It's all I can do to not really strut my stuff and hoist the little shit off the ground in a show of force. I take a deep breath and reign in my temper.

"Listen to me," I hiss at him, our faces inches apart. "Don't push me. You won't like me when I'm mad. Got it? Keep Simon safe."

His glasses have slipped down his nose, and I can clearly see his eyes for the first time. They are so small without the lenses in place, bloodshot and wide with fear, but still resolute. He's well aware how important he is to everyone on this trash heap, and worse yet he knows I know it. On the other hand, he's also intelligent enough to know when to argue and when to settle. He mentioned the Cold War yesterday, and a word from some nearly forgotten government class springs to mind: détente, the relaxation of strained relations, or something like that. We both know we need each other, and it's in our best interests to cooperate. Stifling a low growl, I gently release my grip on his shirt and step back.

"Just make sure he doesn't get hurt, okay?"

Google refrains from smoothing his shirt. He gives me one of those haughty looks of superiority again, one that clearly shows his disdain at my ignorance and lesser intelligence. It's an expression I've seen on him too many times. It's almost enough to make me go at him again, but I don't. That won't help anything, although to be fair it might make me feel better.

"Yes, of course," he says. "I'll do my best."

"Good. I'll be back as soon as I can."

I shift my backpack on my shoulders and turn to leave out when he clears his throat. I look back at him.

"What?"

"Before you go, I thought you might like to see something. Come inside for a moment."

He walks back into his lair, certain I'll follow him, which I reluctantly do. We go to the back of the building, towards his tool bench and the tethered Gray. When we're there, he points to the creature on the floor. It's still wrapped up in the netting, but it's sitting up. There are at least ten empty cans of food stacked next to it. I stare at it. The creature looks… different somehow. Calm. Less ferocious.

"What am I looking at?" I ask. "What have you done?"

He smiles and steps up next to it. I nearly lunge at him to pull him to safety, but the Gray doesn't move. It simply tracks him with its vacant eyes. Google kneels down next to it. The monster doesn't thrash or make a move toward him.

"I fed her," he says simply. "I gave her all the food she could eat, which was an impressive amount, if I do say so myself. Their metabolism is remarkable. And now look at her. She's no more vicious than a child."

Past experience takes precedence over what I'm witnessing now, and I can't make myself take a single step closer. "That's it? You just fed the damn thing?"

"Yes, that's it. Look at her. She's calm and relaxed, no longer a killing machine."

For a few moments, I don't know what to say. Eventually I shake my head. "I can't believe it. That's all it takes? You just have to feed them?"

"Apparently. Think of it, Scout. They are like any other living creature; they get hungry, and need to eat. But they are incapable of finding any source of food. And like any other living being they are programmed to do whatever they need in order to survive. Sadly, unlike normal humans, they lack the intelligence to locate any other source. In the end, they are starving, and they eat the only things they can find — which is us."

As I leave Google's building and trudge through the mud toward my kayak, I'm half in a daze, not even completely sure how I'm putting one foot in front of the next without tripping and rolling down the road. The revelation that stuffing food down a Gray to blunt their murderous tendencies is something I never thought of. Hell, none of us did. We were always too busy either killing them, or trying not to be killed by them, to even give that a thought. And damn if that obnoxious and annoying little shit didn't figure it out in just one day. I'm not entirely sure if, in the grand scheme of life, that knowledge would have made any difference, but it certainly explains so much. They're starving, just like we are most of the time, and they're doing whatever they can to survive.

I reach my kayak. I'm shocked to see BamBam there. His poncho hood is hiding most of his face, but what isn't obscured by shadow is purple with bruising. He's leaning heavily against a boat up on the shore. In place of his beloved bat, he's got a metal pipe. I'm sure it's an effective weapon, but it doesn't have the same aura as his Louisville Slugger did.

"I didn't expect to see you down here today," I say, not unkindly.

Under his poncho, his shoulders move fractionally in a shrug, really just an exaggerated twitch, little more than a hiccup. When he speaks, his voice is a thin whisper, softer than a breeze through fall leaves. He says each word carefully, sparingly, like they're too valuable to waste.

"Me, neither."

I point to the metal pipe. "Sorry about your bat. I didn't mean to break it."

"That's okay. I'll find another. Thanks for saving me. Leaving?"

I nod and untie my kayak. "Yeah. Google found something, and I'm going to check it out. I should be back in a few days, maybe a few weeks. No longer, I hope."

He tries to talk again but winces and puts a hand to his throat. After a few seconds, he gives it another shot. "Scout."

I'm about to step into the kayak, but I stop.

"Yeah?"

"Be careful. Don't trust him."

"Who? Google? Yeah, I know."

BamBam nods, and starts walking ponderously back up the road, the pipe dragging behind him, leaving a shallow groove in the gravel. Did he come down here just to warn me about Google? If so, I'm thankful, but it wasn't necessary. I don't trust the little genius as far as I can throw him, although I could probably toss him pretty far. I could probably put a good spiral on him, too.

Once in the kayak I paddle out about thirty feet, and then start around to the southern side of the massive trash mountain. The steady hissing of the scattered torches follows me as I go, but eventually I pass beyond the southernmost point and aim my little boat south. In no time the monstrous shadowy shape dims behind me until it's lost in the drizzle. The faint sound of the methane torches makes its way across the vast open space like dragons in the distance. All I'm left with is my even breathing and the slapping of my oar against the poisonous water.

With mixed feelings, I wonder if I'll ever see this place again.

CHAPTER
SEVEN

I've been blessed with a pretty good sense of direction, which I guess I got from my mom. She was our navigator on trips, mainly because dad could get lost backing out of the driveway. This genetic gift has come in handy many times since all this began, but even so, paddling for hours in the rain with no landmarks is tricky business. I set my little compass in front of me on the kayak and keep heading south by southwest, which is the best I can do under these circumstances. I've pulled out and studied the map a dozen times, but it's worthless with this new topography that matches nothing. At one point, I row between some thin radio or TV towers topped with dead red lights a few dozen feet overhead. I tap one of the metal structures with my oar when I pass by, and I'm rewarded with a dull thud that barely escapes the grip of the deep dark water. I keep paddling.

Whatever my strange change is doing to me, besides endowing me with incredible strength, quick healing, and my slo-mo power, it's also blessed me with terrific endurance. I can row all day and not get tired. Bored to tears, yes, but not tired. I wish I had some music, someone to talk to. But none of that is possible, so I'm stuck with me, myself, and I — and frankly, we're all getting a little sick of spending so much time together.

However, this rare down time does give me a chance to think, and the most pressing thought now is directed at my slo-mo. More precisely, what happened when it pulled an Elvis and left the building during my last fight at the grocery store? Why didn't it work? Why, after a year of uninterrupted and reliable service, did it suddenly ditch me? I run the fight scene over and over in my head, to the point where I'm not sure I'm remembering actual events or simply embellishing what did or didn't happen. Its failure to manifest at the grocery store is beyond troubling, because if I can't count on my slo-mo to kick in when I need it, my odds of surviving much longer are seriously impaired. I paddle on, peering inward and second-guessing any conclusion that comes to mind, until I circle right back where I started, which is a big fat zero. Angry at myself and the world in general, I row harder, almost flying across the water, the kayak rocking from side to side until I get a little too nuts and the compass nearly slides off. My heart racing at the near loss of this invaluable tool, I force myself to slow down and go back to more measured strokes. Now I'm pissed at myself for being so reckless, not to mention needlessly burning calories that I really can't spare. I slowly cool down, and the failure of my slo-mo takes a back seat for now. But, like any back seat driver, it refuses to quit nagging at me.

After I'm on the water for what has to be at least a few hours, I realize how hungry I am and take a break for lunch. To be honest, I'm always hungry. Drifting in this vast sea of putrid soup, I opt for a can of salmon, which smells a bit funky when I pop the top, but when doesn't canned fish reek a little? I shovel the pink stuff down fast, all while resisting the urge to hold my nose. I can't tell which stinks worse — the fish or everything else around me. I'm tempted to toss the can overboard when I'm done, knowing it will sink and join the rest of the trash so far down below, but old lessons from my parents die hard, and I can't bring myself to litter. Instead, I put it down near my feet, although I'm sure I can still catch a whiff of the funk once in a while. I vow to hold any other cans of the stinky stuff as a last resort. I start rowing again.

A few hours later a dark shape begins to manifest in front of me. I slow down as the kayak eases closer, and soon enough I can make out something solid-looking ahead. I stare at it through the drizzle, but before I can get too excited, I realize it's just a small spit of land barely inching out of the water. The tiny island is little more than a few dozen feet in diameter, but several additional small islands head off to the right, humps of a giant sea serpent undulating into and out of the water. I doubt it's my destination, but these tufts of land give hope that I may be getting close. There's nothing to see on any of the islands except a few dead trees and scrub brush. I row far enough around it to avoid getting snagged on anything below. In no time at all, the clumps of soggy land have vanished in the gloom behind me.

Another few hours of paddling tick by. I'm holding steady on my course, I guess, but I haven't seen anything else to confirm or deny I'm going in the right direction. I'm wondering if I missed the Mound, or if it's even there at all. Shielding the map with my poncho, I try to zero in on the small islands I passed by earlier. I trace my finger around and see a series of tight concentric ovals about two thirds of the way between the Mound and Mount Rumpke, but I'm not sure if circles are the small islands I spotted earlier or not. Over the past year, I've traveled north, east and west of Rumpke Mountain, but I never bothered to try my luck to the south. After all, I've been searching for Lord, and I just can't see how he would have made it down here. Grays can't swim, but would Lord be able to? Or would he have retained enough intelligence to use a boat? Is he even alive? I'm worrying about my brother so much I almost miss the wall of shadow off to my right.

I stop paddling and coast. Through the haze I see what, from here, looks like a slightly darker wall of haze that starts at the waterline and eventually vanishes into the cloudy sky. I can't tell what it is, but it's so massive and out of place in this otherwise monotonous waterscape that at first it didn't register. I almost missed it. My eyes track up and up, and the dark shadow just keeps going until it blends in with the grey sky overhead. I turn my little kayak and cautiously paddle closer.

When I'm no more than twenty feet away the air clears and the shape morphs into a wall. Well, not a wall, but a cliff so steep it might as well be one. It's covered in brown grass and green vines, and it's so tall the top disappears into the misting rain. I consider going closer and tying my kayak up somewhere, but besides the dead grass and vines there's nothing I can tie it to. I drum my fingers on the side of the kayak while I decide my next move and randomly go right.

Keeping close to the cliff I paddle on, but quietly, like the place is a cemetery I'm passing through in the night. If anyone else were here with me, I'm sure we would be whispering in hushed tones to each other, assuming we'd be talking at all. I row in complete silence for what has to be at least half an hour, but there's no change in the scenery on my left, although my compass now says I'm headed more westerly than before. I hate to admit it, but this place is freaking me out, and that's saying a lot after all the weird places I've seen in the last half a dozen years.

Then my oar clunks against something solid below me, and I nearly jump out of my skin.

To this day I don't know what it was, but it doesn't matter. I jerk the oar out of the water like I've been shocked and let my forward momentum carry me in silence for a minute while I take in my surroundings. The cliff on my left suddenly flattens out and opens up. It's hard to make out details in the rain, but it looks like a sloping asphalt parking lot has been cut into the side of the hill. The parking lot is angled up out of the water, and I can make out dirty yellow lines of what has to be hundreds of spaces, maybe more. Tall light posts march into the distance before blurring and becoming one with the mist. I can't see the other end of the asphalt expanse from here, but it has to be huge, Costco parking lot huge. There aren't any cars left I can see, not from here anyway.

Minutes tick by. Nothing moves out there. There's no noise either, except for my slightly rapid breathing. Whatever the Mound is, my guess is I've found it.

I finally get up the nerve to move closer, chiding myself for being so nervous. I dig down for an extra helping of courage and paddle gently forward until the bow scrapes on solid ground, grit and dirt grinding so loud against the plastic hull I jerk just a little. I cautiously step out and stretch my legs, my head swiveling every which way as I hunt for danger, but there's nothing and no one around I can see. I tug the kayak up into the parking lot with one hand, while my other instinctively locates Chuck in his sheath at my side. I leave everything else in the boat and begin walking up the parking lot, concentrating on using my ability to move ninja-quiet.

Three-quarters of the way up the lot, I spot a car parked next to a light pole. It's a late-model Toyota, silver, and covered in mud and grime, looking very sad out there all by its lonesome. Streaks of rust run down its sides like wet mascara. The left rear tire is flat. I peer in the filthy window, but there's nothing to see except a few dozen candy bar wrappers on the passenger side floor. I try a door handle, but it's locked. Still glancing all around me, I leave it and keep going.

Peering ahead I can see the end of the parking lot. At least I think it's the end, because the wall of dead grass and vines juts up again, up and out of sight. I'm wondering why the hell this parking lot exists at all since there's evidently nothing else around: no office buildings, warehouses, or stores. Was it a shuttle lot? A place where people left their cars and boarded busses that took them to downtown Dayton? I'm still trying to figure all this out when I spot a break in the cliff wall over to my right. I venture in that direction so soundlessly it would make a cat envious, my feet picking their way cautiously across the gritty parking lot. When I get closer I see something, and I stop, then take a step back, ready to sprint to the kayak if I have to.

It's a door, but not like any door I've ever seen before. For one thing it's massive, as big as a barn, at least two stories tall, if I had to guess. It's dark green, basically the same color as the vines that are over-grown and dangle down the front of it. It's built right into the side of the cliff. It's actually two doors split down the middle, with a massive locking mechanism at chest level. When those doors are open, I bet a brass band could march right on through and not scratch a tuba on either side. I screw up my courage and ap-proach it, planting my feet just a few paces away. The thing is made of steel, the sort you'd see on a hull of a freighter, with rivets the size of quarters reinforc-ing the hinges and locking mechanism. Whoever built this either wanted to keep something inside very bad-ly, or wanted to make sure something outside stayed there. Either way, I'm pretty sure that nothing short of a cruise missile could dent this thing. There was some classic sci-fi movie my dad used to watch, and al-though I can't remember the name, it had some huge black stone slab in it that freaked everyone out. That's what this door reminds me of, and what it's doing to me now.

I step closer until I'm mere inches away. I gin-gerly reach out a hand and touch the painted metal with the tip of one finger, not knowing what to expect. It's neither cool nor hot, but seems to be the same temperature as the outside air. I gently rap on it with a knuckle, but it's so thick and dense that it doesn't make a sound. I'd get the same response knocking on a boul-der. Still curious, I shuffle a few paces back and survey the thing. I'm calming down now, just staring at it with my hands on my hips, when a familiar Southern voice from behind me says, "Hey, Scout. How y'all doing? Long time no see."

I spin around, and Hunter is standing no more than ten feet away, the round black eye of a shotgun barrel leveled at me. He's smiling, enjoying my shock, the freckles on his pale face clearly visible. His wet hair is pulled back in a ponytail. He's wearing a short black raincoat with the hood tossed back.

"You," I hiss, and I instantly relive the horrifying moment back at Church Island when he shot Singer, the way Singer's body spun and fell into the boat, the bloody wound blossoming across his chest. I can still feel the weight of him in my arms as I carried him back to Jacob at Church Island. My pulse starts hammering behind my eyes and suddenly, I'm no longer concerned with the door, the Mound, or anything else. The bastard who shot Singer is standing mere feet from me, and I'm going to make him pay.

"And I thought we'd never cross paths again," he says, not lowering his gun. "Here I am just out scrounging, and look what I found. But you look mad, Scout. Why is that? Aren't you happy to see me? I'm hurt, I really am."

My hand drifts down toward Chuck, and just then it happens, and it's all I can do not to pump my fist in glee: I feel that familiar buzzing of bees behind my neck, and a smile touches the corners of my mouth. My slo-mo is back! Yes!

Time hits the brakes, just like it's done a hundred times before. A million raindrops seem to almost hover in front of my eyes as they gently drift downward as leisurely as confetti at a parade. The constant hiss of rain striking the pavement is abruptly cut off, replaced with a low and steady rumbling. I slide to the right, away from the potential trajectory of the shotgun blast, just in case he somehow manages to pull the trigger. In slo-mo, I can easily dodge an arrow or a sprinting Gray, but I've never tried my luck with a gun before, and I don't want to start now. I force myself through the thickness toward him, almost grunting with the effort because I'm pushing the limit on how fast I can move. But he's so close! When I'm almost to him, I reach out a hand to grab his arm. I'm going to throw him all the way to the end of the parking lot, farther if I can, and then I'm going to get creative. This is a day both of us will remember, although the nature of our memories will certainly be quite different.

But just as my hand is about to touch his wrist, his eyes flick my way and he turns his head, his smile growing larger.

He lets go of the shotgun with one hand and grabs my arm before I can react. His grip is warm and insanely strong. I gasp in pain as he bears down. In one smooth movement, he twists, throws and suddenly, I'm airborne. I'm spinning slowly across the parking lot with all the elegance of a duck shot out of the sky.

I land twenty feet away and careen across the wet asphalt, finally coming to a jarring stop on my back next to the Toyota. My head is ringing, and I'm dazed and aching in a dozen places. I try to sit up, but I'm so dizzy I almost tumble over. I notice that my unreliable slo-mo has inconveniently shut itself off. My sight blurry, I look up and he's already standing over me, the shotgun now resting over his shoulder. The grin on his face is wide in amusement, but his eyes are thin slits, staring at me with all the warmth of a Gray before it kills.

"And what do you know," Hunter says, spacing each word out, the wonder in his voice as sincere as a politician's pledge. "Little Scout got herself some powers too. And here I thought it was just me."

Still on my back, I wipe rain from my eyes with a shaky hand. Nonplussed. Yeah, that's a word I never thought I'd use today, but it's a perfect fit right now. I'm nonplussed. How is any of this possible? How did Hunter get slo-mo and strength like me? I open my mouth to ask, to say something, but nothing comes out except for a few senseless syllables and a cough. Hunter laughs out loud at my condition, his shoulders bouncing up and down, thoroughly loving my confusion and shock.

"Well, I could ask you the same thing, right?" he finally says when his laughter fades, kneeling in front of me. "When those sons of bitches on Home ran me off, I thought for sure I was a dead man walking. I mean, who lives for long out here on their own? Am I right?"

My head is clearing to the point where I can sit up, although I'm still groggy. His eyes, unblinking, are locked on mine.

"And then stuff started happening. I got strong, like you, I guess. And I got super speed, just like you. Don't ask why, 'cause I don't know. But I've sure been having fun with it since then, let me tell you. This world ain't half bad when you can do what I can. Well, what we can, I guess." He turns his head and spits into a puddle, then stares at me again.

But I'm not looking at him now. Behind him half a dozen shapes are materializing out of the mist, moving slowly toward us. Hunter sees me looking over his shoulder and follows my wide eyed stare. He stands up, his shotgun at his side. I crab walk back a few paces in terror.

"Oh my god, Hunter," I manage to squeak out, my voice a high-pitched panicked whisper, little more than a hiss. My fear of him has been eclipsed by a new horror. "Grays! We've got to get out of here!"

He looks down at me, his body still relaxed, which doesn't make any sense to me at all.

"Oh, don't you worry your pretty little head," he says casually. When he grins down at me again, I'm suddenly more terrified of him than I am of the advancing Grays. All I can think is, Hunter, what the hell have you done?

"W-what? I don't understand," I say quietly.

He waves a hand casually at the approaching Grays. "These guys are with me."

CHAPTER
EIGHT

I want to scream. Or run away. Or better yet, run away screaming.

Seven Grays are shuffling toward me, and Hunter is standing over me with a shotgun with that shit-eating grin on his round face. I remember leaving Rumpke Mountain and wondering if I'd ever see the place again. Right now, I'm not sure I will. In all my travels since the Storm began, I've never felt so certain I was about to die.

A sudden sensation of complete desolation washes over me, like I've been treading water for days and I no longer have the strength to keep my head above water. I have so many people counting on me to find a cure, and if I die it's almost certain they'll follow the same path of everyone else now. And Lord, as hard as I've tried, I've let him down, too. His final words to me echo in my ringing head, "Scout, help me." He's counting on me. Hell, they're all counting on me. But I can't help anyone. I can't even help myself.

In seconds, the Grays have me surrounded. They're all far gone in their changes, although they don't look as hollow and malnourished as most. The only sound from any of them is their feet scuffing on the wet pavement, and an unpleasant moist rasping as they breathe through open mouths. A few are female. None are wearing more than some random scraps of clothing. Most are barefoot, except for one wearing the remains of a frayed tie and what may have been expensive dress shoes at one time. They're all filthy dirty, covered in old blood and grime. The smell coming from them reminds me of something from the bottom of a trash can in summer. I swear I can feel the heat coming off of them, but that's probably my imagination. I've rarely been this close to Grays before without being in a fight.

They start to converge on me, tightening up the circle until I'm completely surrounded. I struggle to my feet, a sliver of resolve gaining traction in my mind. Damnit, if I'm going down, I'm going to go down fighting!

Then Hunter lifts a hand, and they stagger to a stop. He laughs. "I told you not to worry, Scout. This bunch listens to me."

I tear my eyes from them and finally stare closely at Hunter, and after a second I gasp. His hair is streaky with white, bands of it, like a red and white zebra. It's not salt and pepper like mine. Whatever his change is, whatever is happening to him, it's following a different route. I whip Chuck out of his sheath and hold him in front of me, his point aimed directly at Hunter's chest. His emotionless shark eyes, set so far apart, burn into the depths of my soul and trigger a sudden bout of trembling, a primitive response I have no control over. I imagine a serial killer might look at someone this way, as if he didn't give a damn if you lived or died.

"Stay back," I hiss, teeth gritted so hard my jaw throbs. Chuck is shaking in my hands, vibrating faster than a struck tuning fork. "I've taken out hundreds of these monsters before, and I'll do it again."

Hunter's neutral smile doesn't dim. "Easy, Scout. If I wanted you dead, you'd be dead. I didn't expect to see you here, that's all. Let's talk, okay. That's what friends do. They talk."

"Friends?" I shout. "Friends? You shot Singer!"

Hunter's lips compress, and he tilts his head. "Yeah, about that. I do feel bad about that. I really do. That was just the…heat of the moment, you know? How is our favorite musician doing now?"

"What do you mean, how's he doing? You shot him! I had to leave him on Church Island. I don't know how he's doing!" I'm yelling a lot now, but I can't help it. His calm manner is throwing me off.

"And you," he says, still calm, talking to me as if we're old college buddies catching up over a beer. "You were all chained up in that crappy basement room. They were going to keep you there until you went Gray, then they planned on killing you. You'll have to tell me how you got out of that mess. I am intrigued, yes, I am. But first." He motions to one of the female Grays. "Karen, go to her boat and get anything she left there. Bring it to me."

The Gray hesitates for a moment, then heads toward my kayak at a clumsy jog. I'm staring openmouthed at it, shocked to my core. Not only do these things actually seem to listen to him, but he named them! That is wrong on so many levels.

He watches it lope off. "Most of them are as dumb as a bag of hammers, but a few follow orders better than others. Karen's one of the good ones."

In no time at all, the Gray – I refuse to call it Karen – returns with my backpack in one hand, the empty can of salmon in the other. It's licking the inside of the can. Watching all of this play out for some reason makes me sick to my stomach. It drops the backpack at Hunter's feet. He gives it a little nudge with his foot.

"Heavy. If I know you, Scout, you've got a book or two in there, am I right?"

I don't answer him. I've still got Chuck out and pointing at his chest, my eyes narrowed. The shakes have settled down a little. I'm thinking furiously about how to get away from him and these creatures, but I have no idea. They're all just as strong as I am, and Hunter's endowed with slo-mo. I can't fight my way out, and I can't outrun him. I don't know what to do! Hunter purses his lips in thought, then glances back in the direction the Grays came from. He picks up my backpack with his free hand and slings it over his shoulder.

"To be honest, Scout, I'm not sure what we're going to do with you. There's still that matter of you cracking me across the face with my telescope. Which I did not care for, by the way. I loved that telescope, and I've never been able to find another." He rubs his head where I bashed him, then takes a few steps back and points the shotgun at me. "Let's all head back to our boats, and I'll figure something out. After all, I'm still in charge of you. Your dear brother said so. And besides, I still have some business to attend to up north I've been dying to get to. Let's go."

The Grays still have me surrounded, but they start walking as a group, following Hunter's lead. I try to go slow, to give me time to think, but the ones behind me bump into my back and push me along. That son of a bitch is so confident that we're right behind him he doesn't even bother to look back.

And then, just like that, the world goes crazy.

From every light pole across the entire expanse of the parking lot, red lights start flashing and spinning, deafening alarms blast out of a hundred unseen speakers. The riotous noise descends on us from all sides. It's so loud that as a group we all slap hands to our ears and duck our heads to escape it. But there is no escape. The wailing klaxons are a wall of sound so intense it's almost debilitating.

I crack open an eye and see the Grays around me have fallen to the ground and are writhing in pain, or terror, or something else. Hunter himself has dropped to one knee with his hands clasped over his ears. The shotgun has fallen to the asphalt next to him. For some reason this abrupt pyrotechnic onslaught is affecting them more than me. I don't know why, but I'm not going to stick around and find out.

Heart leaping, I jump up and run toward Hunter. Flying by him at a full sprint, I rip my backpack off his shoulder and knock him on his ass, not looking back. My kayak is all the way at the other end of the parking lot, but I don't know where else I can go. If Hunter recovers from all this soon and his slo-mo kicks in, he'll be able to catch me without breaking a sweat.

I'm only a few dozen yards from the fallen Grays when I see motion off to my left. The massive green doors, as solid as the world's largest bank vault, are slowly opening.

Decision time. I glance over my shoulder at Hunter, and see he's already scrambling to his feet. The Grays around him are doing the same. I can't hear a word he's shouting over the noise, but it's clear he's giving them orders. I can pretty well figure out what they are. Damn! There's no way I'll make it to my kayak in time. I take a hard left and head straight for the opening doors.

Halfway there, I risk another look and gasp. Hunter is charging after me, followed by all seven Grays. Terror is a helluva motivator, and I feel my already blistering pace increase from ten to eleven. I can't hear them behind me because the sirens are still drowning out the world, but I can feel them reaching out their clawed hands for me. Hunter hasn't gone into slo-mo, which might mean he can't turn it on and off at will, thankfully. That might be the only thing that's gone my way today.

I'm almost to the door when it stops moving, the opening now no wider than a foot or two, and then it starts closing. I'm nearly on it now, my feet splashing through puddles and my breath loud in my ears despite the sirens. By the time I reach it, the gap is less than a foot wide, and I fly through the narrow opening into pitch blackness. I stop so fast I nearly fall down and race back toward the thinning gap, a twenty-foot vertical line of light against the velvet darkness surrounding me. I sprint back and push on the doors, foolishly thinking I can help them along.

Arms stab at me through the thinning opening as the doors continue to shut. Then Hunter's shotgun barrel pokes through, and I duck out of the way just as he gets a shot off. The white flash of light and accompanying blast momentarily drown out the barrage of sound from outside. I cover my ears and jump to the side, sliding down the nearly closed doors. The gun goes off again, but the shot goes high and well away from me. Hunter tries to yank the barrel out, but it's too late. The doors continue their slow movement, and the black barrel is crumpled flat as the doors shut with an ominous rumbling thud that echoes all around me. Then the sirens stop, and I'm left sitting in the dark, my back against the steel doors. The only sounds are my sobs and panicked breath crashing in my ears.

CHAPTER
NINE

I've never really known what people meant by "the silence was deafening," until now. The rumbling echo of the doors closing is gone as quickly as it came, and the lack of all noise after so much of it is playing nasty tricks on my senses. My ears are straining to figure out what's happening, without any success. When I move my foot and it scrapes across the gritty ground, the sudden sound is so loud I stifle a yell. I'm also reminded of another saying, "It's so dark I can't see my hand in front of my face." I hold my hand up to verify this, and find that it's true, too. I move it so close I touch the tip of my nose, but I still can't see a thing.

Slowly, I grab my backpack and stand up. My face is wet with tears, rain, and sweat. I wipe it all away with my sleeve. My breathing is slowing and my heart is no longer trying to smash its way out of my chest. So, you know, progress.

With Chuck still gripped in my hand, I take a single step forward. For all I know, I'm on the edge of a cliff or next to another wall. I'd pay a million bucks for a flashlight, not that I have a penny to my name, or that anyone would actually care about money now.

Then a few dozen feet ahead of me a single light blinks on. It's mounted to the side of the wall, encased in a metal cage, and the incandescent bulb is bright enough I can see all around me. I'm so happy I almost cry out loud, even though the sudden illumination does nothing to prove I'm in any less danger than before.

The lone bulb shows me I'm in a long, curving tunnel, wider and taller than the steel doors. The walls, floor, and ceiling are all smooth, with sharp inside corners where they meet. This is not a cave, not a natural one at least. It looks more like a manufactured tunnel, something constructed out of concrete and not carved out of rock. I take a few steps forward, and the light goes out, only to be replaced with a second one farther away.

Okay, I'm not always the sharpest tool in the shed, but I'm supposed to walk that way. So, I do. I mean, what choice do I have? There's no way out behind me, especially not with what's out there waiting for me on the other side of the doors.

When I near the second light, it winks out and a third flashes on farther down the tunnel. I have no idea how big this strange place is, but I rowed my kayak around it for hours. It could be miles and miles long for all I know. My footfalls are silent as I pad along. The light ahead is humming a little, a faint buzzing, and it gets louder as I draw closer, growing in volume from a single hornet to a small hive. Then it clicks off and a fourth blinks to life down the huge corridor. My initial terror is easing, since if whoever is doing this wanted to hurt me they probably would have by now. I clear my throat.

"Hello?" I call out, louder than I intended. My voice, sounding stronger than I hoped it would, echoes up and down the tunnel, bouncing off the hard concrete surfaces. I'm actually a little proud of myself at how confident it sounds. Let's hear it for Team Scout. "Who's there?"

There's no immediate answer. I stop and stare ahead into the darkness. Phantom shadows blur and move in the distance, false images as my eyes and mind conspire to play tricks on me. A few seconds tick by. I cross my arms and plant my feet solidly on the concrete floor.

"I'm not moving until you talk to me. Who are you?"

The silence drags on for a few seconds, feeling much longer than that. I'm beginning to think nothing is going to happen, then there's a click, followed by a different humming sound. Someone coughs.

"Uh, hello. Hi," comes a loud voice from all around me, electronically amplified. It's a man's voice, deep and scratchy, as if it's unused, as rough as the Tin Man's in that creepy Wizard of Oz movie my mom used to watch. And don't get me started on the flying monkeys. I can't see any speakers anywhere, but they must be there out of sight in the darkness.

I keep my arms crossed in defiance, or what I hope looks like it. It's hard to project a tough image when you're as small and unimposing as I am. "Who are you?"

Another click. "My, uh, name's Ted. Sorry if I scared you. I didn't mean to. Sorry."

"Uh, that's okay, I guess. My name's Scout."

Click. He clears his throat again, the cough bouncing off the walls like a ping pong ball. "Hi, Scout. Nice to meet you."

This conversation is shockingly…normal, like we just met at church barbeque. It's kind of freaking me out. "Nice to meet you, too, Ted."

A pause, then, "Just keep following the tunnel. It's not much farther."

My mouth works for a minute, but I can't figure out any other options. I'm not sure what he means by not much farther. I glance back over my shoulder towards the huge doors, but all I can see is a sheet of uninviting blackness. "Okay. Oh, and thanks for saving me. I mean, that was you, right?"

"Yes, that was me, and you're welcome. Glad I could help," he replies, and I can tell from his voice he's smiling, which I take to be a good sign. "You looked in a bad way back there."

I start walking again, growing in confidence now. Like I said, if this Ted person had meant to hurt me, he's already had plenty of chances to do so. I mean, he didn't have to help me out. When I get close to the next light, it goes dark and another flicks on farther away, just like before. I don't even slow down now.

Four more times the lights wink on and off, until I've walked several hundred yards. When the next one turns on, the scenery is different. The tunnel has ended in a blank wall, and there's a long, raised platform on the right, like a warehouse loading dock. There are steps at the end of the dock leading to a standard-sized metal door that looks just as solid and imposing as the huge one at the entrance, only people-sized this time. I climb the steps and reach for the handle. When my fingers are close, there's a loud buzzing noise, which I guess means it's just been unlocked. I push on the door and step inside.

Strips of fluorescent lights along the ceiling hum and flicker to life, and there's a camera mounted in the ceiling with a red light next to the lens. I'm in another corridor, although this one is nothing like the cave. The walls are smooth and painted a clean white. There's a drop ceiling made up of those square acoustic panels, and plush tan carpeting like springy moss under my feet. The sensation that the doorway is a passage from one world to another, from the primitive to the modern, is undeniable and so unsettling, I nearly stumble over my feet. I couldn't be more shocked if I had just walked through the cabinet in *The Lion,*

The Witch, and The Wardrobe. The bright lights clearly show me the accumulated mud and grime covering my arms and hands, and I'm suddenly self-conscious at how gross I must look. I try to wipe some of it off without making it look like that's what I'm doing, but the dirt is pretty well ground into my skin and doesn't budge. There's something sticking out of the wall next to me, and it takes me a few heartbeats to realize it's a stainless steel water fountain. More out of curiosity than anything else I push the button. Clear water burbles out and swirls dutifully around the drain. I desperately want to take a drink, but I resist.

There's that click from overhead again, but not as amplified in here. "Go ahead and take a drink," Ted says, his voice coming from a round speaker near the camera. "The water's fine. It's okay. Trust me."

I don't know why I should, but he hasn't done anything yet to give me a reason not to. I hesitate for a second, then bend over and drink. The cold water hitting my teeth is like a punch to the mouth, such a shock to my senses I nearly sputter and gag. But I don't. I drink long and hard, slurping loudly, enjoying it much more than I should. Some people say that water is water, and it all tastes the same. I say to hell with that. This stuff is pure, clean and amazing! It's all I can do to stop gulping it down. Ted may have chuckled, but that was probably my imagination.

Another click. "See? I told you."

I wipe my mouth on my sleeve and resist the

urge to burp. At the end of the corridor is another door, a normal one this time, white with a standard round doorknob. I do what any tired, hungry, and scared girl in a crazy underground complex would do. I twist the doorknob and push. The door opens easily, and I step inside.

The room is big and square, lined with long wooden tables with black tops. If they had Bunsen burners they would have been identical to ones in my old science lab in school. Tall stools are scattered about. Different types of equipment are covered with plastic sheets and lined up against the walls. I peer closer but can't figure out what any of it is. Some of the equipment is tagged with red labels. At first glance, it would appear this stuff was either being packed and ready to be shipped out, or was in the process of being brought in. I have no idea which, not that it really matters. The far end of the room is one large glass wall with a glass doorway leading inside. I head in that direction, sidestepping the stools and tables as I go. When I get close, I see a plaque on the doorway that says "Clean Room." I tug on the door, but this one's locked.

"Ted? You there?"

Click. "Yes. Just a sec."

Beyond the glass, in the Clean Room itself, I see more tables, some dated-looking control panels with lots of lights and knobs, and dozens of gauges. All the gauges are dark. TV screens are mounted on the walls above the control panels, showing scenes from the tunnels, the hallway with the drinking fountain, and the parking lot. I peer with heightened interest at that one, seeing if Hunter and his band of merry Grays are still around, but all I see is the open space and, in the distance, the lone car I spotted earlier. A few of the screens are dark, blank rectangular eyes that reveal nothing but reflections of the overhead lights. Of more immediate interest to me, there's also about a thousand candy bar wrappers and empty cans of Coke and Mountain Dew littering every flat surface. My mouth fills with saliva at the sight of it all, and without even realizing it I give the unyielding door another jerk.

Then a guy I assume is Ted walks into view from the left, and my unconscious yearning for the candy bars is blown away.

The man standing on the other side of the glass is old. Not just in his late teens or early twenties, but actually old. I've only seen people my age or younger in over six years. I'm so thrown I can't even figure out his age right away. He smiles at me and pushes a button near the door on his side.

"Hi, I'm Ted. It's, uh, good to see you. Freakin' good to see anyone, really."

He's tall, well over six feet, even though he's a little hunched over. His cheeks are sagging, his eyes droop so low I can see red on the lower lids. He's completely bald on top. The hair on the sides of his head is dirty-blond and long, down to his shoulders. When he smiles, his lower teeth show, which for some reason I find fascinating and weird. If I had to guess, I'd say he's in his fifties, or maybe even older, but I could be way off. He's scarecrow skinny, and his jeans and filthy white T-shirt hang on him like drapes on a window. To my untrained eye, he doesn't look very healthy, but that might just be his age throwing me. I remember seeing homeless people on highway exits begging for money who looked better.

But how is he even here? I mean, he's almost ancient! Seriously, he should have gone Gray long, long ago. He sees me staring and smiles, a sheepish smile that shows he understands my very evident confusion. Literally, how is he even here? How is he alive? Ted hesitates, then takes a small step forward and pushes the intercom button again. His voice is still scratchy, his vocal cords like an old piece of machinery asked to run after being mothballed for years. He looks me up and down, then glances down at himself. His lined face reddens as he plucks at his grimy T-shirt.

"Uh, sorry. I wasn't expecting any company. I'm a bit of a mess."

I have no room to talk. I just nod at him and try not to draw his attention to how awful I look. It's clear both of us have been a little negligent in the personal hygiene department for quite some time. But that's not what I'm wondering about now. He nods and pushes the intercom again.

"I know, right? If you're asking yourself why

I haven't changed like everyone else, I'm not really sure." He spreads his hand. "But here I am."

I realize I'm staring at him with my mouth open in what I have to imagine is a really stupid looking expression, and it's all I can do not to physically push my lower jaw closed with my hand. I shake my head. "I'm sorry, but I haven't seen anyone like you in, well, years. I don't understand."

He shrugs and smiles sheepishly, hands out at his sides. "Me neither."

I'm starting to get my wits about me again, although it's a slow process, as slow as waking from an unexpected nap. I blink a few times to give me a chance to gather my thoughts. We're being quite patient with each other, which I'm sure both of us appreciate. I know I do. It's plain to see he's as shocked to see me as I am to see him.

"I'm sorry," I repeat. "But please understand this is coming at me kind of fast. I mean, you, this place, what happened outside. It's all a little much right now, you know?"

"I get it. And to be fair, it's freaking me out to actually be talking to someone. I've been alone down here for so long now. Well, like you said, forever."

"But how? And what is this place?" I shake my head. "My god, I don't even know where to start. And possibly more important than anything else, I see you've got candy bars in there. Got any of those to spare?"

Ted kicks at some of the wrappers on the floor, then leans against the glass that separates us. He sighs, before picking up an empty can of Coke from the table next to him and staring at it blankly. His mouth curls into something between a sneer and a frown.

"I'm so sick of this stuff. You have no idea."

Turns out that for the last few years he's been living almost completely on Coke, Mountain Dew, and candy bars. Just like the map said, he tells me, this place is called the Mound, or, more appropriately, the Mound Laboratory. It was, of all things, a nuclear research facility during and after the Cold War, and was actually a part of the Manhattan Project. It was named after the nearby Indian Mounds in the city of Miamisburg. It supplied detonators and stuff like that for nuclear bombs. I guess that explains the huge steel doors and the fact that it's underground. If one of those things blew up, they needed it to be contained here. The place was officially shut down about a decade ago, but the cleanup was still underway when the Storm first hit. I feel a little ignorant, seeing as I've lived my entire life in Ohio and had no idea it even existed.

"I'm part of the cleanup crew, I guess you'd call us," he explains. He glances away a lot when he talks, for some reason not comfortable looking right at me. I get the impression he was a shy guy before all this, plus not seeing anyone for years hasn't helped. "Or, I was. I was the last guy here, you know, working over a weekend for some overtime, when the rains started. My car got waterlogged and died in the parking lot, and I just decided to bunk down here for a few days until it stopped. Which it never did, of course. By the time I figured I had to leave, I couldn't. The roads were flooded, and the power was out all over the place. Before I knew it, I was stranded up here."

"And then the Grays came?"

"Grays? Is that what you call them?" He tilts his head in thought. "Interesting. I just called them 'Crazies,' since that's kind of what they are. But with the grey hair and the color of their skin, I get why you call them that. Anyway, I was stuck here. You can't see it from where you're standing, but there's a full cafeteria in the back, showers, bunkrooms, and everything. And I've had power this entire time. Generators or solar power, or something. I really don't know." He sighs. "But all the good food ran out a long time ago. For the last year or so I've been living on this crap. I swear to god, if I have to eat this garbage much longer I'm going to starve to death. I can't stand it. I used to love all this junk food, but not anymore." He makes a face and kicks at the wrappers again, the paper at his feet flying up in the air before slowly settling around him.

I feel sorry for him, for sure, but I would be more than happy to take some of them off his hands. I can almost smell the chocolate on the other side of the glass wall. Sitting here talking to him like this reminds me of some prison movie, where the inmate is seated behind the glass and begging his lawyer to get him out. And that makes me feel even more sorry for him, because he really is a prisoner here.

He tells me his full name is Ted Hilliard, and he's originally from up the road in Dayton. Unmarried, no kids, kind of bounced around to different jobs a lot. He'd been working at some insurance company in one of the suburbs before the Mound advertised for people looking for a good wage and not terribly concerned about working in a decommissioned nuclear facility. Office life with so many people wasn't really to his liking, and this opportunity with a small team of people was right up his alley.

"So that's pretty much it. I've got a few dozen DVDs to watch, some books I've read about a thousand times, and not much else. There are some cameras aimed at the parking lot I can watch, but nothing really ever happens, at least not until today. Sometimes a group of Crazies will walk by, but nothing much else. Until you came along, that is. Just a lot of 'me' time. Way too much 'me' time."

There are a zillion other questions rattling around my brain, but tops on my huge list is his age. "Uh, just how old are you, anyway?"

He thinks for a moment, counting off on his fingers. "Well, if I kept track correctly, I turned fifty-seven last month."

Fifty-seven. Some quick and probably inaccurate math in my head means he's around 680 months old. That's an incredible number, and more than triple my age. I can't believe I'm standing in front of someone who's been around so long. He's basically my parents' age.

"What about you?" he asks.

"Me? I'm two hundred and ten months old."

He tilts his head at my answer. "You keep track of your age in months?"

"Well, yeah. No one lives more than 240 months any more. Well," I catch myself, "at least we didn't think so. Everybody goes Gray by the time they hit 240, some a lot sooner, so we track our ages by months because it's more accurate. Makes it seem longer, too."

"Two hundred and forty months. That's it? That's not very long."

"No, it's not," I admit. "Trust me. It's just about all we think about.."

"Christ, I would think so. That's awful."

The more we talk, the more at ease he becomes. He's leaning against the glass wall now, peppering me with questions. What's it really like out there? Does it really rain all the time everywhere, or just here? How many Crazies do I think are out there? Is there any form of government still in place? I patiently do my best to answer him, even though some of my answers are simply "I don't know." I'm pretty sure he could go all night and into tomorrow if I let him.

"So what about me?" he asks, pointing to himself. "How did you find this place, or even know I was here?"

"Well, to be honest, we didn't know what I might find. We figured out the number station and the lady reading off the numbers."

"Number station? What's that?"

"Ted, aren't you the one who's broadcasting something from here? The shortwave radio? Isn't that you?"

He screws up his face for a minute, the deep crevices around his eyes made even more defined by the stark lighting. There's a fleeting expression on his face I can't quite figure out. "I don't know what you're talking about."

"You know, the lady going on and on with numbers, and how they eventually repeat? Total monotone? The number station."

He wags his finger as he glances back, over his shoulder. "Oh, right, the radio. Wow, that thing actually works, eh? A few years ago I found some old equipment in a back room and finally decided to turn it on. I heard that lady rambling on with the numbers, but never knew what it was. I was hoping she was a real person, but nothing I did made her answer me. That stuff must date back to World War II. It was covered with some old tarps and smelled so hot when I turned it on I thought it was going to catch on fire. I have no idea what it was or what it did. Once I turned it on, I didn't think I should shut it down. Is that how you found me?"

I take off my damp poncho and lay it over a stool. For the next few minutes I explain what Google discovered, that the numbers were tied to Bible verses, and how we traced them to this place.

"Google? That's his name?"

"Well, no, not really. I don't know what his real name is. He just goes by that. In fact, most of us don't go by our real names."

"Interesting. Well, anyway, it's impressive he was able to figure that out. To be honest, I was afraid to mess with any of the dials, so I just left it alone. I left it turned on in the closet and forgot about it. I'll be damned."

Our conversation lags for a moment, long enough for me to wonder why a Number Station here would be directing someone to come to the Mound. It doesn't make much sense. If what Google told me about these ham radios is accurate, they were supposed to help deep cover agents during World War II and the Cold War with messages and directions and stuff. It doesn't make any sense one of these things would have been set up for that decades ago, much less now.

But I can't stay focused on that right now. All I can think about is the potential for scoring a few dozen candy bars and cans of Coke. I sincerely hope he has enough left over to share. But instead of going there, I try to park my greed and concentrate on him and his situation.

"This whole thing is amazing. I mean, you've been trapped here this entire time, all by yourself. Granted, you've got heat and light, and no Grays are trying to eat you, so it's not all bad. And a bunkhouse and TV? I gotta admit, I'm a little envious."

Ted thinks about it for a moment. "Yeah, I guess. And you wouldn't know it to look at me, but there are showers and toilets and all that, too."

Toilets? Showers? I'd almost swap Chuck for a hot shower and some clean clothes. Actual hot water? Soap? That sounds like heaven.

"I'd love to come in and see everything back there," I tell him. "You have no idea how bad I want to brush my teeth. Got any toothpaste?"

Ted blanches and backs away from the door so fast he nearly stumbles, the whites of his eyes huge against his already pale skin. I've seen fear plenty of times since all this began, and Ted couldn't be more terrified than if a thousand Grays just burst through the door. After a moment of clear indecision, he reaches back out and stabs the intercom button again, his finger trembling. He shakes his head very fast back and forth.

"Oh, no, you can't do that. This room is hermetically sealed. The air and water here are purified. Nothing gets in, and nothing gets out. Whatever is changing people into those Crazies might be airborne, and I'm not going to take any chances."

Hermetically? I don't know that word, and please don't ask me to spell it, but I can pretty much figure out what he's talking about. He shakes his head again, and his body language has changed. He's as close to bolting as anyone I've ever seen.

"Nope. No freakin' way. I'm not coming out. And no way are you coming in."

CHAPTER
TEN

It takes some time and more gentle words to convince him to step away from the ledge, so to speak. When he's finally chilled out to the point where I'm no longer afraid he's going to sprint out of the clean room, we spend the next few hours talking. Well, I'm talking and he's listening, if I'm being honest – although I'm bummed I won't be satisfying my sweet tooth or blasting off a few layers of grime anytime soon. He's fascinated with what's been going on outside his glass cage since the Storm began, which makes perfect sense when you consider he's basically been here in solitary confinement the entire time. I tell him everything that's happened to me since Lord and I left Cleveland, skipping over the more painful details about our parents. I haven't related all this to anyone in so long I keep surprising myself at some of the details I dredge up, like places we've stayed, people we've lost, and what we've had to do in order to survive. Some of it is shocking to hear out loud, even to me. Eventually I slump down on the soft carpet with my back to the wall and rest my head on the wall. I feel a weighted blanket of fatigue begin to force my arms and legs down. I keep forgetting what a long day it's been and what I've been through. Even though he can see I'm exhausted, he keeps pressing for more. With his baggy clothes and wild hair he could be a scarecrow weirdly animated by a strong wind. He's especially interested when I show him my salt and pepper hair, and what happened when my own change began.

"I don't understand," he stops me at one point. "What do you mean, you can go into 'slo-mo' when you're attacked. What's that?"

I describe this enhanced ability as well as I can, along with my increased strength and endurance. It sounds funny when I talk about it out loud. I explain the tingle in the back of my head when it's about to start, and how it works. The way that sounds are muffled with all the high notes chopped off. The ravenous hunger afterwards. For the first time in a while, he doesn't move or talk. He crosses his arms and looks at me, his eyes narrowed.

"I'm sorry, Scout, but I gotta call BS. That doesn't sound possible at all," he states. "Can you do it now?"

I shake my head, still leaning heavily against the wall. I'm so tired I'm lucky I'm stringing words together in coherent sentences "No. It only happens when I really need it, usually when I'm really scared. Well, most of the time. It's been a little hit and miss lately. But the strength part, that's all the time. That doesn't go away."

"Really? Can you show me? Pretend I'm from Missouri."

I have no idea what he means about being from Missouri. For some reason, I'm a little annoyed at his skepticism, maybe because I'm pooped, but maybe not. But I get it, I guess. With a sigh, I push myself to my feet and look around the room at all the furniture and equipment scattered about. I pick up one of the tall stools. It's heavy with thick metal legs and a green padded seat. I grab one of the legs and yank, pulling it cleanly off with a loud snap. Out of the corner of my eye, I see Ted jump. With very little effort, I bend the metal leg a few times, twist each end, and muscle it into the rough shape of a misshapen chrome pretzel. I hold it up for his inspection then toss it on the floor, where it bounces with a pronounced thud and comes to rest near the door. Ted's eyebrows lift comically. He takes another step back. His face is a screwed-up mixture of confusion and disbelief that borders on comical.

I smile at him, trying not to be too smug and probably failing. "See? I could just as easily pick up one of those tables and toss it across the room if I wanted to."

"That's amazing. I mean, it's really freakin' amazing. But if you're so strong and have this 'slo-mo' thing, why couldn't you save yourself from the Crazies and that guy with the red hair?"

I sigh and glance away, staring at my nearly

transparent reflection in the glass. Wow. I really do look like hell. To truly explain this to him, I'd have to get into the complicated and personal history of me, Singer, and Hunter. Especially that jerk Hunter. That time he groped me, standing over me and declaring his perceived authority over me, is still too raw and personal. It's not something I'm ready to share with a guy I just met. Not even a guy who saved my life.

"You saw the guy with the red hair? The one that didn't look like a Gray already?" I ask him, and he nods. "Let's just say he and I have a history together, and we didn't part on good terms. I never used to think this, but some people are inherently bad, you know? Hunter's one of those.

"But I will tell you this," I add. "All Grays are super strong, just like me. Some have slo-mo, like me. We call them 'fast Grays.' Hunter somehow has all of that, too. But he also has some ability to control Grays, and that's something I've never seen before. I have no idea how he does it, but the fact that he can makes him even more dangerous than ever. In fact, he could be the most dangerous person alive right now. And that scares the hell out of me." I pause and point at the TV screens behind him on the walls. "I just wish your cameras could tell me where he is right now and what he's up to."

Ted stands up a little straighter and his eyes light up. He's almost dancing in place, bouncing from one foot to the other. He really does possess a lot of energy. Must be all the candy and Coke. "Well now, what if I could tell you exactly where he is, and what he's doing? What would you think of that?"

I'm suddenly much more awake, the fog of my exhaustion blown away by the winds of his excitement. "I would like that very, very much. But how can you do that?"

Instead of answering, he almost sprints over to one of the consoles, the one below the blank TV screens. I didn't notice it earlier, but this console has a newer look to it, much more modern than the ones flanking it. He flicks a switch and the middle screen shudders to life. The image is nothing but a blurry smudge of gray and black. But then Ted fiddles with a pair of toggle switches that look like video game joysticks. The image on the screen swiftly changes. It takes a second for me to realize what I'm seeing is the top of the Mound, and it's quickly receding while I watch. In seconds, I'm looking hundreds of feet down at the entire complex, including the parking lot and the endless water surrounding it. Holy crap.

"Yeah," he says proudly, pushing another intercom button on the console. "I've got a drone, complete with cameras. In fact, I've got two. I call them Larry and Curly."

As I stare in amazement at the view, I think he should have led with this bit of information. But that's okay. He's got drones with cameras!

"That's awesome," I blurt out, my hands flat on the glass, and my nose squished against it. "I'm not even going to guess why in the world this place has drones, but I'm not going to complain about it, either."

He doesn't take his eyes off the screen. "I wondered that, too. In fact, I didn't even know they were here for the first few years after I got here. I was too scared to mess with any of the equipment, you know? I guess it was an added level of security or something. Another way of keeping track of who was coming and going."

He works the joystick, and the drone slides to the side, away from the parking lot. That thing is fast! The picture is clear most of the time, but once in a while goes blurry with rainwater on the lens. Either there is no audio, or if there is, I can't hear anything through the glass.

"Like I said, I have two here. I had a third, but I took Moe out too far and it died before it could make it back. It crashed into the water about a mile away. Since then, I've been much more careful with Larry and Curly."

"How far can they go?" I ask, still mesmerized by the view, even from here behind the glass. "What's their range?"

"It's pretty impressive, really. I think it's about twenty miles. Well, twenty miles out, and another twenty back. I wouldn't want to go any farther than that. Any kind of inclement weather, winds or heavy rains, can really impact their flight time."

He keeps working the joystick, never taking his eyes from the screen above him. After a minute goes by, he stops. He doesn't actually say "voila", but he may as well have.

"There. See that movement down there? I'd say I just found your Hunter."

I want to tell him he's not my Hunter, but I think it's implied now. It's killing me that I can't get closer to the screen so I can see better, but from where I stand I think I see what he's talking about. I can make out some movement way down below, tiny shapes on the open brown water. It's a boat, a good-sized bass boat with figures moving around and heading away from the Mound. I can't tell from here, but the person at the bow looks like he has red hair. Hunter. And his minions.

"Looks like him," he says. "And he's got his Crazies, too. Didn't you tell me they don't like water?"

I don't answer for a moment, enthralled with what I'm seeing. "Well, yeah. They can't swim, and they're too stupid to know how to work a boat. But somehow that son of a bitch taught them how to row."

While we watch, another boat comes into view. No, not just one, but six more. Each filled with people. More minions, boatloads of them. Chills run up and down my spine as an uneasy feeling fills my gut. I don't want to watch any more, but I can't look away.

Not only does Hunter know how to control Grays, but he's got more of them.

A lot more.

CHAPTER
ELEVEN

It gets to the point where I just can't keep my eyes open anymore. Ted, however, is fully caffeinated and showing no signs of slowing down. He's desperate for company and wants to keep talking, but I'm pooped and have to get some sleep. The day has taken its toll on me, and I need to get some rest before I fall over. He's clearly upset I'm tapping out after being by himself for so long, but I assure him we'll talk more tomorrow. After bringing the Larry drone home, he dims the lights in the clean room and leaves by a back door. I slide my backpack under my head and close my eyes, the carpeting soft and dry beneath me.

Of course I can't sleep. Even as wiped out as I am, my mind is in overdrive and refuses to call it quits for the night. All I can think about is Hunter, that he's now got my powers – and more. Somehow that lunatic can control the Grays around him, and that terrifies me. He's bad enough on his own, sure, but to be able to direct Grays to do what he wants, well, that's another level of horrible. With abilities like that, no one is safe. And I mean no one. My eyes fly open.

Not even Church Island.

I suck in a sudden breath when what he said finally drills through the shell of my exhaustion, right before I got away. "I still have some business to take care of up north," or something like that. My god, I can only imagine it's just a matter of time before he heads back there to finish what he started when he shot Singer. He's certainly vindictive enough, and I'm sure his desire to get even for them kicking him out won't let him rest. If it were just Hunter by himself, I might stand a chance of taking him. But there's no way I can overcome that nut job and his standing army, too. Nobody on Church Island is safe with him out there. Not Jacob, Mim, or Annie. Or even little Carly.

I've got to get back there and warn them, as soon as I can.

Correction. I need to get back to Rumpke Mountain and warn them first, then haul ass and prepare Jacob and the rest. I can't think of anything that would stop Hunter from getting revenge. That's just the way he is, and the way he thinks. I have no doubt vengeance is the fire that drives him.

I know I should leave now, but I'm so tired I'd probably fall asleep on the kayak and tumble overboard. My head knows that, but my heart is trying to push me out the door. My head wins, barely, especially with the beginning of a plan in place. I'll just catch a few winks, and then get going again. As I lay there, I'm finally able to shut down my brain enough to go to sleep. I suffer through a few nightmare visions of Hunter and his Grays staring down at me with dead eyes, but I'm so tired I sleep right through them.

When I finally wake up, the lights in the clean room are on, and Ted is sitting in a chair by the door. He's been watching me sleep, which creeps me out a little, but again I give him the benefit of the doubt. He's been here for years by himself, and even though he seems to be something of a natural loner, seeing anyone must be a treat for him. I sit up and knuckle grit from my eyes and look him over.

He's taken the time to get cleaned up, the lucky duck. He exchanged the nasty T-shirt for a clean white one, shaved, and his long blond hair is tied up in a ponytail. He looks less like a homeless guy and more like an aging hippie. It's an improvement.

"G'morning," I mumble through a yawn. "How long have I been asleep?"

His finger stabs the intercom button. "Almost ten hours. You must have been really freakin' tired."

Ten hours? Damn that's too long. I should have left here hours ago! I quickly hustle to my feet and rummage in my backpack and retrieve a can of salmon. While Ted watches in uncharacteristic silence, I pop the top and devour the pink meat, licking the can clean when I'm done. I've still got another can of salmon and a few larger cans of beef stew. I'll save those for later even though I'm still hungry. I feel bad for eating in front of him, knowing what he's stuck with for food.

"Did you sleep well?" he asks, the words tumbling out in an excited rush, a big grin across his lined face.

I nod, smiling back. "Yeah, thanks. I don't often have such a nice place to crash." I'm looking for somewhere to toss my empty salmon can, but I don't see one. I stuff it back in my pack for later.

"That's good. I'm glad. You really needed it."

I hate to break it to him that I have to leave already. The poor guy has been alone so long, I can't imagine he'll take it well when I tell him. But what choice do I have? I need to get back to Church Island.

"Uh, Ted, I hate to tell you, but I have to go," I say, and hurriedly explain why. He doesn't know Hunter and what he's capable of, but I do my best to make him understand. When I'm done, his head drops, but after a moment he nods. His eyes are shiny as he fights to hold back tears. I feel terrible that I'm putting him through this.

"Yeah, I don't know this Hunter person and everything he's done, but I had a feeling that might be the case after what you told me." He sighs, wiping his face with the back of his hand. Then he perks up and holds something towards me. "Here, while you were sleeping, I dug through the storeroom and found something that might help." In his hand he's holding something black and rectangular, about the size of a pack of cigarettes but with a long antenna on it.

"What is it?"

He spins a knob on the top of it, and a red light glows. "It's a hand-held shortwave radio. I've got a couple of them. I figure you can take one, and I can keep one. We should be able to talk to each other. I don't know what their range is, but I think it's pretty far."

I step up to the glass, and he holds it out to me. The word Baofang in silver script lettering is printed across the top, right above a lighted LED screen. Below the screen are smaller buttons numbered zero through nine, and a few others I don't understand.

"I can use the drones to see what's going on out there, and let you know," he continues, his mood changing for the better. "I'll be your eye in the sky. I can keep track of where you are, and what's going on. That should be helpful, right? Right?"

A wave of hope washes over me. "Ted, this is amazing! If you can see what's coming at me, or what I might be headed into, that could be so helpful."

He smiles, showing more lower teeth than upper ones. Yeah, still weird. "I thought you might like that," he beams. "I just wish I could do more."

"But – but wait. How are you going to get one to me? You said nothing goes in or out of your room."

In his other hand, he holds up a clear cylinder with rubber ends. I've seen one of those before, back when mom and dad would go through the drive-through at the bank. The teller would always slip a sucker in for me. He flips a small latch, and the cylinder pops opens at one end.

"This place has a pneumatic delivery system for sending documents and stuff to other parts of the complex. I've got one in the back room. I can stuff a radio in here and send it to you." He pauses and taps the side of the clear tube. "There's only one problem."

"Yeah, what's that?"

"Well, I don't know where the tubes go. I'm guessing they come out in the building upstairs, but I don't know for sure."

The fact there's a building upstairs is news to me. "What building?"

He looks up and points to the ceiling. "Up there, on top of the hill. There's a building up there, with some offices and a guard shack. If you can get up there, I'm hoping that's the other end. Just do me a favor and don't send it back afterwards."

Oh, yeah, that makes sense. The whole "hermetically sealed" thing again. But I have to think that whoever designed this place was smart enough to know that, too. I walk close to the glass, the closest we've been so far. I'm getting so used to talking to him this way I barely notice it anymore.

"Thank you, Ted. Thanks for saving me from Hunter, and for what you're doing now. I really appreciate it. You're amazing."

He beams at me, and his voice trembles when he answers me. "You're welcome. And are you freakin' kidding? I've had nothing to do for six years besides watch the same damn DVDs and read the same books over and over! At least now I've got a purpose, something to do. This is the most excited I've been since I got locked up in here."

I gather up my backpack and look hard at him. "How much more food do you have back there? How long can you last?" I ask him.

His manic behavior bottoms out and doesn't match his answer at all. "Don't you worry about me. I'll be fine."

I'm not sure I believe him, but like so much else in this world, there's nothing I can do about it. I wish I didn't always feel so bad for things that aren't my fault, and I have no control over, but I can't. I slip on my poncho and shoulder my pack, jiggling it a few times to get it comfortable. I pat Chuck, who is securely strapped to my thigh.

"Okay. But before I go outside, please do me a favor and make sure nothing is out there."

He makes an okay sign at me. "Way ahead of you! I've been up for hours and scouring the whole area with the drones. There's nothing near this complex but you and me. The parking lot and all the water for miles around are clear. But there's a heckuva storm out there now, and I had to bring Larry back a little while ago."

"Thanks, Ted. And we'll keep talking, I promise. Okay?"

He gulps heavily, his Adam's Apple bobbing up and down. With tight lips, he nods at me. "Just be sure you don't touch any of the settings on the radio. I set the frequency to match mine." He holds the radio close to the glass and I see a series of numbers on the LED screen: 145.110 on top and 146.160 below it. "You spin this knob to turn it on, and push the red button to talk. The batteries are fully charged, and should be good for a long time."

"Got it. Don't touch the buttons."

"Memorize the settings in case something happens. If those change and you can't put them back, we won't be able to communicate. Okay?"

"Okay. Promise I won't mess with anything."

Tears are forming in the corners of his eyes again. I still feel like crap leaving him alone like this, but I have to go. A saying my dad used to say pops unexpectedly into my mind, "We're burnin' daylight." Thinking of him both warms my heart and saddens me at the same time, like it always does.

I force a smile I don't feel, and give Ted a two-fingered salute, just like Lord would do. I pull open the door and head into the hallway. I stop for a moment and drink deeply from the water fountain one more time. The pure water is so cold it gives me a touch of brain-freeze, but I don't mind. I turn and wave at the camera in the corner. As I near the heavy-duty door, I hear the buzzing sound, and I pull it open. The tunnel is completely lit up this time, but even so it's so long I can't see the other end. It's hard to grasp how massive this place must be.

I make my way down the tunnel until I'm standing at the huge doors. I turn and say, "I'm here!" Somewhere over my head I hear machinery start to hum, and the massive doors creak open. It gives me great satisfaction when the smashed barrel of Hunter's shotgun clanks to the concrete floor. When the huge doors are open wide enough, I kick the barrel aside and slide through. I'm back in the parking lot again. The sky is the same uniform and dismal grey it always is, and rain pours down around me. I flip up the hood on my poncho and step outside.

CHAPTER
TWELVE

Old habits die hard. Even though Ted just checked for Grays, once I'm in the parking lot I spend a few moments scouring the area. The rain is coming down hard, waves of it sweeping across the empty asphalt expanse like an aurora borealis dancing in front of me. I'd love to wait this out in the shelter of the massive doors, but I can't afford to waste time. I pull the strings to snug my hood tight around my face and step into the torrent. Thank God for good boots.

I skirt along the edge of the parking lot, the hill next to me way too steep to climb, even if I could hold onto the vines growing thick everywhere. The wind is to my back, and the force of the storm is enough to push me along. Weather this bad is something new. I've never seen wind and rain like this, not since the Storm began. Up ahead I can see where the asphalt ends, and I'm getting concerned there's nothing there. When I reach the edge it's a sheer drop off. I peer down, and see the familiar brown sludge about twenty feet below me. Small waves, driven by the rain and wind, lap like warm tar against the side of the hill. Frustrated, I turn and head back the other way, the rain smacking me in the face now and stinging my exposed skin.

I pass the huge doors and keep going around a bend. A few hundred feet up I see something, an irregularity in the hill. Whatever it is, the vines have taken over and have almost completely covered it up. I rip a few away, and a dirty slab of concrete peeks out from the sea of green. I yank more away, and a narrow set of steps is revealed. Okay, this is encouraging. I start up carefully.

This stairway is narrow, only wide enough for a single person, and a skinny one at that. There's an obvious and critical lack of a hand railing. A dozen steps up I spy what looks like a sign on a post. Peeling back the vegetation, faded red letters say "Warning. Authorized Personnel Only." The rule follower in me chuckles when I barely slow down.

After a few minutes of climbing, I wish that I had counted my steps, just for fun. I think back to the time I went with my family to a Cleveland Indians baseball game. I was little, no more than seven or eight, and our seats were in the nosebleed section behind homeplate. I remember putting my head down and climbing for what seemed like an eternity, at least for a little kid. Each step seemed huge and almost insurmountable to me. I never did make it to the top, and my dad had to carry me the rest of the way. And wouldn't you know it, I had to pee the minute we got there, and we had to do it all over again.

My head down, I keep going. The steps go

through a few zig zags up the hill. Several times they are so overgrown I'm not even sure I'm still on them. One time I miss a step completely and catch myself right before I tumble down the steep slope. More gingerly now, I keep putting one boot in front of the other, cautiously making certain I'm on solid concrete before fully committing myself. The downpour increases, the rain slapping at my back so hard it threatens to sweep me off the staircase. Without my increased strength and endurance, I'm not sure I could make it.

Head down, I'm concentrating so hard on my incremental progress I don't realize when I arrive at the top. In fact, I pick my boot up and I'm shocked when there's not another step to take. I shake the water out of my face and look around. I'm on a large plateau, and the wind is so strong up here I have to spread my legs to brace myself. Looking down behind me all I can see are the dark green vines vanishing into the rain, like I'm a god perched in the clouds on top of Mount Olympus. This would be cool if I weren't so soaking wet and miserable.

I walk on a little, and up ahead I see a hazy shape. It's square, and completely out of place here on this otherwise featureless plateau. I duck my head and push ahead. The shape firms up and becomes a small building with a flat roof and walls with lots of windows, with some sort of tall antennas sprouting from the roof. There's a glass door on the far side. I skirt around the building to the door and give it a tug.

It's locked. Painted on the door is a similar warning to the one I saw below. With the same casual disregard I gave to the sign's threat, I give the handle a strong yank, and the lock gives way with a metallic crunch. I pull it open against the force of the wind and step inside, struggling to shut it behind me. The wind and rain continue to lash the world outside, but sudden and total calm inside is such a shock I stand there, panting, and revel in the peace and quiet.

After I catch my breath, I look around. There's not much to the place. A few desks, a control panel the same vintage as the ones in Ted's clean room, and some chairs. Pictures of someone's family are propped up on the desk, along with a notebook and pens in an empty coffee mug with the Ohio State logo on it. At the back of the guardhouse, there's another one of those very solid and imposing doors, identical to the one from the loading dock to the hallway. I assume it goes to either stairs or an elevator. As strong as I am, it would take a dozen of me to budge that thing. I rap on it with my knuckle, and it's as solid as a bank vault. Okay, breaking that open might take more than a dozen of me.

I prowl around anxiously, searching for the tube system Ted was talking about. What was the term he used? Pneumatic. Yeah, that's it. If I were designing this place, where would I put something like that? I start by checking out around the desk, inspecting the walls, and even poke around at the floor itself, but I can't spot anything. I'm really getting concerned now since I was really looking forward to that radio. On the back wall is a cabinet. The doors are locked, but only until I give them a hearty pull. Inside are some shelves filled with paper, stacks of forms, and small badges with the word "GUEST" printed on them.

The sinking feeling I might not find it is growing in me, but then I notice a panel on the back of the cabinet with a handle near the top. I pull on the handle, but nothing happens. I stare at it for a moment, then push it down. It slides down smoothly and stops with a solid clunk, revealing a single slot for a carrier like the one Ted had - but it's empty. A sign in small print says "Receive Only," which makes sense. I can't send a tube back to Ted from here, which is how they keep the clean room sealed. Clever. There's a red light next to a button, and without hesitating I push it. I'm greeted by a long hiss of air and after a few seconds the light turns green and a carrier pops into place with a thud. Eagerly I grab it and flip open the end. Inside is the radio, just like Ted promised. It's heavier than I thought it would be. The antenna has been detached to make it fit, which makes sense. But Ted also sent something else. Two somethings, to be precise. I hold the Milky Way bars with trembling hands, and I have to choke back tears of joy and gratitude. I clutch them to my soaked chest.

I screw the antenna back on the radio and spin the knob on the top. There's a burst of static, which is loud in the small space. I take a breath and press the red button on the side, careful not to touch any other buttons.

"Ted? You there?" I ask, my voice catching.

A few seconds pass, and then I hear another burst of static, followed by his voice. "Scout? Is that you?"

"Yeah, it's me. Ted, you didn't have to send the candy. Don't get me wrong. I love it. But you shouldn't have."

A few seconds pass. "Don't worry about it," he replies, and I can tell he's smiling. I'm sure his lower teeth are showing.

I smile back at him, even though he can't see it. "Thanks again. I'm going to dive into one of these, and then head out. The weather is horrible, but I can't wait. I'm going to save the battery and turn it off now, but I'll check in later. Oh, and don't try to send the drones out now. They wouldn't last a second."

I'm sure he wants to talk more, but he gamely says goodbye. I turn the small radio off and zip it up carefully in my backpack. Then I sit at the desk chair, deliberately open one of the candy bars, and take a first bite. And yes, it's so delicious I'm pretty sure I moan out loud as I force myself to chew slowly, savoring every bit of it, rolling the gooey goodness all around my mouth. Even when it's gone and I've run my tongue around and around my mouth and teeth, the chocolate and caramel taste remains. I sit in the chair longer than I should, my head back, while the sugar careens through my system. Nothing I've eaten since all of us were holed up in that office building last year can compare to this. My eyes lock on the second bar, but I resist temptation and hurriedly pack it away with the radio before I have a change of heart. Contrary to popular belief, at least in this case, out of sight is definitely not out of mind. I slip my backpack on and cinch up the straps.

With my new-found treasures safe and sound, I brace myself and step back outside. The winds have eased up a bit, but the rain is coming down even harder than before. I retrace my steps and eventually locate the stairway again. Going down is much harder than going up, and I have to take it nice and slow, so I don't take a tumble. I slip a few times, but manage to catch myself before anything nasty happens. Head down, feet placed carefully, I trudge down the narrow staircase and eventually set foot in the parking lot. I see the lonely car and I grin, knowing now that it belongs to Ted. I remember how many candy bar wrappers littered the inside of it. I pass by it and continue walking toward the kayak. Thankfully, I had pulled it far enough into the parking lot that it hasn't simply floated away, which could have happened with all this rain. But there it is, waiting patiently for me. I dump the accumulated rainwater out, climb in, and begin paddling. My compass once again perched in front of me, I aim the nose of the craft north by northeast, and pray I'm not too late.

CHAPTER
THIRTEEN

On my way to the Mound, since I really didn't know where I was going or what to expect, I pretty much took my time, playing it cautious and safe. That's all changed. Now I'm paddling so fast the nose of the kayak is out of the water, and I'm actually creating a wake behind me, an ever-widening V that is quickly erased by the rain. My arms are aching and my breath is coming in great gasps, but I can't slow down. I need to get to Church Island before Hunter does. My mind keeps devising horrible things that Hunter and his minions could be doing. The problem is that any and all of them could be accurate. Nobody except me knows what he's really like.

My immediate target, however, is Rumpke Mountain. My directional sense tells me Google's home is almost directly on the path to Church Island. I'm afraid Hunter will stop there first. I try to tell myself I don't care about anyone there except Simon, but deep down I know that's not the case; there are dozens of innocent kids living on that filthy trash heap, and, like it or not, I know we could use Google and his freakish intelligence. As I found out when I was tricked into capturing that Gray for him, the mad little genius sometimes has his own agenda, and he's got the personality of a stump — but saving him is the right thing to do. I'll need him, I'm sure of it.

But I have to get there first.

Before I know it I'm flying past the dead antenna towers, the ones I saw on my trip out, and I'm heartened I'm on the right course. I don't slow down, although if my arms simply fell off from exhaustion I wouldn't be surprised. I pause for a moment to catch my breath, my heart threatening to punch out of my chest, then I'm back at it again. My paddle smacking into the putrid water is loud. It's the only sound besides the rain and my heavy breathing. Thankfully the downpour has slowed down a little, and the winds have almost stopped. Still, visibility is next to nothing so I can't ask Ted to risk one of the drones for me. All I can do is trust my innate directional sense and the compass that sits dutifully in front of me. I hope I've pointed the kayak in the right direction.

Another hour or more goes by, and I'm starting to worry if I missed Rumpke Mountain altogether. As huge as the thing is, I can't believe I would, but I can't see more than a few dozen feet in front of me. Panic begins to chip away shards from the edge of my once rock-solid confidence.

Then I smell something foul, something stomach-turning and horrible, burned eggs mixed with pig manure and something else that even a skunk would run from. I know then I'm not far away. While my nose is screaming at me to get the hell out of there, my heart leaps. I'm getting close. The speed and ferocity of my strokes actually surprises me, and before I know it I'm almost flying across the water, travelling faster than I ever have before, the hull of the little kayak skimming as smoothly as a skipped stone.

Up ahead and way to the left I see a smudge of light. One of the flares on the flank of the mountain. I change course slightly and charge toward it.

Good god, I almost missed it. If I hadn't gotten close enough for the stench to hit me, I may have paddled right by the place. But now I head directly at it, the geyser of flame becoming more solid the closer I get. I aim the nose of the little boat directly where the road should be, the spot where BamBam is eternally stationed. As the mountain looms ever closer, I'm relieved to see that the only other boats tied up are the ones that were there before, the Jon boats we used for the grocery store raid. I don't see any that I don't recognize, which is a positive. The kayak runs aground, and I'm going so fast the entire thing ends up on the gravel and out of the water. I jump out, my fatigue forgotten.

"BamBam!" I scream, running up to the mounds where he hangs out. "BamBam, where are you?" I spin around, but he's nowhere to be seen.

Anxiously, I run up the wide gravel road, my poncho fluttering like a cape behind me. Halfway up I see something on the ground. It's a baseball bat, a black one with dents and scratches all up and down it. I quickly snatch it up and keep going. BamBam must have found a replacement, but he wouldn't have dropped it if he didn't have to…

A few dozen feet farther up the road, I spot something else on the ground, something that at first looks like a messy pile of red clothes. I stutter to a halt because I don't want to get close to it, but I can't help myself. Edging closer I'm pretty sure it's what's left of BamBam. Pieces of him are scattered all over the road, like he was being dragged by a mob as he was killed. Bones and blood and meat, that's all that's left of him. I've seen so many horrors like this I shouldn't be bothered by it, but that's not how I'm wired. Thick, hot sweat breaks out across my face, and I fall to my knees and puke, my gut heaving with the effort. I stay that way for a few seconds, head down, spitting out hot, thick mucus that's stuck to the back of my throat. When I'm done, I wipe my mouth with my sleeve, pick up the bat, and start back up the hill, not looking back. I increase my pace with each step.

When I reach the plateau, I sprint past flattened tents and the leveled remains of tin covered shacks. Peering into the deep holes as I run by them, I don't see or hear anything. But as I get closer to Google's building, I dodge around more tattered and bloody piles of human remains, trying to convince myself I don't see a mangled hand there or somebody's torso over there. I'm so horrified at everything I see around me I almost trip over a decapitated head, its nose and ears chewed off. I slap my hand over my mouth to smother a scream. My god, they never stood a chance. It was a massacre. No one, not even Google, expected Grays to be able to make it to Rumpke Mountain, especially not in these kinds of numbers. But then, no one expected a vicious bastard like Hunter and what he would and could do. I nearly throw up again when I'm forced to detour around the horrible remains of a dozen kids piled on top of each other, gnawed rib cages exposed to the elements. I can't help myself, and I feel terrible for it, but I utter a silent prayer of thanks that I haven't seen any bright blond hair among the shredded bodies.

I skid to a stop outside of Google's building. The grisly remains of several more bodies are strewn around the entrance, and I can only imagine they were trying desperately to get in when they were attacked. The cinder block walls still stand, but the steel door is scraped and decorated with several shiny new silver dents, deep round ones with the paint blasted off, something that can only be caused by bullets fired from close range. But the door held. The whole building held. This is one brick house that the big bad wolf couldn't blow down. I try the doorknob, but it's locked, not that I expected otherwise.

"Google!" I yell, pounding on the door with my palm. "Google! It's me, Scout! You in there?"

At first I don't hear anything, but then there's noise behind the door. Some clothes rustling. A foot scuffing the floor. Whispers. No, several people, whispering and arguing.

"Scout? Is that you?"

I close my eyes and lean against the door, my knees momentarily buckling under me in relief. For the second time in as many minutes I say a prayer of thanks, and then chastise myself for being such a damn hypocrite for only praying at the worst of times.

"Simon, is that you? Are you okay?"

I hear some more arguing coming from within the building, two distinct voices now, clearer than before. My name is mentioned several times.

"Yeah, it's me," his small voice says. "Are…are you alone?"

I rest my forehead against the metal door. The rain has picked up again, and with my hood down the water is flowing into my eyes and mouth. I'm pretty sure I'm crying, but it's hard to tell.

"Yeah, I'm alone. There's no one else out here. Whoever was here is gone."

There's a buzz and a click, and the door inches open. Simon's pale face peeks out through the crack, his blond hair a tousled mess. When he sees me, he throws it open the rest of the way and leaps into my arms. Sobs wrack his small frame, his shoulders jerking up and down. Behind him stands Google, his eyes huge behind the thick glasses. He's awkwardly holding a pistol, like it might be radioactive, his hand trembling so hard I can't believe he hasn't dropped it. I'm sure he knows the mechanics and physics of how a weapon like that works, but I'm equally sure he has no practical idea how to use it. I finally peel Simon away from me, staring into his red-rimmed eyes.

"What happened?" I ask softly, although I'm sure I already know the answer. I can tell that neither of them is comfortable with the door open, especially with the gruesome remains of their friends scattered around the entrance. Simon quickly drags me inside, and they lock it behind me. It's stifling hot in here, like usual, but that's the least of my problems now. I reach out and take the pistol from Google's hand before he shoots himself in the foot. I place it on one of the dozens of shelves that line the walkway. My soaking wet poncho drips on some of his precious electronic equipment, but he's in too much shock to care. Both of them slump down on the shelves.

"I…I don't know what happened," Simon starts after taking a deep breath. His voice cracks, and he has to clear his throat to keep going. When he talks, his eyes don't focus on me, or anything else, really, except perhaps on the memory that is permanently wired into the fabric of his brain. "I mean, one minute I was in here," he tilts his head toward Google, "doing some work for him. Cleaning up the storeroom and stuff, taking inventory. And then there was all this shouting and screaming. We couldn't see much because of the rain. But people were running and yelling, and then we saw all these Grays. They were everywhere, and they were tearing people apart, and eating them!" He stutters to a halt, and tears begin pouring down his dirty cheeks, each one leaving a path of clean skin behind, as if they were trying to wash away the horror he's seen. They roll off his cheeks onto the ground at his feet.

I take a deep breath. "Okay, what happened next?" I urge softly, although I can imagine what it must have been like. I've seen what Grays can do to people.

He exhales through pursed lips and runs a hand through his hair. "I don't know. Not really. We were standing in the doorway here, watching, trying to figure out what to do and if we could help. But we couldn't! I tried to shut the door, but a Gray crashed into us and knocked me down. It picked up Google by the neck, and I swear it was about to start pulling him to shreds, and then she came out of nowhere and attacked it."

I turn and stare at him, focusing on what he just said. "She? What are you talking about? Who tackled it?"

Simon points to the back of the room, near the workbench. There, sitting on the ground with its arms wrapped around its knees, is the Gray I captured earlier. The netting is gone except for some shreds of it around its ankles and neck. Somehow it broke free of the nets. As far as I can tell, nothing but air is keeping it restrained now. It's just sitting there, staring at us with its stupid, dead eyes.

"She killed the other Gray," Simon tells me. "She ripped it to pieces."

Now it's my turn to sit down, although to be honest my first reaction is to whip out Chuck and end this monster's life right now and add to my tally. In my head, I hear a voice say *two hundred and forty-three*. I shove some equipment aside and perch my butt on the edge of the shelf. I point to the Gray, and I'm surprised to see Chuck is in my hand, his deadly point aimed directly at the creature.

"You're telling me that thing saved you two?"

Simon nods. "Yeah, she ripped it to pieces and threw it outside. I've never seen anything like it. And that gave me enough time to close and lock the door. Grays started banging on it outside, but they couldn't get through. Then someone came and was yelling at us to open it up. Whoever it was even shot it a couple of times, but they couldn't get in. After a while, all the noise stopped. I guess they went away. We've been hiding in here ever since. Until you got here."

"You said someone was yelling. Did you see who it was?"

He shakes his head. "No. I never did."

I try another angle. "This guy who was yelling. Did he have a southern accent?"

Simon thinks for a minute. I'm not sure he would know a southern accent if he heard one. He doesn't answer, but Google finally breaks his silence.

"Yes. Yes, he did. Very pronounced. You know who it was, don't you?"

My head falls into my hands and I stare at my feet. My boots are covered in mud tinged with red. "Yeah, I know him."

I never told Simon or Google much of what happened to me before I first showed up at Rumpke Mountain. It didn't seem important. Google knows about Lord, but I never wanted to talk about Hunter. The memory of who Hunter is, what he did to me and the rest of us, is too raw. Looking back, perhaps I should have, but I'm not sure it would have made any difference.

Google is slowly rejoining the land of the living, his distracted, distant expression coming back into focus. Just looking at him, I can see his mind is waking up behind his thick glasses. He's raised one eyebrow, thinking.

"So, you're telling me this Hunter person has all your powers, plus more? He can somehow control his group of Grays? His – what did you call them? His minions?"

Simon snorts, the recent horrors momentarily forgotten, supplanted by a happier memory. "Minions? You mean like those funny yellow guys in that movie?"

Okay, apparently Simon has seen *Despicable Me*. "Well, yes. Kind of. Bad guys have helpers. That's what a minion is. I don't know what else to call them. Slaves? His army?"

"Minions will do fine," Google says.

"So yes, it would seem he can. I don't know how, but somehow they do what he wants." I explain what happened when Hunter captured me on the Mound, and what Ted and I saw from the drone, with Hunter and his boats of obedient Grays. I choke back a sob, feeling my eyes well with tears again. The guilt of my absence pushes hard against my chest. "I was coming here to warn you about him. If I had gotten here sooner, none of this would have happened."

Google, ever Mr. Practical, shakes his head. "I doubt that. All that would have happened is that you would likely be dead, too. As you said, you could possibly take on Hunter by himself, but a small army of Grays would have been too much. We were doomed the moment they set foot here. Some others may have made it safely inside here, but who's to say?"

I know he's not trying to make me feel better, because that's just not the way his mind works. But he's right – against a concerted force like Hunter's, I don't know what I could have done. We would have been outnumbered and overwhelmed. I'd probably be dead now, too. I nod and wipe my face. I'm thankful for the excuse, even if I don't feel like I deserve it.

"Yeah, probably. I guess. I don't know."

Google stands. "Not probably. It's a fact. Now we'd better get ready to go."

If there's one thing Google is good at, which he's demonstrated time and again, it's catching me off guard. "Go? What do you mean? Go where?"

"It's clear we can't stay here. Right? This Hunter person knows where we are, and could come back at any moment to finish what he started. We need to pack up as much equipment and food as we can and leave for your Church Island. It's the only safe place to go."

My head swivels from him to Simon, and they're both staring back at me. Simon tilts his head and nods.

"He's right. We can't stay here."

"From what you've told me," Google continues, "that island is fairly well-fortified. They are trained and armed and can likely hold their own against Hunter and his army of Grays. We'll pack as many boats as we can with supplies and leave immediately. We've got to get ahead of them and get there first."

Damn, if he isn't right. Hunter could come back and attack at any moment. Plus, the system Google set up here has been wiped out. No more people, no more digging, no more scrounging raids, no more barter system. It's over. He could stay holed up here in his cinder-block lair for a while, but it's just a matter of time before he runs out of food. I nod at him.

"Okay. I agree. Let's get packed up and go. We'll leave as soon as we're done." My gaze drifts back toward his workbench where the Gray is watching us in silence. "What about that thing?"

Google doesn't hesitate. "Susan? Oh, we'll take her, too."

"Yeah," Simon agrees. "She saved our lives. We take Susan, too, or we don't go. All for one, you know?"

Susan? Oh, god. They named the damn thing.

CHAPTER
FOURTEEN

Agreeing we have to leave is the easy part. What's hard is convincing Google to abandon all his treasures and take only food. Well, food and weapons.

He's incensed when I tell him flat-out he can't take any of his salvaged electronic gizmos. They're heavy, and take up too much room. They're basically worthless. We don't need any of it. He rants and stomps around with his hands up on the sides of his head. The only way I finally get him to see it my way is when I remind him the Grays could come back any time. That stops him in his tracks, and he exhales so long and hard I don't know how he simply doesn't deflate. I'm not sure, but he may have actually sobbed once. Then he wordlessly turns away, and begins gathering up cans of food from his accumulated stores.

We make lots of trips down to the boats and back. I figure we'll load up three of them. Simon and Google can row one and tow my kayak; I'll lash the other to mine and pull it behind me. We won't break any speed records, which worries me, but without supplies we won't make it very far. It's a long way to Church Island. We'll stick to the water the entire way and hope we won't have to portage anywhere.

We're about ready to go when Google points to his shortwave radio.

"We have to take this," he states flatly. "We can leave the rest, but we have to take it."

I shake my head. "No. Absolutely not. It's too heavy and it'll take up too much room. We don't need it."

"I disagree. Those radios you have are only good for line-of-sight communication and have very limited range. They probably won't work beyond ten or fifteen miles. With a proper antenna and the right atmospheric conditions, I can communicate with nearly anyone around the world. Even with that Ted person at the Mound. Something like that could be invaluable."

I eventually give in to this final demand, although I have my doubts. But if this is what it takes to move him along, then so be it. With sure movements of his small hands, he disconnects several wires one at a time and hands me a stack of metal boxes, including the receiver. The antenna looks like a miniature version from something on the roof of a house. He folds it up and stashes it away.

"Really? All this?" I ask, hefting the equipment. The battery is particularly heavy, even for me.

"Yes. We'll need the receiver, the power supply,

battery, speaker, and the rest. This unit is sophisticated and expensive. It probably cost thousands of dollars." I resist rolling my eyes, and quickly lug the awkward equipment down to the boats, then cover everything with a plastic tarp and lash it all down nice and tight. The three boats are riding low on the water, and that's without any of us on board. My two companions are going to have a helluva time keeping up with me once we're underway.

A few minutes later I'm back. Somewhere Google conjured up a map of Ohio, and has it spread out across his workbench. I peer over his shoulder and reach down.

"We're here," I tell him, pointing. Then I slide my finger due north several inches. "Church Island is way up here. It'll take us at least a week or more to get there, and that's if we don't run into any trouble."

Simon is staring at it, too. I'm not sure if he understands the relationship between where we are, where we're going, and how challenging it will be. I doubt he's ever seen a map before. I leave them inspecting it and take one more look around the building. I'm tempted to grab more supplies, but I resist, although it's killing me to leave all this behind. Finally, we're all standing together, ready to go. I tilt my head toward the Gray.

"What about that thing?" I ask, refusing to use the name they gave it.

Without a word, Google opens up two cans

of tuna and dumps them on a plate. He takes it to the Gray and places it on the ground at its feet. With quick motions the Gray scoops up handfuls of the white meat and shoves it into its mouth, barely chewing. Then it licks the plate clean and stares at him. Google ties a thin rope to its wrist and tugs.

"Come on, Susan, let's go," he says.

The Gray dutifully allows itself to be led along behind him. He turns to me, deadpan, like having an obedient Gray on a leash is an everyday occurrence. I couldn't be more shocked if the little genius had sprouted wings and drifted into the air. Simon glances between the two of us, smiling at my slack jaw and arched eyebrows.

"Now we're ready. Let's go," Google says, with another light tug on the leash.

I shake my head, completely blown away that this little man has a full-grown Gray on a leash, and it's not happily tearing him to shreds. We leave the building, and Simon pulls the door shut behind him. Google takes a small device from his pocket and pushes a button. I hear a buzzing sound as he remotely locks the door. That's handy. No one will be raiding what we're leaving behind, apparently.

Doing everything we can to ignore the death all around us, we march in single file down to the boats. There are no vultures overhead yet, but there will be. As we pass by the flaming methane torch, the Firebrand in me wishes we could somehow capture and take some of that blessed flame with us, but we have no way of keeping a fire going. The warmth of it as we move beyond it is fleeting, as it always is.

Once we're underway, it only takes a short time on the water to figure out our arrangement isn't going to work. Google has the upper body strength of a garden gnome, and while Simon tries like hell, he can't row for very long before he's panting and exhausted. The Gray is seated behind them in their boat, and I fleetingly wish I could teach the stupid creature to row, like Hunter did with his minions. My earlier estimation it would take a week or so to get to Church Island is way off. At this rate, our supplies will run out long before we get there.

"Sorry, Scout," Simon says, panting as he falls back into the boat. "This is a lot harder than I thought it would be."

I can't be mad at them, although for some reason I am. Without a word, I pull my second boat up close and climb in. I carefully step to the back, thankful I've been blessed with good balance, and toss them a rope. Simon catches it on the first try.

"Here. Tie this to yours, and I'll see if I can pull everything. You guys do what you can to help."

They lash their boat to my second one, and we've got a waterborne wagon train: mine, followed by my cargo boat, then theirs, with the kayak bobbing gently behind them. I slot the two oars into the locks, turn around backwards, and start rowing. At first it feels like I'm simply exerting a lot of energy and anchored in place, but eventually all four crafts line up and we start inching forward. I've got my compass on the seat behind me to make sure I keep my bearings, and once the convoy is moving, I put my head down and keep going. The sequence of movements soon becomes my new normal: lean forward, dip oars in the water, pull back with my arms, back and legs, lift the oars out of the water, and start all over again. It's monotonous, but at least we're making progress. I glance up once in a while, and each time I do I can tell Rumpke Mountain is shrinking in size behind us. Soon enough, distance and the misting rain has obscured it from view, and we're alone on the water. I'm not sad to see it go.

We do this all day long. At one point I call for a break, and we eat some food. Google feeds a can of something to the Gray, and I try to hide my resentment that he's giving valuable supplies to that thing. There's not much talking, mainly because I'm pretty pooped, but also because I think Simon is a little ashamed that he can't do more to help. I take this opportunity to carefully pull the small radio out of my backpack. I twist the top knob and push the red button.

"Ted, are you there?"

Almost immediately there's a burst of static, and Ted's excited voice says, "I'm here, Scout. Everything okay? What's going on?"

I'm sure he was parked on a stool in the Clean Room, hunched over the radio, just waiting for me to call and break up his monotony. I briefly fill him in on what's happened so far, not going into any detail surrounding the massacre we left behind. But what I'm really interested in is what's ahead of us.

"Can you take one of the drones out and find us?" I ask. "I just want to make sure we're not headed into any immediate danger."

"Sure. Larry is charging in its cradle right now, but Curly is ready to go. Keep your radio on, and I'll be back in touch soon. Hang tight."

I really don't want to wait, and I tell him that. "We'll keep going, but I'll turn the radio back on once I hear the drone."

Google perks up for a moment. "Larry? Curly?"

"Yeah, he named them. I don't know why."

Simon perks up. "Larry and Curly? What about Moe?"

I tilt my head at him. "How did you know the other drone was named Moe?"

He laughs, and it's a great sound, fun and happy, and something we don't hear nearly enough. "The Three Stooges? You guys don't know who the Three Stooges are? Old time black and white TV show? Funny as hell?"

I'm beginning to understand Simon must have enjoyed a lot of television before the Storm.

"Me and my brother watched them all the time with my dad. They were hilarious," he continues, pleased that for once he knows something we don't. Google and I exchange a look, and I shrug.

"Nope. That's a new one to me. "

For the next few minutes, he regales us with stories of these three morons his family used to watch together. To me it seems like a lot of unnecessary violence, with too much punching, slapping, and people getting beaned on the head with cast iron skillets. But it's clear Simon liked them, and he's cheerful for once, and that warms my heart. Still, no wonder my parents never let me watch them. My mom would have hated it.

The break over, I grab the oars again and we move out. Quite a while later I stop, because I swear I hear something. A weird buzzing noise, high in the sky. I look up, but I can't see anything. I turn on the radio to a burst of static.

"Scout, I see you. Three, no, four boats with you at the helm?"

"Yes, that's us. I hear the drone but can't see anything."

"Hold on," he says, and seconds later the buzzing gets louder, and then I see a black shape, a rectangular body with four arms topped with whirling blades, hovering above us. I'm impressed with how steady the little craft is in the air. The whole thing is no bigger than a dinner plate. Behind Google and

Simon, the Gray starts to thrash around, making the boat list dangerously from side to side. I'm tempted to pull my own version of the Three Stooges and crack the thing on the head to settle it down.

"Do me a favor and fly ahead a few miles and make sure nothing's in front of us."

"Will do," he answers.

The drone tilts to one side and buzzes off. As soon as it's gone, the Gray settles back down. Interesting. Google and I exchange another look with each other, and he shrugs at my unspoken question. I start rowing again. The constant drizzle runs down my face, but it feels cool on my skin, and I'm okay with it. Sometime later, my radio crackles again.

"Ted?"

"Nothing up ahead for miles, Scout. I went all the way up past where downtown Dayton used to be, and it's all clear."

I thank him, and promise to check back in again. He wistfully says goodbye, saying he'll keep looking around until he's got to bring Curly back to charge. We sign off.

"Those drones could be undeniably useful," Google states. "Impressive."

I nod. Having the ability to scout ahead really eases my mind. For as long as I can remember, we've never been able to know what we're about to get into, good, bad, or ugly. Knowing what's ahead, and what to avoid, will make this trip so much easier.

Even so, I honestly don't know what I'll do if we come across Hunter and his Grays. I can't fight them, not on the water. And Hunter is such a good shot he could probably pick us off from a distance. I could quickly unhitch the boats and row like mad, but that would only be a short-term solution. No, right now I have to rely on the drones to make sure that doesn't happen. Avoiding them now is our only hope.

"Did you see what that drone noise did to the Gray?" Google asks.

"Yeah, I did. I was going to ask you about that. Why would it act like that?"

"I don't know why it would, but it's good information. Maybe we can use it to our advantage sometime."

"They didn't like the noise in the parking lot, either," I recall, thinking out loud.

I row until the dim light starts to fade and even my arms have begun to ache. As strong as I am, I have my limits, too. We grab another bite to eat, and Google feeds his pet Gray again. As we tug our ponchos over us for the night, I stare at the creature as it finishes its meal. I'm not at all comfortable with it back there in the other boat with Google and Simon, especially not while they sleep.

"You two," I say, pulling their boat alongside mine. "Come over to my boat and sleep here tonight. I don't trust that thing."

Both of them start to protest, but I'm not giving in, not this time. With some low grumbling from Google, both of them clamber over to my boat and make themselves as comfortable as they can in the tight space. They squirm around until they're almost nose to nose with each other, their legs curled up underneath them. The Gray doesn't seem to care that it's got the boat to itself now. I force myself to stay awake for as long as I can while the two of them fall asleep, making sure that monster doesn't try anything. Despite my best intentions, eventually I drift off, the gentle hiss of the rain surrounding us like soft static. The last time I had to sleep in a boat in the rain I had Singer snuggled up beside me, his arms holding me tight against what could have been a total meltdown on my part. I desperately wish he were here again.

CHAPTER
FIFTEEN

The next morning is just like any other, rainy and dismal. I'm sure the sun is up in the sky somewhere, but it's playing hide and seek behind the leaden blanket of clouds, like it always does. We grab a bite to eat, and I realize how spoiled I'm getting with all this food. It's basically three meals a day, with a snack or two tossed in for good measure. Soon after, I start rowing again. Anyone else's arms and back would be screaming in agony from yesterday's work, but mine feel just fine. Bless you, healing power.

True to Ted's word, we soon pass by downtown Dayton, the top of the black skyscraper mere feet above the waterline. The last time I came here was after we captured the Gray, and BamBam was so badly injured he could hardly move. I try to put the memory of that quiet, kind kid out of my mind, but I'm not at all successful. His bloody and gruesome remains on the road will haunt me for the rest of my days, however long that will be.

Memory is a funny thing. So many of the good

times I shared with my family before the Storm have faded, like they've lost their edge and have grown fuzzy around the corners. Half the time I'm not sure if my memory is correct, or if I'm trying so hard to recall events I'm actually making things up. I have vivid recollections of certain things, like going to Kings Island and riding the roller coasters, or a day at the beach up on Lake Erie, but so much of the rest is either a blur or simply gone. In fact, there are times when I can barely remember what my mom and dad looked like. I mean, I have a general idea, but many of the specifics are gone. My dad told me he broke his nose in college, and I know it was always a little crooked, but I can't remember which way it was bent.

Balance that with events that have happened since the Storm began, and those mental visions are as clear as if they happened yesterday, like those pathways of my mind are forever frozen in place. I will never forget every single detail of what took place on Rumpke Mountain, the mangled bodies and heaps of blood-soaked clothing. I can also remember any little detail I want for each Gray I've killed, like what gender each one was, or what shreds of clothing they still had on. It's not fair, that's what it is. I can easily recall what I don't want to, but can't remember the good stuff. I wish for the hundredth time I had taken some pictures of my family with me when we fled Cleveland. I try to convince myself there was no time, but that does nothing to ease my pain.

Dayton is behind us now, the remains of the skyscraper long gone. Before, when I found the grocery store on the hill, I headed west here. But now we keep going due north, following what is probably Interstate 75, the main highway that used to go from upper Michigan all the way down to Florida. In the distance to either side of us, we can see the dim shapes of hills peeking out of the water, but they're far away and nothing we want anything to do with. And if memory serves me correctly, which I'm pretty sure it does, the farther north we go, the flatter the land becomes, which is a good thing. Flatter land means more consistent water cover, and that means fewer Grays.

Fewer Grays, that is except for Hunter and his minions. I'm still coming to grips with all that. I can't for the life of me figure out how that SOB is controlling them, much less how he taught them to row a damn boat. I can't wrap my head around that.

I glance up from my exertions and check out the Gray behind Simon and Google. The creature is sitting with its head down, doing nothing at all, its long white hair dangling in front of it and covering its face. Just seeing it there makes me anxious. I stare at the thing, concentrating as hard as I can. I'm not really trying to make it do anything, at least I think I'm not. Honestly, I don't know what I'm trying to do. But I keep staring at it, my eyes boring holes into its head. Suddenly its head jerks up, its dead eyes staring right at me. It tilts its head to the side, like a dog listening to barking in the distance. My steady rowing abruptly stops when one of the oars pops out of the rowlock holding it in place. I apologize to no one under my breath and fit it back in, then start rowing again, although my cadence has been shot. I'm not at all sure if something happened there with that Gray, or if its reaction was just coincidence, but I'm uncomfortable just the same.

"You all right, Scout," Simon asks from his boat "You look a little pale. Need a break?"

"No," I assure him. "I'm fine. Just keep rowing. Every little bit helps."

I chance a look up again, and the Gray is still staring at me with its creepy, empty eyes. I lower my gaze and concentrate on getting back into the right rhythm again, purposefully ignoring the creature. Whatever just happened, if anything, has shaken me for reasons I don't understand.

Morning slowly leaks into afternoon. We take a few more breaks, and at each stop Google feeds his pet Gray. I still don't like it, but I've come to grips with it. A fed Gray is content, and the last thing we want is to be trapped on a small boat with one that's hungry, like that kid in *Life of Pi* who was stuck on a boat with a tiger. Still, it irks me that so much of our food is being given to that thing. Several times I visualize the creature accidentally tumbling overboard and sinking like a stone to the bottom. I'm sure I could make it happen if I tried, but I don't need Google and Simon pissed at me. Or do I? Would it even matter? This train of thought keeps me occupied until we stop for the night again. And just like we did the night before, I make both of them get into my boat. We toss our ponchos over us and bed down for another lousy night's sleep. The Gray sits in its boat by itself, not moving.

This goes on for days. We don't talk much, because we ran out of things to say early on in the trip, and I'm too tired. The days are so void of events we've got nothing new to discuss. I talk to Ted once in a while, and I've heard one of his drones overhead a couple of times. He insists we're headed in the right direction, and there is nothing of concern ahead of us. I soon lose track of the days, and don't know how long we've actually been out here. The boats are getting lighter as our food and water supplies dwindle. That's one positive, I guess.

A few days later we spot a smudge in front of us, a long, low ridge of ground that stretches from one dim horizon to the other. I ask Ted if there is any way around it. To my dismay, he says there isn't.

"It's a long, low hump of land with some buildings on it," he says, studying the view from several thousand feet up in the air. "There's really no way around it that I can see. Did you cross over this the last time you came through here?"

I shake my head before I remember he can't see me. "No, I don't think so. I think I went more to the west last time. This doesn't look familiar to me."

He tells us to hold tight while he checks it out. What has to be half an hour passes before he comes back online.

"I looked around as well as I could, and I didn't see anything dangerous. Just a few buildings. But I had to get Larry back before he ran out of juice. Want me to send Curly out and look some more? It will take a while."

I hesitate, considering. "You didn't see anything?"

"I took Larry down closer before I had to bring him back. Like I said, it's a thin strip of land. The buildings I saw are an old farmhouse and a barn. Several miles away there's the remains of a small town, but that's way out of your way."

I don't want to wait while his other drone makes it here. That could be hours I don't want to waste.

"We're going to keep going. How wide is it?"

"Um, if you go east a little bit, there's a section that's only a few hundred yards wide. Near the barn and house. That's your best bet, I'd say."

I drum my fingers on the gunwale while I think. "That barn and farmhouse. How'd they look? Maybe someplace to sleep tonight out of the boats?"

A pause. "Yes, from what I could tell. And not far from the water at all. I've been watching the whole area for a while now. There's nothing moving down there for miles in all directions."

I glance at my two passengers, noting how wet and miserable they are. Okay, we're all miserable. Sleeping in puddles in the bottom of a boat for nights on end will do that to you. We've got piss-poor attitudes, and I actually heard Simon snap at Google earlier today, which is totally not like him. I wouldn't even consider risking a night off the boats without our eye in the sky. But we could be warm and dry for once, and perhaps even start a fire in the house or the barn, maybe even cook some food. The temptation of being dry and sleeping under a roof with a fire is too much for me to pass up. Plus, I'm exhausted and sick to death of these damn boats.

"Do me a favor and send the other drone out to keep an eye on things. In the meantime, we're going to head in that direction."

"Okay," he answers. "But you'll be there before Curly will."

"I know. But you're sure it's clear for miles around, right?"

"Yeah."

"I can't imagine Grays would have any reason to travel all the way out here." I turn to my two passengers. "You guys heard all that. Have any problem with this? We'll spend the night and leave first thing in the morning."

Simon has no problem following my logic or my lead, and the potential for being off the water rings home with him, too. Google is less enthusiastic, but nods his agreement. Not that they need to know, but I probably would've done this without their consent. Even so, it's nice to know we're all on the same page.

Whether it's the thought of being off these damn boats, or the remote possibility of a hot meal, I actually begin picking up the pace, moving us along faster. Simon and Google have given up any pretense of rowing, since most of the time they do more harm than good, and they just hang on as we cruise across the water. As we near the thin ribbon of land, the buildings begin to materialize ahead of us. I can pick out the barn, a dirty white one with most of its roof still intact. Snuggled next to it is a two-story farmhouse, also a dirty white with dark windows, the window glass still intact. Sections of fencing stretch from the barn and dip into the water, vanishing below the brown surface. Tucked next to the house a tall TV antenna sticks straight up, piercing the low clouds as cleanly as a hypodermic needle pierces skin. Nothing moves that we can see.

"So we're going to spend the night here?" Google asks from his boat, voicing some second thoughts. "Are you sure that's wise?"

I'm not at all sure. Any time I set foot on solid ground I'm afraid I'm going to be attacked within seconds, mainly because that's happened to me in the past. Technically, we could quickly portage the boats and supplies over to the other side and head right back out on the water, but I don't want to. I take a long, measured look from one side of the ridge to the other, and as far as I can see before the brown land fades into the mist in either direction. The thought of a fire, a real meal, and a roof over our heads is just too tempting. Plus, Ted is bringing his other drone back as soon as he can, and that gives us a huge advantage.

"Yes, I'm sure. I'll check the area out before we do anything else. If it's clear, we'll take the boats and supplies over to the other side now, so they'll be ready first thing in the morning." Or, I add in my head, if we need to make a quick getaway. I keep that thought to myself, although I would imagine the two of them are thinking along the same lines.

I row us up to the shoreline and step out of the boat. I wobble for a second while I get my land legs back, then slide Chuck from his sheath.

"Stay here," I tell them unnecessarily, neither one showing any inclination to leave the safety of the boats. "I'll be back soon."

For the first few steps, the ground is soft and squishy under my boots, and I sink down a few muddy inches in the slop. The ground itself is covered with dead grass that has gone flat and brown from so much dismal weather for more than half a decade. As I move higher up the slight hill, the soil firms up and walking gets easier. The barn is closest to me, so I aim for it first, always scoping things out right and left like my head is on a swivel.

I ease close to the barn and walk cautiously

around it first, peering inside the huge open doors and windows as I go. I have to hop over two different sections of broken-down wooden fencing. Satisfied that there's nothing outside, I take a slow step in. Immediately, I'm plunged into deep shadow, and the sound of the rain pattering against my poncho ceases. The sudden silence is strange to ears used to the constant white noise of rain. As my eyes begin to adjust to the darkness, I can see there are built-in stalls along both walls, thick, heavy-duty ones made of solid wooden planks and thick posts. Up top, above the stalls, is a storage area loaded with straw or hay bales. There's an office of some sort at the other end, taking the place of one of the stalls.

I'm getting a good vibe from this place, so I slip Chuck back into his sheath and climb a ladder to the upper level. Prowling around, I quickly discover there's nothing up here but me and the bales and a lot of cobwebs, most of which end up in my hair and face. Once I'm back on the ground, I stick my head in each stall, one at a time. There's a pleasant, musky smell in here, a lingering scent of large animals and feed. Horses, I would guess. It's nice. The office is nothing more than a desk and a toppled over chair. A faded calendar with a scene of horses grazing in a pasture is on the wall. Whoever lived here took good care of this place. I like it.

I head out the other door and wave at my two companions. Simon waves vigorously back. Heartened that we're probably alone here, I jog over to the farmhouse and circle around it. On the back side, away from the water, I notice some long narrow areas of turned dirt. Unless I'm mistaken, and I don't think I am, it's two separate rectangles of what is probably a pair of graves. One is older than the other, the ground flatter and with a few determined weeds, while the other is relatively new, the soil not yet completely smoothed over by the constant rain. And the plots are long, not graves for kids. Okay, so who in the world buried them here? Someone took the time and effort, and that someone might still be hanging around. Internal warning lights go off, and I begin to proceed more cautiously than before, my earlier optimism tempered.

I ease into the back door of the house through a screen door, a metal one that's discolored with age. It creaks a little as I open it and I wince. I slip farther into the first room, a small mudroom with an ancient washer and dryer tucked in the back. Old boots line the wall, and a mat with a large "WELCOME FRIENDS" is thick with dried mud from people tramping in from outside. The mudroom leads to a tidy kitchen, full of knick knacks on shelves, little figurines of all shapes and sizes, happy little people full of smiles and in different poses. I gently pick one up, a little angel with outstretched wings, white with gold trim. A window over the large white sink looks out over the yard with the barn beyond that. I'd guess this was a kitchen of an older couple, someone who was probably happy living day to day, just getting by. My grandparents died when I was little, so I never knew them, but mom and dad said they lived on a farm at one time. I imagine they might have called a place like this home.

The rest of the house is cozy, but threadbare. Armchairs with cushions sunken down from lots of butt-time, carpet worn in paths where the owners walked from room to room, old photos of smiling people and their pets. I pick up a picture of an older smiling couple, sturdy in their advanced years, gray hair and glasses. At their feet are two Border Collies, and it strikes me how much I miss the companionship of dogs. The remainder of the first floor is this living room, complete with a fireplace on the outer wall and a small bathroom with just a toilet and a tiny sink. Carefully, I go up the narrow stairs to the second floor. I walk on the outside of the steps, trying to minimize any creaking. There's not much up here, just two bedrooms with small beds, still made up, and another bathroom with a claw-foot tub. I peek into each closet and under each bed, but there's nobody here. Somehow, and I don't know how, but I can tell I'm alone here, and I breathe a sigh of relief. I make my way back downstairs.

Glancing around the living room, I'm impressed at how well kept the place is. It's a modest home, but the roof is intact and the entire house is dry and cozy. Honestly, I haven't been in anything this nice in months. Hardly any structure like this survives six years of constant rain, total neglect, and desperate groups of people like me. In my mind, I've already picked the bed I'm going to sleep in tonight.

I look around one more time just to be sure there's nobody else here. I'm in the kitchen again, and I notice a door I didn't check out before. Opening it up, there are narrow, dark stairs leading down to a cellar. In a horror movie, the horrible monster would be hiding down here, waiting for the stupid, big-boobed teenagers to go down there. Plus, I don't like basements, not after what I went through on Church Island. I clamp down my discomfort and force myself to put my foot on the first step on the groaning stairway, holding onto the railing that's smooth with age and the grips of a thousand hands. With each step I take, the air temperature drops a few degrees, until it can't be much over a very cool and comfy fifty-five degrees at the bottom. Tiny windows reluctantly permit some dusky light in, enough to see the floor is packed dirt, and shelves line the rough stone walls. Each shelf holds several dozen Mason jars, their oxidized silver lids barely visible in the gloom. Inside the jars are pickles, green beans, and all sorts of other vegetables. How has nobody found this place yet and picked it clean? If the previous owners knew their stuff and canned all this correctly, we'll be eating well for weeks. I mutter a soft thanks under my breath. Excited to share the news, I hustle back up the steps and out into the yard. My two companions aren't as excited as I am about the canned goods, but I think it's because they're too young to know what I'm talking about.

An hour later, and I've portaged the boats and most of the supplies to the other side of the ridge. Ted was right. It's only a few hundred yards wide, and the view from the other side is more open water as far as I can see. Simon and Google helped carry a lot of the food, although I got stuck lugging the short-wave radio over myself. Google tied his pet Gray up to the fence, and it watched us make a dozen trips back and forth. It sat with its back against a post and did little more than dig in the dirt and pick at the grass nearby. I try to ignore it, but having a Gray so close still makes me twitchy.

Before the meager sunlight fades for the day, we hear a buzzing noise above us, and we spy one of Ted's drones overhead. I dig the radio out of my pack and fire it up.

"Hey, Ted, we see the drone. Anything to report?"

"Nope. Nothing that I can see. I went all up and down the ridge just to make sure. You guys spending the night there, right? You sure that's a good idea?"

"We'll be fine," I assure him. "We've got the boats all set for a quick getaway if we need it. We've got several guns, too. We're not going to be here long enough for anything to happen."

Ted doesn't sound convinced, and although I don't blame him, our minds are made up. Well, mine is. We talk a little more, then he gooses the drone and off it goes to scout around some more before he has to charge it back up. The three of us watch it buzz away, then head into the house for the night. The screen door as it slams behind us is a wonderful, homey sound that takes me back to happier times.

Inside, Google prowls around the kitchen and living room. Behind a picture on the mantel, he picks something up and holds it high, as proud as a runner lifting the Olympic torch to the skies. It's a red Bic lighter, something so commonplace in the old days, but so very rare now. He flicks the wheel and a tidy yellow flame dances on it. A huge smile breaks out on my face, and apparently it's such a novel expression that these two stare at me in wonder, as if I've lost my mind. Do I really not smile that often?

"Come on, guys," I tell them. "It's an actual working lighter! We can have a fire tonight! How great is that?"

There's still logs stacked next to the fireplace, like the previous inhabitants just up and left one day. There's no kindling of any kind, so I rush out to the barn and grab a handful of dry straw. Within minutes I've got a nice little blaze going. I might be concerned someone might see or smell the smoke, but it's dark outside and Ted assured me there's nobody around. Memories of better times with Lord and Singer along with my stint as the Firebrand flood my mind and fill me with a different kind of warmth. We retrieve some old pots from the kitchen and fill them with cans of beef stew. Within minutes, the wonderful aroma of food fills the small living room, and it's all I can do not to stick my face in and devour it right out of the pot.

Simon has located some colorful ceramic bowls, and we ladle the steaming stuff into them, all the way to the brim. Each and every one of us burns our mouths as we shovel the too hot beef stew into our mouths, but we don't care, laughing at our joint misery. I bring up some jars of pickles from the cellar and crack one of them open. There's a hissing pop, and the tangy aroma of vinegar fills the room, overwhelming the warm smell of the main course. We devour all of the stew, including every drop of thick broth, plus several pickles each, then sit back and do nothing but stare at the fire as it pops and snaps beyond our feet. As the light outside fades away, my radio crackles and Ted's voice breaks the silence.

"I gotta get Larry back," he says apologetically. "As soon as Curly is charged I'll send him out to keep an eye on you guys. But it'll be a few hours, at least."

My feet are hot and my stomach is full. I'm completely dry for the first time in days. My eyelids drooping, I assure him that it's okay. We're going to bed down for the night soon. He signs off, and I turn my radio off to save power. The three of us are in no hurry to move. To be fair, I'm not sure we could if we wanted to. The Gray is tied up in the kitchen, out of sight of the fire and away from us. Finally, Simon stirs.

"I'm going to bed," he mumbles around a yawn so huge I'm surprised he doesn't crack his jaw. "I'm pooped. Anyone got dibs on the beds?"

"I was going to claim the one in the far room," I tell him. "But I've changed my mind. I'm going to stay down here and keep the fire going. You two head upstairs."

I get no argument from either of them. I hear the two of them clomping around upstairs for a little while as they get ready, and some murmuring as they say goodnight to each other. I'm left downstairs with my fire. I tenderly place a few more logs on it, then sit back and lean against the couch. My mom called a couch a davenport for some reason, I remember. I smile at the memory.

The fire dancing at my feet, I close my eyes and drift off, content for the first time in ages.

CHAPTER
SIXTEEN

When I was the Firebrand, I had this uncanny ability to wake up during the night to feed the fire. I say it was uncanny, because it was. In all the time I was in charge of the fire, I never overslept to the point where it was too far gone to revive. It was a point of pride that I never let my companions down. But, there's a first time for everything, right?

I crack open an eye, and the windows on either side of the fireplace are rectangles of dim light. Of course, I have no idea what time it is, but enough light is coming through the dirty glass that I can tell it's late morning. Cursing to myself, I scramble over to the fireplace where I'm greeted with nothing but cooling ash and the stubs of a few blackened logs. I growl under my breath for being so irresponsible, until I remember we have an actual lighter and I can start another fire if I want to. Hell, we could start a hundred of them! Still, I'm the Firebrand and I shouldn't have let this happen. I stand and stretch, and once again I'm amazed at how good I feel. My ability to rejuvenate myself so quickly still astounds me.

I hear a noise from the kitchen and stick my head in. The Gray is standing and pacing back and forth, moving only as far as the tether will allow it. The stupid thing could snap that leash with a strong yank, but for some reason it hasn't. Regardless, for some reason it's agitated and I'm half tempted to yell up to Google to get down here and take care of it. The dumb creature is probably getting hungry or something.

"Hey," I bark at it. It stops and stares at me. "Quit it. Settle down or you're going outside."

Not waiting to see if it had a clue what I was talking about, I head to the little bathroom. Once there I turn on a spigot, hoping to see water to pour out, like the drinking fountain did at the Mound. Sadly, nothing at all happens. I don't know why, but I'm mildly disappointed by that. The rest of the place is in such pristine shape I half expected the silly thing to work.

Back in the living room, I take my time and stuff my few belongings in my backpack. My book is still safely tucked away, along with my precious Milky Way bar. Without really thinking about it, I turn on the radio. I jump when Ted's panicked voice streams out.

"…to get out of there now! Scout, there are Grays heading your way!"

I frantically push the button over and over, but

this thing's not like a phone, and I can't transmit until he stops talking. Finally, there's a pause while he catches his breath.

"Ted! Ted!" I yell into the break. "This is Scout. What's happening?"

"Oh, my god, Scout! Thank god! Where have you been, young lady? I've been calling for an hour! Grays are headed your way. Dozens of them! Maybe more! They're coming from the town!"

Still grasping the radio, I run to the bottom of the stairs. Cupping my free hand around my mouth, I scream upstairs.

"Google! Simon! We've got to go! Grays!"

I can hear thumps and running feet on the floor above me, then the two of them tumble down the steps and into the living room, eyes wide, still pulling on their clothes.

"What's happening?" Google shouts.

"Ted just told me Grays are coming from the town. A lot of them. Grab your stuff and let's go!"

We sprint into the kitchen. I don't wait for Google to untie his creature. I grab the leash and snap it in two. The Gray, still agitated, follows us out the back door, the screen door banging loudly behind us.

The boats are right there where we left them. I'm faster than my companions, but I slow down to let them get ahead of me. I glance to my right, and my heart skips a beat at the sight. Grays, dozens of them, are charging towards us at full speed. I can't see them all, but the ones in the lead appear to have just recently changed. They aren't nearly as thin and hollow looking as most. But I don't have time to think about that now, because they are less than fifty yards away, so close I can hear their feet splashing in the mud. As I watch, they swerve slightly to cut us off from the boats.

"Google! Simon! Run faster!"

I slow down and whip Chuck out of his sheath. Damnit, I have to get to Church Island and warn them of what's coming, but there's no way I'm going to let these monsters touch Simon! I don't know how much damage I can do before they overwhelm me with their numbers, but I'm sure I can take out a few, hopefully enough to slow the rest down. I stop completely and take a deep breath, setting my feet on the slippery ground. Chuck is in front of me at the ready. I should be terrified, but I'm strangely calm. My breathing is steady, even after that mad sprint.

"Come and get me, you sons of bitches!" I scream as loud as I can to get their attention.

Just as the first one closes in, there's a blur to my left. Something moves fast from behind me. Google's Gray launches itself at the lead attacker, hands extended and its fingers curled into claws. I had forgotten how big it is compared to most. It slams into the lead Gray and flattens it, a tsunami of mud spraying in the air from the impact, then leaps to its feet and goes after two more. Before they can figure out what's happening, those two are flung into the air as it heaves them aside. The rest of the rushing Grays are momentarily confused, and their frenzied assault stutters to a haphazard halt. I don't dare look away, but I can hear my companions reach the boats and push off in a panicked jumble of activity.

Then the Grays charging toward us stop completely. I've never seen a group of them do that before, not when there's a meal standing right in front of them. But seconds later, I realize it's not me they're interested in. They look over their shoulders, and as one they take a step aside as smoothly as synchronized swimmers parting. Why do I suddenly have a bad feeling about this? Through the gap lumbers a lone Gray, a huge one, bigger than any of the others, stalking toward me with a singular purpose. Unlike any other Gray I've ever seen before, this one is thick with muscle and as solid as a boulder. Before this I'd only seen these things work in packs or three or four, and there was never a leader of any kind that I could tell. But this group is different, and my earlier optimism that I might live through this begins to slip away.

Google's Gray spots this newcomer and rushes it. The huge leader snatches it out of the air by the neck, our Gray kicking and swinging in silence. Effortlessly, the leader lifts it up, studies it for a split-second, and then slams it to the ground. There's an audible thud I feel through my boots as it smacks into the mud. I don't know if it's dead or not, but I don't see how anything could live through an impact like that. Then the huge Gray lifts its shaggy head, long white hair hanging in front of its eyes, and takes a step towards me. I know I should run. I really do. But for some reason my feet have grown roots, and I'm stuck in place watching it advance. Chuck seems very small and insignificant in my shaking hand, no more deadly than a butter knife.

The massive Gray steps closer until it's no more than ten feet away. Then it stops, staring at me with eyes that are much more alive than any Gray's should be, eyes so intense they bore into my head and punch twin holes out the back of my skull. It opens its mouth, working its lips carefully, like it's not accustomed to moving its face like that.

"Scout," it says, its voice the sound of gravel sliding out of a dump truck.

I jump back a step, because now that he's spoken, I suddenly see it. I'm so used to looking at these beings as monsters that I missed it. While so much of him has changed, the fine details of his face are the same: the spacing between his eyes, his thin nose, the shape of his face framed by the long white hair. Someone who didn't know him like me might not recognize him, but I do. He even carries himself the same way as before, the essence of confidence packaged in a body that moves with smooth efficiency, even though that body is now crisscrossed with scars that weren't there before.

It's my brother. It's Lord.

"Leave," he growls, the words so thick and unused it's hard to understand him. "Leave now."

I'm torn between running away in horror and rushing into his arms. My brother is still alive! He's much more Gray than before, for sure, but he's not nearly as far gone as he should be. I've never known one of these things to live more than a month or so after the change, but here he is, more than a year later. I stare deeply into his eyes, and there's more than a spark of my brother still in this massive creature planted in front of me.

"Oh my god, Lord," I shout, my voice leaping up a few octaves. "It's you! I finally found you!" I'm trying not to cry out of sheer happiness and relief, but to be fair I'm not doing a very good job of it. Tears of joy burst from my eyes. Several Grays around him take a menacing step my way, and he leaps between us. With a snarl, he smacks each one of them with such force they stagger backwards. I quickly realize his command over them is far from complete. I reach out for him, but he takes a step back.

"Leave," he repeats, lifting a massive arm and gesturing around him. "It's not safe here. You're not safe."

"Lord, I don't understand. What is this place? Who were the people living here?"

He moves his mouth, as if forming words is hard for him. "This place. We protect it. We protected them. They were…special."

Now it dawns on me who must have buried the people that lived here. For some reason they were being watched over by Lord and the rest of these Grays. And when they died, he must have been the one who buried them. But the graves are so large, adult-sized, and from the looks of the inside of the house, the inhabitants were clearly older. Probably very old. Grandparent old. And if that's the case, how did they live so long? Were they immune? Did they do the impossible and die of old age? Is that why he took care of them, why he said they were special? I have so many questions! But as much as I want to know all about these people, my immediate concern is the more pressing threat of Hunter.

"Lord, please help me. I haven't found a cure yet. I told you I would, and I've been trying, but I haven't. But right now we need your help even more. Hunter is trying to kill us."

He doesn't speak, but his ashen face turns down into a scowl that's so like the one I would see when we were kids, when he was pissed off at some injustice. His open hands clench into fists and a deep snarl leaks from between his lips.

"Hunter?"

I hear a click behind me, and I whirl around. Simon is standing in one of the boats with his pistol leveled at Lord. The oversized gun is shaking in his small hands. He's lining up to take a shot.

"No!" I scream at him, my hands in the air,

palms up. "Put that down. I'm okay. It's okay." I'm proud of him for trying to protect me, but he doesn't understand what's going on. How could he? I don't wait to see if he's complied before I turn back to my brother.

"Yes! Yes, after you took a hike, we all made it to an island. There was a church. We lived there, safe from Grays. But Hunter shot Singer and would have killed me, too, if he could have. Hell, he tried again last week. Now he's going back there to get revenge. Carly, Annie, and Tiny are there. And maybe Singer. Come with me and help me stop him!"

"Church. Island. I know it."

"Yes, Church Island. Come with me. We'll find a cure and stop Hunter. Together!"

Behind him, Google's Gray is sitting up and shaking its head, dazed but alive. Somehow it gets to its feet and starts shuffling toward the boats. None of the others make a move to stop it. It wobbles by me, its footfalls heavy and clumsy, the stagger of a hardcore drunk on his way home at two in the morning. To be honest, after that thumping, I'm not sure how it's even standing, much less walking.

Lord shakes his head. "No. You are the Firebrand. You must find a cure," he says.

"Then help me. We'll do it together!"

"No. I can't leave. I made a promise to protect this place. You have to go. It's not safe for you here."

Frustration and anguish collide in my heart

and threaten to shatter it, like hot water poured over the ice of my hope. I've spent the last year searching for Lord, trying to find him so we can figure out how to combat whatever this affliction is that turns all of us into monsters. It's been my sole commitment and guiding purpose, the one reason that got me out of bed each day, even when I desperately wanted to stay there and pull the covers over my head and do nothing but read. All those Grays I killed, all two hundred and forty-three of them, died simply so I could continue my quest to find him. So we could be together again. Every single thing I've done these past months was geared toward finding him.

And now that I have, he's rejecting me.

My knees get weak and wobbly, and I nearly fall over. Chuck tumbles out of my limp grip and sticks point first in the ground with a moist thud. My hands cover my face, and I start crying again, although this time all joy has left me and only crushing sorrow remains. Then my legs call it quits and give out altogether, as I sink down to my knees in the mud, convulsing with sobs I have as much hope of controlling as I do of stopping the rain from falling. Of all the scenarios that I've played out in my mind, this is not one I ever imagined would happen.

Lord stays where he is, although the scowl etched into his face softens into something else. Compassion? Maybe pity? His broad shoulders slump, but he makes no move to comfort me. Instead, after a few seconds he turns to face his Grays and points in the other direction, back the way they came. Slowly, as if they heard an actual command from him, they turn and begin walking away, and I can see all of them share the same look of a recent change. Lord watches them go, and several moments pass before he gives me a final look over his shoulder. Our eyes lock.

"Don't come back. Please." He levels a finger at me. "Go. Be the Firebrand. Save us all."

My brain is a thick fog of despair, neurons no longer firing the way God intended. I hear his final words dimly, as if my head has been shoved under the putrid water that surrounds us. I know in my heart I won't return here. I will leave this place, and him, and I'll never set foot on his spit of land again. When I lift up my head, he's already a few dozen yards away, his broad back receding with every step. He may have given me a two-fingered salute, but I can't be sure. I watch through blurred eyes until he's lost in the hazy distance, and all that's left is me sobbing, alone, on the cold wet ground.

CHAPTER
SEVENTEEN

I have almost zero recollection of the rest of the day. The hours are a timeless blur of rain and the tinny sound of brown water smacking against the hull. I'm emotionally spent, my chest aching so badly that having my heart physically ripped out would be a blessing. I barely have the energy to keep from tumbling out of the boat. What do I do now? How can I go on in this horrible world now that Lord has rejected me? The goal of finding him, of being reunited with my brother, is what's kept me going. Now that's gone. I'm completely deflated, a sack of skin and bone that's empty of all emotion except misery. I'm as devastated as I was when we first realized he was going Gray, back in that office building. That feels like several lifetimes ago, although only a little more than a year has passed.

Simon does his best to comfort me, but I'm beyond help right now. Even Google tries in his clumsy fashion to lift my spirits, and his awkward attempts at conversation might have been funny if I weren't so out of it. But nothing is funny now. It's just me, a hollow shell, slowly breathing in and out because my body does that much on its own, with no thought about what I'm going to do next.

Later that evening I finally manage to drag myself back to now. I no longer have the overpowering urge to throw myself into a bottomless Sparta pit, like the one in that movie *300* Lord watched with his friends like a zillion times. I wipe tears and snot away from my face and see my two companions have made almost no progress at all. In fact, we're still so close to the ridge of land I can make out the faint shape of the barn through the misting rain. I mumble at the two of them to switch boats with me, and I throw myself into rowing. The mechanical activity serves to occupy a small sliver of my mind, which leaves less of my gray matter to focus on everything else. I have to concentrate on my strokes, and once I get into a good rhythm, Simon and Google sit back while our convoy of boats glides quickly across the brown water. I row harder and harder, throwing myself into the task. I'm not concerned with our destination. I just want to put as much distance as possible between us and the tract of land that quickly vanishes from view. I'm pulling so hard on the oars I'm peripherally worried I might hurt myself, but I don't care. I'm not sure we could go faster if I had a real motor on the back of this thing.

Night time comes, but even that doesn't slow me down. Eventually, it becomes so dark we can't see the compass anymore. Simon clears his throat.

"Um, Scout, why don't you save your strength and call it a night?"

I stop so fast the muscle memory of rowing makes my arms twitch. Without a word, I toss my poncho over my head and throw myself down in the bottom of the boat. The sound of them eating and getting ready to bed down for the night barely registers. I'm so physically and mentally exhausted I'm out before I know what hits me, a fitful sleep that's punctuated by visions of Lord before he changed, back when we were kids.

In the morning I stir early, before the others. The night's darkness is receding, the morning just beginning to be reclaimed by the obscured rising sun. I'm famished, and while I don't feel like eating anything, I know I have to keep my strength up for the good of the others. I mechanically eat two cans of cold beef stew and sample some dried pineapple from a plastic bag, not tasting any of it. The image of my brother, of what he's become, keeps barging into my mind like an unwanted guest.

As my companions begin to wake, my thoughts return to what Lord said. We protect this place. These people. They were special. I'm convinced it was an older couple, likely a lot older. They probably lived their entire lives in that house. For some reason, they didn't go Gray like everyone else. Somehow, and I don't know how, they must have been immune to the change. My brother must have thought they were so unique they needed to be protected from all of the dangers of this world. And when they died, he felt the need to watch over what they left behind as well. I don't understand it, but I suppose he had his reasons, reasons that are so dear to him that they wouldn't let him leave with me.

"Um, Scout," Simon says quietly, concern written across his face and in his gentle motions. "How you doing today? Better?"

I manufacture a small smile I don't feel, lips upturned in something that couldn't possibly fool anyone. "Yeah, better. Thanks, Simon. Let's just not talk about it, okay? Not yet."

If anything, he looks relieved. I keep forgetting how young he is. He's just a kid. Sure, he's had to deal with a lot during his short life, but bizarre family dynamics like this would certainly be new to him. Hell, they'd be new to anyone. Me, included.

Google feeds his pet Gray. Watching the two of them interact, I can't get over how the stupid creature went after the attackers yesterday. Was it trying to protect him, or all of us? Does it have enough sense to do that or was it operating on pure instinct? We feed it, so we must be good. The others were obviously trying to kill us, which would have cut off its food supply, so they were bad. Is it actually smart enough to add two and two together like that? I don't know, but I do know I'm in the damn thing's debt no, and I don't like that one bit.

The others finish up their breakfast, and wordlessly we get ready to go. With a sudden pang of guilt, I turn on the radio and squeeze the broadcast button, realizing how concerned Ted must be. In all the confusion none of us thought to contact him yesterday after we were attacked. That was a cruel omission on our part.

"Ted? You there?" I ask.

Immediately his voice blares out of the small speaker. "Holy crap, it's about time! Where have you been? I've been worried sick about you!"

I apologize and give him a condensed version of yesterday's events, including my encounter with Lord. He deserves that much. We weren't together in the Mound long enough for him to know my entire backstory, but he gets the gist of it.

"Damn, I'm sorry, Scout. That must have been awful."

I stare at the radio in my hand and don't answer him. There's no way he can understand, and I doubt I could explain everything to him. But I thank him anyway, a perfunctory thanks that lets him know I don't want to talk about it anymore.

"What do you see ahead of us?" I ask, changing the subject. I'll never come to grips with the fact my brother is gone for good, but there are other people counting on me. They're not my own flesh and blood, but I love them all just the same. I can't come completely unglued now. We still have a job to do, even though in my current state I'm afraid I won't be much good to anyone. Hopefully that will pass in time, a wound that slowly heals but leaves a visible scar.

"Well, I'll take Larry out as far as I can, but you guys made some good progress yesterday. I'm afraid you've just about got to the limit of the drones' range. I won't be able to scout ahead for you much longer."

"Okay, do what you can. We don't need any more surprises. I'll check back in with you later."

"Will do."

He signs off, and I power down the radio. Simon and Google are in their boat, staring at me like I'm a bomb that could go off if they suddenly twitch or cough. The concern on Simon's face is easy to see. Google, on the other hand, is observing me with a more clinical gaze, like a science experiment that has gone wrong, or a computer that needs to be rebooted. The guy might be super smart, but his people skills will always be subpar.

"First of all," I assure them. "I'll be fine. Thanks for your concern. That meeting with my brother just threw me for a loop, okay? Second, that doesn't change why we're here or what we're doing. We still need to get to Church Island before Hunter and warn them. All this means is Lord won't be here to help us. Okay?"

They both nod, and Simon grins at me in relief. He doesn't know any of the people we're trying to save, but he's happy to see me back amongst the living. I can't forget I must be as dear to him as my friends on Church Island are to me. That improves my mood, if only a little bit.

"So, we're good? Okay, let's get going."

I grab the oars, and within seconds our little convoy of four boats is moving across the water at a good clip. I row for what must be an hour before we hear the humming of Ted's drone overhead. It's too high to spot, buried in the clouds hanging low today.

"What do you see, Ted?" I ask him a few moments later.

"Um, it's hard to tell," he answers, his voice cutting in and out between bursts of static. "The clouds are thick as pea soup, and I'm afraid to go much further than this. I think there's some more land ahead, but I can't be sure. I wish I could take Larry farther, but I'm already pushing the limits of his range."

"Okay, take it back before something happens to it. We'll keep heading north."

I pack the radio away, concerned our airborne advantage has been lost. Not just that, but that static on the line makes me think we're nearing the end of the radios' range, too. Google warned me these things would be limited to little more than line of sight. Apparently, we must be nearing that limit, too. I'm afraid Ted will soon be alone once more, and that makes me sad.

Several hours later, we break for lunch. I'm famished, but our supplies are starting to noticeably dwindle, so I restrict myself to a single can of cold soup. I check the compass, make a slight course correction, and start rowing again. The wood on the oar handles has been worn as smooth as glass from my work, and may even be dented in the shape of my fingers from my constant exertions. I keep my head down and maintain my cadence. The convoy moves ahead smoothly. The boats are noticeably lighter now, which makes my job easier. That's both a blessing and a curse. A little later on, Google clears his throat to get my attention.

"What?" I ask, not slowing down.

"Are you ready to fill us in on what transpired between you and your brother? What exactly did he say?"

I sigh, and realize I owe them an explanation. They heard what I said to Ted, which was actually very little. I take a few minutes and relay our brief conversation. "He told me he and the others protected the people who lived there before. I have a feeling they were somehow immune to the change. I don't know that for sure, but I'd bet I'm right. They still protect the place for some reason. He said something about making a promise, or something like that. I don't know."

Google nods and purses his lips in that thoughtful way he has. "Maybe he assumed their immunity was transferable. Perhaps he thought staying close to them and keeping them from harm would somehow be beneficial."

"Who knows. Maybe that would explain why he's still alive? I've never seen a Gray live as long as he has."

He's quiet for a moment, wheels in his head spinning away so furiously I can almost hear the humming. "Perhaps they were able to share their immunity with him? I can't say, since I've never seen anyone who didn't eventually change."

"Neither have I," I reply, then stop myself. "Well, that might not be exactly true. We think we almost ran across someone else who was immune and had a kid." I tell him about Tiny, how we found him in that abandoned house by himself. We always wondered who would or could have a child, and whether his parents could have been immune. And if they were, would they have passed that gift on to their offspring? I'm about to mention this to him, but he beats me to the punch.

"So maybe Tiny will never change, either. Interesting. But I'm not sure I accept your original premise that only someone older than us would or could have a baby. It would be physiologically very possible for someone one hundred and eighty months old to give birth to a child. However, I do agree that doing so would be very unlikely."

I do the math in my head without even thinking about it. One hundred eighty months is fifteen years old, or quite a bit younger than me. I shudder at the thought of bringing a baby into this horrible world. Who would do such a thing? Sure, accidents happen, but still. And being pregnant and fighting off a pack of Grays? How would that even work? I don't know if anyone older and more mature would think differently, but it's not something I'm interested in, thank you very much. Surviving each day is enough of a challenge now.

"Okay, so maybe I was working under a bad assumption about his parents, or maybe not, but we won't find out about Tiny for another two hundred months, and we'll be long gone by then. I'm not sure it makes a difference."

He falls silent, but I can see he's mulling this over – and now I am, too. Would it make a difference if Tiny were immune? Is that why Lord was protecting those people? Was he hoping to benefit from their immunity in some way? Or was he just being Lord and taking care of people, like he always did? I shake my head and keep rowing, keenly aware I'll probably never know. But still…

As dinnertime approaches, Simon spots more land in front of us and I nearly groan out loud. We're not going to take any chances this time, not after what happened back at the farmhouse. As we near the shore, we see a few dozen houses ahead, some half in and half out of the water, collapsing from the elements, furniture visible through the tumbled down walls and fallen roofs. They are larger homes originally built on a hill, probably part of a subdivision of some kind, but even the ones out of the water aren't in much better shape. They rarely are. I get my boat close enough to wade to shore, and needlessly tell the others to wait for me. Again, I get no pushback.

Just before I step out, I click on the radio. "Ted? Are you there?" I release the button, but the only sound from the tiny speaker is light static. There might be a fraction of a word buried in the hissing here or there, but it's nothing that makes any sense. With a sigh, I repack the radio. We're on our own from here on out.

The portage over the hill is thankfully uneventful, although we don't spend any more time there than we need to. A few of the huge homes are kind of intact and inviting, but considering what we went through yesterday, none of us have an appetite for sticking around. Moving everything over to the water on the other side takes an hour or more, but I've got Simon stationed high up in a house with a lot of windows keeping watch. Nothing is going to sneak up on us this time.

On the plus side, he finds an unopened bag of cat food in a cupboard in a garage. Some rodents nibbled on a corner of the green bag at some point, but the rest of it is unspoiled and very edible. Cat food has all the appeal of old sawdust, but it will fill our bellies if needed. Besides, Google can feed it to his pet Gray all day long, and the stupid thing will munch it down like it's Cap'n Crunch cereal. That will leave the good stuff for us.

I know it doesn't sound like it, but we've been lucky so far. The two bits of land we've had to cross have been narrow and easily navigated. We won't always be that fortunate, I'm afraid. And like I tell the others, the farther north we get and the flatter the land becomes, the less land masses we're likely to encounter. Neither one of them would agree we've been all that fortunate, but for most of their short lives they've been holed up in the relative safety of Rumpke Mountain, surrounded by the safety of water. We're not likely to enjoy anything like that on the rest of the trip.

But we take each day as it comes, because we have no choice. We sleep in the boats another two nights, rain pattering down on us in a constant drizzle that would be soothing if we were inside somewhere. I'm feeling better mentally, slowly improving each day. On the morning of the third day after our last portage, we spot a long, strange structure in the distance, and whatever mental progress I've made is suddenly in jeopardy.

"It's a highway overpass," Simon says, squinting to see. "No, I take that back. It's more than that. It's one of those big cloverleaf things. Like where two major highways come together. I've seen those before, on road trips with my dad and brother."

"Hmm," Google adds, not concerned in the least. "That shouldn't give us any trouble. We'll just go under it."

That's easy for him to say. I tell them about the time Dog was attacked when we went under an overpass, and that makes them sit up straight. Their faces turn so white I swear it's like a plug in their heels has been pulled, and all the blood in their bodies gushed out. First hand stories of your friends almost dying has that effect on some people.

"We'll go under it because we don't have any choice, but we'll do so carefully," I tell them both.

We row closer, and with every stroke my anxiety skyrockets up to new heights, into the atmosphere where the air is too thin to breathe. My stomach starts to ache. Land and portions of old highway dip into and out of the water on either side of the cloverleaf as far as the eye can see. I don't like this. I stop when we're a few dozen yards away, the rest of the boats clunking into mine as their momentum lets them catch up. As I stare up at the huge man-made structure ahead of us, my gut goes from the annoying ache to performing the kind of nervous flip-flops I remember suffering during roller coaster rides at Cedar Point. Not for the first time do I wish Dog and his miracle nose were here. Some of the swooping arches of concrete soar almost a hundred feet over our heads, like an immense alien construct. It's magnificent in its own way, a true testament to humanity's past grandeur and ability, like the modern-day pyramids of Giza. There are no vehicles moving above us, but I imagine I can hear the thrumming of thousands of tires as ghostly cars and trucks roar by overhead.

"What are we waiting for?" Google whispers.

I shush him with my best teacher to student glare, and his mouth closes with an audible click. I direct my gaze up and down every inch of the vast series of swooping overpasses, determined not to be taken by surprise again. There are so many places to hide! The mental image of that Gray leaping down and knocking Dog off the boat is sharp and clear in my mind; the screaming as Dog went under, the helpless panic we all suffered as we stared at the churning water. Singer was there to save him that time. I'd bet no one on these boats would have the nerve or daring to do that again, including me.

"I'm not taking any chances. Both of you inspect every inch of this place to make sure we're alone. We're not moving until we're sure."

Five or more minutes pass, and the two of them are getting antsy to get going. I'm more patient than they are, mainly because I've been around longer and seen more than either of them. But, as my mom used to say, patience is a virtue, and while I rarely listened to her back then, her words ring true now. I finally turn to them.

"Here's how it's going to go," I inform them, my tone so stern all three of us are taken aback. "Each of you have a pistol ready. Simon, you watch to the right. Google, you look left. If you see anything at all, yell out a warning. And for god's sake, shoot first and ask questions later, okay? This is not a time to be stingy with ammo."

Simon nods, his head bobbing up and down faster than if he were strapped into a speeding car on a bumpy road. Google can't seem to look away from me, as if he's attempting to translate a foreign language and failing, then nervously digs around at his feet for a gun. When each of them is armed and as ready as possible, I take a deep breath and start rowing. I put my back into it. The convoy straightens out, and we surge ahead.

Within seconds, we're sliding under the first overpass. The wide expanse towering above us throws the boats into an uncomfortable slice of shadow, and the slapping sound of my oars hitting the water bounces back at us in warped echoes. We pass by several concrete pillars as thick as the trunks of sequoias, moss and scum covering the portions near the waterline. Google and Simon are scanning above them as diligently as anti-aircraft gunners on the lookout for enemy bombers. In less than a minute, we leave the first shadow behind, and we're back in the dim daylight. I don't slow down.

We repeat that exercise three more times, and each time I'm more certain than ever that Grays are going to rain down on us from above. But after we clear the final shadow and the cloverleaf is in our wake, I finally release a deep breath and ease up. My two companions exhale and smile, the tension leaving their slight bodies. They're grinning at me, no longer watching for trouble, and Simon holds his hand up for a high-five. Google doesn't understand the gesture, and I almost laugh. Then I tense up.

"Look!" I shout, pointing behind us at the final overpass, one that was only a few dozen yards overhead when we passed under it. They spin around in their seats and follow my finger. Simon raises his gun with both hands, the barrel quivering as he tries to locate the danger. Google's pet Gray begins to tug at the leash around its wrist.

There, watching us from the lip of the last overpass, are two Grays. One has something dark around its neck, and the other is nearly bald, a white fringe of hair just visible. They make no move to attack us, but stare at our convoy blankly, unmoving and still. I'm about to switch into high gear with the oars, but I stop when the creatures turn and run off.

"Holy crap," Simon whispers, slowly lowering his gun as they disappear.

Holy crap, indeed, I think.

CHAPTER
EIGHTEEN

As much as I've learned and as long as I've been sur-viving in this "me versus them" world, I have to admit, I'm not really sure what happened back there. Why didn't those two Grays come after us? Were they smart enough to understand that by attacking us they would almost certainly die? Perhaps they were aware their chance of getting us was pretty much nil? But if either one of those answers were true, that would give those things a lot more credit in the brains department than I've ever seen before. The creature that attacked Dog wasn't worried about it, so why would they be? Or did they just get there too late to do anything?

"Well, that was lucky," Google says with a sigh.

Simon is still staring where the Grays were. "My dad always said he'd rather be lucky than good, and I gotta agree with him."

I'm not convinced. In the last week, I've seen more bizarre behavior from Grays than I have since the Storm hit, and this just adds to the tally. So, no, I'm not convinced it was luck, but I don't have a better answer, either. If I can't accurately predict what these things are going to do, we'll continuously be at an even greater disadvantage. That conclusion does nothing to ease the pain in my gut.

"Let's just keep going," I eventually tell them, still unnerved by the close call.

The open water in front of us is clear as far as we can see, and I put my back into it again. Google and Simon are still giddy with relief at what just happened, both filled with nervous laughter and talking louder than usual, but I'm not watching them. My eyes are locked on Google's Gray. It's no longer twitching and tugging at its restraint, but is sitting still and staring at the bottom of the boat, back to its status quo. Each time since it's been with us and we encountered Grays, it seemed to know they were near. Whether it can somehow hear or sense them before we do, I don't know. But I do know I'll be watching it more closely from now on.

We pass close to several tall antenna towers, then between the tops of green highway signs a little farther on. I call for a break, and ease up to one of the huge signs and try to read the white writing that should be several feet below the surface. It's not easy, since everything underwater is covered in thick green scum. I try to scrape away some of the slime with an oar, but the stuff is sticky and gross, making it harder than cleaning burnt eggs off of a skillet. Thankfully the white lettering begins to show through, if just barely.

"I think it says Sidney, next exit," I tell the two of them. They look at each other and shrug, since that means nothing to them. I retrieve the paper map from my backpack and unfold it in my lap, shielding it from the rain. I locate Rumpke Mountain near Dayton, then trace my finger up I-75 to Sidney.

"Is that good?" Google asks, leaning over to see.

"It's not bad. Once we get north of Sidney we'll be getting close to the remains of the Great Black Swamp. That's good, because that's where the land really flattens out. We shouldn't run into much high ground then, hopefully nothing we can't go around. Church Island isn't far from there either. It's here, near the town of Cedar Ridge."

Two more days and nights pass. Or has it been three? I'm afraid I've lost count since nothing else has happened to break up the monotony of rowing, eating, and sleeping. The Gray is perfectly content to eat the cat food we found earlier, and that helps stretch our shrinking supplies. My two companions don't have much to say to each other, that is until Simon starts playing 20 Questions with Google about his favorite television shows. Google, as smart as he is, apparently didn't spend much screen time mesmerized by a TV, and fails miserably each round.

"How do you know these things?" he drills Simon at one point, having just lost again.

Simon smirks quietly, happy to be able to baffle the little genius. I'm only partially listening to the exchange since I'm concentrating on keeping our course, but even I'm stumped most of the time and I was quite the TV-holic as a kid. For the most part Simon's shows are older ones that he watched together with his brother and dad, programs like *Happy Days* and the *Dick Van Dyke Show*, ones where I know the title and not much more. The constant chatter and Google's mounting frustration starts to get on my nerves a little, but it's keeping them happy so I hold my tongue and leave them to it. Too bad they're not playing this game with the Harry Potter series, because I'd clean up there. What's truth serum called? Veritaserum. What was the name of Harry's hippogriff? Buckbeak. We spend another miserable night in the boats, and after rowing for several hours the next morning, I stop when Simon says something.

"What is it?" I ask him.

He points behind me, and I turn around. Directly in our path is the dim outline of a huge hill, and on the hill is the shadowy remains of a city. It can't be Sidney, since we certainly passed over that submerged town miles ago. It's some other little burg, and the hill it's built on stretches for miles and miles in both directions. My heart sinks.

"That doesn't look good," Simon mutters.

No, it doesn't. I wish again we had Ted's drones to help us out. Without them to show us the way, we could go hours or days out of our way without finding a path over or around it. I don't say anything as I study this new obstacle.

"What's your recommendation, Scout?" Google asks, even though he's smart enough to know there's only one answer.

I drum my fingers on the gunwale of the boat, the clinking of my chipped fingernails on the metal loud in the silence. Now that we're a little closer, I can make out individual structures and a few roads that vanish in between buildings or suicide into the water. It's a sight we're all used to now, but it had to be horrible to the people who lived there as most of their town slowly drowned before their eyes.

"Well, we don't have much choice, do we?" I say. "Much as I hate to say it, we're going to have to go through there and hope the water starts again just over the hill. I don't see any other option, although I'm open to suggestions. Anyone?"

We all know there are no other options. Both of them are getting used to the drill now, and grab their guns. I glance at the Gray, but it's still motionless, staring at the hull of the boat. At least that's a good sign.

"Okay, then. I guess we have to go."

I row up to the nearest road and step into the thick brown sludge. This close to a town the water is filled with floating plastic bags, water bottles, and other trash, like always. There used to be a lot of dead fish near shorelines, but they've all rotted into nothing by now.

"Simon, move the boats twenty or thirty feet offshore and wait for me. I'll go check it out."

Simon dutifully takes the oars from my outstretched hands and paddles backwards. Once the convoy is a safe distance away, I turn away and stare at the remains of the town before me. I stand stock still for a few hundred heartbeats, listening and looking. Far off in the distance to the right, I see vultures circling overhead, which is a bad sign. Something dead is there, and more often than not that something was killed by Grays. Instead, I head straight into town on the main road, always making sure I bear left when I can.

Like every place I've been in since the Storm, the place is a wreck. It doesn't have that tornado ravaged feel to it. Nothing like that. No, it's more like a slow disintegration caused by neglect on top of time and the persistence of the elements. Is entropy the right word? I think it is, but promise myself I'll look it up the next time I get my hands on a dictionary. I keep walking, my footfalls silent on the wet pavement. I look down and find Chuck is securely in my right hand, and I don't even recall drawing him.

Cars block portions of the street, rust eating away at their sheet metal hides in random patterns of bubbling, scabby skin cancer. Windows on all of the shops are either broken or dark, their once gleaming gold letters fading and lifeless. Most of the buildings are two or three stories tall, like in most midwestern small towns. My guess is businesses inhabited the first floor, while apartments or storage took up the remaining ones. I pass a once quaint meat market on my left, then a drug store with a green sign that's crashed to the sidewalk. Next to that is a tiny appliance outlet that somehow survived the corporate competition from the big box stores.

I quietly dodge around a few SUVs that block the sidewalk in front of some diner called The Bistro, its door open and hanging there by a single hinge. Some movement up high catches my attention, and I see I'm heading closer to the vultures than I like. I turn left at the next street to steer away from them and find myself between the sides of several three-story buildings, a box canyon made of red brick. If I were in a war movie, this would be a great place for an ambush, with soldiers hidden high on the rooftops waiting to pick us off. That image does nothing to calm my percolating nerves. I try to wipe my sweaty hands on my wet poncho, which does nothing except make them wetter. I'm not usually this nervous when I'm out, but recent events have changed that.

I soon clear the box canyon, and on either side of me are parking lots, probably for the shops uptown. Abandoned cars litter the asphalt lots, some smashed into others like they were contestants in an adult-sized bumper car ride. I keep walking, my gaze jerking as quick as a bird this way and that, scouring the area for tell tale movement of Grays.

Two more blocks pass, and then I'm out of the downtown and into a residential area of huge old homes. They are magnificent structures, all brick, stone, and stucco, no two alike. A few have those orange tile roofs that makes me think the architects couldn't make their minds up if they wanted the finished product to be elegant, or to look like something from the Far East, and said what the hell, let's do both. As much as I'd love to explore inside some of these grand old homes, I resist and keep going.

Four or five blocks later, the houses thin out and the road inclines slightly. Hopeful that this means the city will stop and blessed water will begin again, I increase my pace. I'm almost running when I reach the top, but as soon as I do my heart deflates and my chin falls to my chest.

Ahead of me is nothing but more open land, unbroken except for a few houses scattered here and there among fields of dead grass, weeds, and a few skeletal trees. The trees all bear a striking resemblance to ones from any horror movie ever produced, full of gnarled branches and naked of leaves. There's no water as far as I can see, which means our relatively safe and easy passage has come to an end. This is the worst thing that could have happened.

From here on out, we travel on foot, visible and vulnerable to whoever or whatever is out there.

CHAPTER
NINETEEN

Before I admit defeat and head back to the boats with the bad news, I explore some more, hoping against hope I'm wrong. I'm not. As far as I can see through the haze, there is nothing but more land in front of us, flat fallow fields that must have been beautiful in their day, filled with rows of soybeans or corn swaying in the breeze. With a sigh that's about eighty percent curse, I retrace my steps to the boats. I motion for my companions to paddle in, and Simon eventually man-handles the awkward convoy to shore.

"Bad news," I tell them. "We're going to have to walk for a while."

Google's eyebrows raise comically high above his eyes, quickly understanding the gravity of the situation now that he's been off Rumpke Mountain and in the "real" world for a while. Simon doesn't grasp the awful ramifications right away, but I'm sure he will soon.

"How far?" Google asks.

I give half a shrug. "I don't know. If we weren't

in such a hurry, I'd consider heading back out and seeing if we could find a way around. But we don't have that much time."

"Okay, so we walk," Simon chips in. "Let's carry all the supplies we can and get going."

I glance back the way I came. The vultures are gone. I don't know if that's good or bad.

"It's not that easy. We have to bring at least one of the boats with us. Eventually, we'll get to water again, and there's no way of knowing if we'll be able to find another one. We can't take that chance."

"And we have to take the shortwave radio with us, too," Google states.

"We're not lugging that damn thing with us," I snap at him. "It's too heavy and we don't need it."

But same as before, he's adamant we don't leave his precious equipment behind, and after several minutes of arguing I throw up my hands in defeat.

"Fine! But you're carrying the stupid thing!"

Using some of the ropes that lashed the boats together, I fashion a crude harness and hook it to one of the boats. Being "crafty" like this really isn't where I shine, but I do the best I can, ending up with something more like a belt than a harness. While I'm doing that, Simon is transferring as much of the supplies to it as he can. Google is working on something with his pet Gray, but I'm pissed at him and studiously ignore whatever project he's focused on. I thread my arms through the rope straps of my harness, tie the rest around my waist, and take a few tentative steps. The boat lists to one side as I drag it partway out of the water, and some of the loose cans tumble off the top of the heap.

"Hold on a minute," Simon says, replacing them carefully. "Now try it."

I start tugging again, and the remainder of the boat slides out of the water. The hull scraping against the wet asphalt makes a sound as pleasant as a car grinding along a concrete retaining wall, but I'm strong enough to pull it along without too much trouble. This is not going to be fun or easy, but it's doable. I've put up with worse.

Google, meanwhile, has worked up his own intricate harness that is way more complex than mine, and he's slipped it onto his Gray. Wrapped up inside it is every piece of the shortwave radio, including the battery. I'll be damned if the mad little genius hasn't turned the creature into his own private pack mule. He tilts his head and his closed lips turn up in a grin, his huge eyes gleaming behind the thick lenses in pride. I wouldn't mind punching the smug bastard right now, but I'm the picture of restraint, and I don't.

Simon has his pistol out, and I can see Google's is tucked into his belt, the black handle sticking halfway up his stomach. We're as ready as we'll ever be, so I nod at them.

"Let's move out."

I start pulling, and the boat scrapes along behind us, making less noise than a jet engine but more than a broken down lawn mower. I quickly try to gauge the amount of effort this is taking, and come to the conclusion I should be able to pull this makeshift sled for quite a while if I have to. We head up the street, back the way I came, Simon a few steps in the lead. Before we get too far, I tell Google to take his pet up ahead of me, so I can watch it.

"Why?" he asks, mystified.

"Because each time we've seen Grays, that thing gets all antsy and nervous. I don't know if it happens every time, but it sure seems to. I want it in front so I can watch it."

This observation must be news to him, but like a scholar presented with a new premise, he tentatively accepts my theory for further review. The two of them move up ahead of me, next to Simon. Google looks like he wants to talk about my revelation, but the noise of the boat scraping along the road makes conversation impossible. I don't like having that creature behind me, anyways. I can't help it. I'm much more comfortable where I can keep an eye on it.

We're quickly back uptown, and while it's somewhat familiar to me, it's all new to my companions. Neither of them has likely been in a place like this for years, or perhaps ever. They peek into the storefront windows as we pass, sometimes stopping for a second to peer through the glass with their hands cupped on either side of their faces. The Gray pays no attention to any of this and shuffles docilely along, the heavy weight strapped to its back causing it no trouble at all. I remind myself the damn thing is just as strong as I am, which makes me want to keep it in front of me all that much more.

We turn the corner into the box canyon street, the boat screeching along behind me as we step up onto the sidewalk. My companions stare in concern at the lips of the roofs far overhead. They may not be able to relate to the whole war movie cliche I imagined before, but they can sense how exposed and vulnerable we are right now. We thankfully clear the tall buildings and skirt by the parking lots. Within a few minutes we're in the residential neighborhood. I take this opportunity to drag the boat up onto the small front lawns, where it glides almost quietly over the muddy ground. The silence after so much noise is a blessing.

We head up the hill, and I'm just about to let myself feel relieved when Google's Gray lifts its shaggy head and its entire body starts to twitch. Its hands flutter like twin birds in a cage.

Oh, shit.

"Get the harness off that thing!" I shout as I struggle out of mine. Google freezes where he stands, cursed by the swift understanding of what's coming. Simon doesn't get what's happening yet, but sees our companion won't or can't follow my command and rushes over to help. With tiny whimpering noises leaking from his mouth, he manages to strip the ropes from the Gray with hands clumsy with fear and haste. I finally get my last foot out of mine, and I whirl around and around, trying in vain to locate the danger. Where are they? My heart is pumping so fast I'm not sure why it doesn't simply explode and leave a gaping, bloody hole in my chest.

Google finally thaws out and gestures behind us, downtown, where I spotted the vultures my first trip out. The motion is so fierce his glasses nearly tumble from his face, and he has to shove them back onto his nose.

"There! There they are!"

Four Grays are pounding down the middle of the street toward us. I frantically search for some protection for Google and Simon, but we're in a nearly empty stretch of open land with just a few homes here and there on either side of the street. I spin around, and my eyes are drawn to the boat. I quickly flip our improvised sled on its side, dumping the supplies on the ground in a crash. Cans go spinning away in all directions. I kick a few stragglers out of the way and pick it up, its weight nothing compared to my frenzied strength.

"Both of you. Get under the boat. Now!"

For a split-second Simon is about to protest, but with my free hand I manage to shove both of them to the ground. I slam the upside down boat over the pair and pray that I didn't just hurt either of them.

Of course, whatever I may have done pales to what the Grays will do if they get their claws on them, and I promise to apologize if we live through this. Once the boat is in place, I jump on top of it and hold it down with my slight weight. Chuck is in my hand. His blade gleams as if he's happy to be in business again.

"Come on, you bastards!" I yell.

The four of them are less than half a block away when Google's Gray storms past me. In seconds it targets the leader and takes it out with a flying tackle that sends both of them tumbling down the street, arms and legs everywhere. The others ignore the two of them struggling and keep coming straight at us.

"Come on, slo-mo," I whisper to myself. "Come on, come on, come on. Please don't fail me now."

When the remaining three are almost on me, I think of Simon below me, only marginally protected by the thin aluminum hull of the boat. My impromptu plan will only work if I stay alive and in place. If I can't stop these creatures, both he and Google will be dead in moments. I am NOT going to let that happen! Not to Simon!

And then I feel it, the blessed tingle, the wonderful sensation of bees buzzing behind my neck, and I almost whoop in delight. The sprinting Grays stop in place, like I just hit the pause button on a DVR. Two of them are caught with both feet off the ground and in mid-air, reminding me of a pair of hurdlers photographed during a race. The one nearest to me has its mouth open, yellowed teeth visible between peeled-back lips, its hands stretching forward. I jump off the boat and slowly land ten feet away, nearly on top of them, lighting on the ground as gradually as a soap bubble on a still day. Pushing through the wet concrete of resistance, I get close enough to the lead Gray and slice below its ear, putting all my strength behind it. Chuck cuts through the skin and bone so smoothly I almost completely separate its head from its body, a flap of skin the only thing keeping them connected. *Two hundred and forty-three.* I shove the fresh corpse away and deliberately turn to the next one. Out of the corner of my eye I spot three more Grays in mid-gallop towards us on my left, heading in our direction from behind a house. Now there are seven of them! Even with my slo-mo fully engaged I've never had to take out this many at one time before. My math skills have never been above a C level, but I do my best to calculate which ones will arrive first, and how to get to the next ones before they reach my makeshift shelter. But there are so many, and I'm restricted to how fast I can move. If I kill the remaining two on the street, not counting the one Google's pet has occupied, I'm afraid the other three will get to the boat. Likewise, if I go for the second group, that leaves a clear path for the others. This two-pronged attack exceeds even my abilities, and it dawns on me that I may not be able to deal with them in time! In fact, I'm almost certain I can't.

And then another horrible variable is introduced to this already complex equation.

Two additional creatures appear on the left, and right away I can tell they're the ones from the overpass. One is bald, and the other is wearing some goofy-looking dickey around its neck. How in the hell did they track us here? I can see them moving in slo-mo, which means they're fast Grays. Shit! They force their way through the wet concrete way better than I can, moving with a kind of swimmer's grace I can't copy. They'll be on me in seconds, even in slo-mo. Without a thought, I ignore the others because I have to. Desperation and fear rush to the forefront of my consciousness, but I compress and smash it into a small ball and shove it aside, to be dealt with later. Because I have to. Because I have no choice. This must be what it's like for a soldier in battle, just act, and react, and don't think, because you can't, because you don't have that luxury. Tap into the primal need to survive, and then later you can look back and wonder what destructive muse guided you through the fight.

The two fast ones aren't coming right at me, which is odd, so I shift left to intercept them. I swing at Baldy with Chuck, but it ducks back and dodges to the side. The second one reaches for me, and it doesn't fare as well when Chuck opens up a ten inch gash that exposes the white bone of its ribcage right below the filthy dickey. But that gives an opening for Baldy, and it grabs my wrist in a searing grip so intense I'm convinced my skin must be charred. I don't even have time to scream at the heat and crushing pain, because it flicks its arm like it's shooing away a fly, and I soar away from them. I tumble through the air with all the poise of a passenger ejected from a car crash, and seconds later land in the front yard of a house. I roll and spin through the mud, until I'm brought up short when I crash into a brick landscape wall near the front of the house, cracking my head.

Dazed, with bright flashes of light popping in my vision, I struggle to sit up. No! My slo-mo has switched itself off again, just like it did when I fought with Hunter. My vision is still blurred from the impact, and I briefly wonder how many concussions someone can suffer before there's permanent brain damage. I struggle to my feet, weaving, mud and dead grass falling off of me in wet clumps. Slo-mo or not, Simon and Google are still in terrible danger under the boat, and I can't tap out of the fight yet. Chuck is miraculously still in my right hand. Without slo-mo I don't stand a chance, but I take a deep breath and get ready to attack.

Then I realize I don't have to.

I've always wondered what one of my slo-mo fights looks like to someone in normal time. Well, check that one off my bucket list. Mesmerized, I watch the two fast Grays tear into the others, literally ripping them limb from limb. I can't see it happening, not in normal time, and to be honest any description I come up with won't do it justice. But I stare in grisly fascination as the two of them systematically shred the others in a flurry of pink mist and flying body parts, like a pair of Tasmanian Devils spinning faster than the eye can follow. Not real Tasmanian Devils, which are actually kind of cute when they're not pissed off, but the Looney Toons kind, all teeth, claws, and slobber, with voracious appetites that one smart-aleck rabbit could never satisfy. The sight is both horrible and immensely welcome at the same time, that car crash you pass on the highway you can't tear your eyes from. One moment there are seven rampaging Grays threatening me and my friends, then with a snap of my fingers, nothing is left but severed limbs and mutilated bodies all around me, steam drifting up from mangled torsos that were whole just moments ago. Blood spurts from a few of them, their hearts not yet getting the urgent message they're actually dead. A wood chipper couldn't have done a more thorough job of wiping them all out. And the most amazing part is, besides the moist splats as pieces of flesh and bone rain down onto the wet road, there's an almost complete lack of noise, like the chipper was shielded behind soundproof plexiglass.

Google's Gray is off to the side, unharmed, but dripping in gore from the friendly fire that just exploded all around it. The two fast Grays stand there, not even winded, their hands and faces covered in blood.

Tatters of flesh hang from their mouths. The one I sliced open hasn't paid the least bit of attention to the huge wound across its chest that has already stopped bleeding. Baldy spits a severed finger out of its mouth onto the street, where it bounces into the gutter. The two pairs of dead eyes look my way, freezing me where I stand, and stare at me for what could have been a second, or possibly a decade, then in eerie unison they turn and walk unhurriedly toward downtown. Their bare feet leave a ragged red trail on the wet asphalt as they go.

CHAPTER
TWENTY

I flip the boat back over, and instantly duck sideways when I find myself staring down the barrel of Simon's gun. There's a loud boom as the pistol fires, and I swear I feel the bullet crisp some stray hairs near my ear.

"It's okay!" I shout, hands up. "It's okay. It's all over."

Simon falls back and the gun clatters to the ground. Both of them burst into tears, Simon with his arm flung over his face, and Google sitting there with his ass soaked from the wet pavement.

I quickly kneel down to comfort both of them, wrapping my arms around the pair, all while repeating, "It's okay," over and over, because I don't know what else to do. I'm reminded again of how young they are, and how the attack would have scared the shit out of them. I'm aching to get away from this place, but I also realize they're going to need a few moments to calm down.

Eventually, they both stop crying and smear

the tears and snot across their faces with their hands as they try to clean up. Simon retrieves his pistol and stands up, his young face so pale it mirrors the color of his blond hair. He stares in mute shock at the remains of the slaughter all around us. Google is more clinical, and ventures a few steps away from the boat to get a better view of the gruesome remains. He toes gently at a severed arm near his foot, as if not really believing it no longer poses a threat.

"Scout," he says softly, his voice filled with either awe or disbelief, I can't tell which. "What happened here? I don't understand. Did you do this?"

I start loading the boat up with our scattered supplies, anxious to get going. "No. It was the two Grays from the overpass. I've never seen anything like it before." I explain what I saw, what I did, and what the two fast Grays did. I omit some of the goriest details because knowing them can't do anything but add to their nightmares, but I recount everything else that happened as well as I can. Even listening to myself go through it, I almost can't believe it.

"But why would those two help us?" Simon asks, still so pasty white and trembling that I'm afraid he may be going into shock.

I shake my head. "I have no idea. Unless…" I stop, my voice trailing off.

"Unless they were sent by your brother to keep you safe?" Google chimes in, accurately finishing my sentence for me.

Is that even possible? Lord certainly was able to control his group of Grays, that much was apparent back at the farmhouse. Hunter could, too. Could my brother have sent those two to keep us safe? Could he have that much control over them? Would they be able to follow his commands like that? Again, I have so many questions, all of which remain unanswered.

"I just don't know," I finally say, staring at the bloody tracks that lead away from us. "I suppose so. I've just never seen these creatures act like this before. This is all new to me, too."

As much as I want to dig into this, I know we have to get the hell out of here. We survived this time, but that's no guarantee we'll be that lucky if it happens again. There's too much open land and not enough cover around here. Plus, we can't be certain that our guardian angels will be back again if we need them. All of this is way too unpredictable.

"We can talk more about this later," I tell the two of them. "But right now we have to get going. It's not safe here. Not at all."

I struggle back into the harness while Google does the same to his pet Gray. I hear him talking to it, speaking in soft, low tones, like he's praising a puppy that just pooped outside for the first time. Listening to him almost turns my stomach. Doesn't he get that these things are monsters? This one may have helped save us again, but they are not to be trusted. I still can't comprehend the weird relationship the two of them have, and to be honest, I don't want to.

Once I'm lashed to the boat, we set off. I'm able to stick to the front yards of the houses until those yards are gone and we're in the open fields. I move away from the road to where the field meets the berm, and there's a natural trench here that fits the V of the hull very nicely. We make pretty good time, and before I know it the town behind us is out of sight. Good riddance.

Simon steps up next to me, head down. We walk for several minutes until he finally clears his throat. "Uh, I'm sorry I almost shot you," he whispers after a few dozen steps.

I figured this was coming. With a smile, I reach out and lay my hand on his head. "Simon, you did exactly what you were supposed to do. Suppose that was a Gray? I told you to shoot first and ask questions later, right? That's just what you did. I'm proud of you."

He perks up a little at the praise. I am really proud of him. He acted just as he should have, although I'm happy his aim was lousy. He already saved me once in the grocery store parking lot, and he showed his mettle here again. I tussle his blond hair.

"But next time, if there is a next time, promise me you'll aim a little better," I say, kidding him.

His smile is honest, if a little bruised. He's not sure how to take my joke, but he nods and we keep walking in silence. I'm sure he's still reeling inside from what he almost did, but I have to hope he'll get over it. He doesn't have any choice, really. Checking him out as he plods along next to me, the innocent face that's way too thin, his blue eyes the color of ocean water, the kind of water that's far from shore and not muddied up by sand, the eyebrows that are so fair they're nearly invisible, I again vow to do whatever I can to keep him safe. He deserves that much. And anyway, I owe him.

We trudge along all day, following the trench next to the road, only stopping long enough to eat and drink. The road itself is laser straight, a two lane country highway with dead fields on either side of us. From what we can see of the sun behind the clouds, we're headed due north, which is perfect. There are abandoned cars and trucks in the ditches, blocking the road every so often. Here and there we spot a tumbled-down farmhouse and a barn or two down long lanes, but we don't stop. The wide open landscape offers us zero cover, but that works both ways. We would see any Grays the same time they would spot us, so that's something, I guess. We press on, the nearly invisible sun dipping lower in the sky to our left. Google's pet is next to him in the lead, and when I'm not watching where I'm placing my feet, I'm studying it for any telltale signs.

Evening is not too far off, and I know we're going to have to stop soon. As strong as I am, even I have to rest once in a while. The Gray, while not lugging nearly as much weight as I am, doesn't appear to be tired at all. Do these things sleep? Do they have to? I've never thought about it before. They were human once, and all humans have to sleep. I wonder if they've changed so much they don't have to any longer. That seems like something we should know.

The concealed sun dips ever lower toward the horizon, while the sky to the east visibly darkens. As I watch, a huge flash of lightning momentarily highlights the black and grey clouds in that direction. A few moments later a rumble of thunder shudders past us. Where a second ago there was no breeze, now a strong gust of wind ruffles our hair.

"Thunderstorm coming," Simon says. "Should we find cover?"

Weather events like this one are not something that happen often since the Storm. In fact, the one that battered me on top of the Mound was the first one I remember. It rains virtually all the time, sure, but we don't have storms. Drizzle, downpours, and mist, yes. But storms? And if this one is anything like that, I do not relish the thought of being caught in the open again. That one nearly blew me right off of the top of the Mound.

"Google, did you guys have a bad storm while I was at the Mound?"

He answers without hesitation. "Yes, we did. It filled all the pits with water and made it impossible to work. It also flattened some of the tents. Why?"

"When's the last time you had one? Before that, I mean."

"Never. Not that I can recall. Why?"

I stop pulling the boat, my hands on my knees as I take a break. "Well, no reason, I guess. It's just weird, that's all. If this one is like that, then we'll definitely need to find some shelter."

Heads nod in unison as more lightning crashes at the horizon. We start walking again in the fading daylight, but faster now, the ominous rumbling of thunder becoming more frequent and intense. The flash bulbs to the east keep popping, giving us brief glimpses of angry clouds churning like boiling mercury. The Gray in front of me doesn't react to the onrushing storm, but my two companions are getting more visibly anxious by the second, jumping every time there's another flash. There's nothing I can do about it now, except to keep pulling.

Darkness is nearly upon us when Simon points ahead with a shout. He's gesturing at a farmhouse less than a mile away. Like all the rest of them around here, it's a two-story white frame house, plopped down in the middle of fields. Also, like most of them we've seen so far, the roof is partially caved in and open to the elements. Next to it are the remains of a barn, a single wall, and some structural supports. To me it looks like a swift kick would topple both of them over, but we don't have any choice.

"Head for the house," I scream, my words shredded by the wind that is growing in intensity by the second. Our ponchos snap around us like capes.

We hurriedly splash across the muddy field, the outline of the house hazy in the quickly fading light. The first wave of rain smacks into us, and it's so fierce all of us are nearly knocked over. Lightning arcs across the sky so close I can almost feel the electrical charge pass through me and out the soles of my feet. The thunder that follows hot on its heels is so powerful it's like a full body punch. I pull Simon and Google close.

"Go!" I shout at them. "Go and find shelter! I'll be right there!"

Simon shakes his head no, but Google is smart enough to take me at my word. He snatches at Simon's sleeve and together the two of them sprint as fast as they can towards the house, his adopted Gray loping along behind them. I put my head down and increase my pace, until another tremendous gust of wind hits me, and I'm yanked off my feet and onto my back. Laying there in the mud, I wonder what the hell just happened. Then there's another tug on my back, and I'm pulled a dozen feet through the muck. The boat is caught in the fierce wind and flopping around behind me like a kite on a string, and I'm still connected to the boat. I quickly rip off the harness, snapping one pesky rope that won't cooperate. As I gain my feet, leaning into the wind, I see our makeshift sled spin on its axis and take off across the empty field, cans and bags of food tossed high in the air and soaring after it.

We need that boat, but we need me alive even

more, and I'm pretty sure only one of us is going to make it through this. I watch in dismay as it bounces end over end away from me and flutters off, its silver hull flickering as thick shafts of lightning are etched across the black sky. The few remaining cans of food are thrown clear and vanish in the rain. It's nearly out of sight when I put my head down and run as fast as I can toward the house, leaning nearly forty-five degrees to my right just to stay on my feet. Another wall of rain slams into my side. I'm temporarily blinded, but I don't stop.

Seconds later I skid to a halt next to the house. All the windows and doors are long gone, rain hammering inside unhindered. Above me a section of the roof is snatched off and follows in the wake of our boat, wood and shingles shredding as it flies away in pieces, then exploding as it smashes into the ground. Whatever this storm is, it's worse than the last one. I remember someone once saying a tornado sounds like a freight train coming at you, and suddenly I'm very uneasy that I can't recall exactly what one of those sounds like.

I run around the outside of the house shouting for Simon and Google, but my screams are nothing more than a drop of water in a raging ocean. I round a corner of the house and spot something on the ground, something almost flat and attached to the foundation of the house, and that creepy Wizard of Oz movie my mom adored bursts into my mind again.

It's a storm cellar, Auntie Em. Those doors lead to a storm cellar under the house. Before I'm whipped into the sky like the Wicked Witch on her bike, I rush to the doors and pull on the handle as hard as I can. The door flips open with a bang, but the wind catches it and slams it shut. I yank again, but hold it this time, tumbling down the slick concrete steps into Simon's outstretched arms. The door crashes shut behind us, and I reach back and slam home a heavy metal bolt I feel more than see. The howl of the wind stops like someone cut the power, and I slump down on the cool concrete steps, the storm raging unabated overhead. The windowless cellar is as dark as a cave.

Gasping and panting, I finally manage to ask, "Everybody okay? Are we all here?"

"Yeah, we're all here. Thank god you made it," Simon yells, the noise outside getting louder again.

"And everyone's okay?" I ask, my breathing finally slowing.

"Yeah, I think so," he answers. "Google? You okay?"

There's a small white flash, then a yellow flame illuminates a tiny bubble of space around us. Google stands there holding the Bic lighter. His hair is standing up at crazy angles from the wind and rain, and his glasses are crooked on his face, but he nods once, which I take as a good sign. The Gray is cowering back in the corner, as far away from us as it can get, its eyes locked on the flickering flame. Whether it's the lighter it's afraid of, or the raging storm, I don't know. I'm about to say something reassuring, like I'm supposed to, when a rumbling roar drowns out all other sounds. It's the guttural, primal scream of a thousand Tyrannosaurus Rexes, and it's followed by a horrible crashing and splintering over our heads that seems to go on and on. As one, we duck down low and cover our ears. The roar grows in ferocity and strength until it's all around us, inside us, and then it comes rushing back to me. Oh, yeah, that's what a freight train sounds like.

There's a final crash that drowns out that tremendous howl, and Google drops the lighter. Simon screams.

CHAPTER
TWENTY-ONE

I'm huddled on the cold wet floor with my arms locked around my body and my head clenched between my knees, making myself as small as possible, just like our teachers taught us to do during tornado drills in elementary school. Nearby, someone is whimpering, a mewling animal noise so soft it's barely audible over my own panicked breathing. My first guess is that it's got to be Simon, but then realize it might actually be me. I clamp my lips shut and the sound cuts off. Yep, it was me.

The thunderous roar has stopped, and the only thing I can hear now is water dripping from somewhere overhead into a fresh puddle near my feet. I slowly unwrap my arms from my knees and crack open an eye. Dim light slants down into the cellar where a few sections of our ceiling are gone, ripped off during the storm. It's light enough now to see my companions huddled close to me. Both of them are shaking so hard I'm surprised they don't dislocate something. The Gray hasn't budged and is still cowering in the corner.

"You guys okay?" I ask, my voice a cemetery whisper. "I think it's over."

First one, then the other, lifts his head. Simon pats himself all over, and I'm pretty sure he's checking to make sure he's still in one piece. He spots the opening overhead where the dripping water has now increased to a steady stream. He nods at me to let me know he's okay, his blue eyes shiny with moisture.

I squeeze each of their shoulders in reassurance and stand up. My poncho is twisted around me so completely that my hood is now under my chin, so I take a moment and tug it back into place. I reach up and slide back the bolt holding the doors and give them a shove. They slam open with a crash that makes all of us jump. I head up the steps cautiously and peer around.

The house is gone. And by gone, I mean it's been completely wiped off the planet. There's nothing left but the floorboards and a handful of bricks from the chimney. The scraps of the barn that were there earlier suffered the same fate, the concrete floor the only reminder there was once a building there at all. All the vegetation around us has been blown flat in a giant comb over. The sky overhead is a back to its uniform grey, all smooth and featureless, a single sheet of suspended slate. To the west the storm continues boiling away, lightning touching down several times a second as it rumbles forward in an elemental purge of civilization. I feel my two companions ease past me to a higher step so they can see out.

"Damn," Simon whispers. "What was that?"

"My guess is a tornado passed right over us," Google says, back to his calm and assured self. "I'd say an EF5 judging from the damage it did. We were fortunate to find this shelter. I can't see how we would have survived otherwise."

I don't know the difference between an EF5 or a Z100, but he's right. There is no way we would have survived that. Nothing living could. Nothing at all. And then it dawns on me.

"Come on," I tell them in a rush. "We have to go. Any Grays around here gotta be dead and blown away. I don't know how much time that gives us, but we need to take advantage of it."

"What about the boat? And our supplies?" Google asks.

I point back the way we came. "I'm sure some of our canned goods made it, even if our boat is in Kansas by now. We have to assume it's long gone. Go scrounge what you can, and then we move out. Come on!"

We hustle out to the fields, sloshing through muddy water that's inches deep. When anyone finds something worthwhile they hold it above their heads and let out a shout. In a matter of minutes we locate a dozen random cans and a few bags of dried fruit. It almost becomes a game, a welcome diversion from what could have been. When we've got all we can carry, we hurry through the muck to the highway and begin where we left off, Google's pet in front and leading the way.

I was wrong about the sun setting. Now that the storm has passed, I figure we've got enough daylight left for another hour or two of walking. Even when the darkness finally settles over the devastated countryside, it's easy enough to stay on the asphalt road and keep on course. There are no stars or moon to help illuminate our way, but we make decent progress anyway.

What has to be several hours later, we pass an old SUV in the ditch. I try to peek through the dirty windows, but the darkness inside is absolute. I crack open a door, half expecting a putrid wash of decayed flesh to smack me in the face, but nothing does, just old, stale air with maybe a hint of pine air freshener. I rifle through the glove box but find nothing of interest. Without a word we resume our march, Simon and Google's shuffling footsteps to either side of me.

A little later on, Simon trips and falls. I rush to help him up.

"You okay?"

"Yeah," he mumbles, the single word thick with exhaustion. "Just tired, that's all."

I drag him to his feet, but several steps later Google follows suit and tumbles over. I keep forgetting that my endurance is so much greater than theirs.

They've been through way too much and have to be dead on their feet. Nearly dying twice in one day will wear you out like that.

"Let's take a break for a few minutes, okay?" I suggest. "We'll find somewhere to stop soon. I promise."

Five minutes turns to ten, then fifteen, and then I reluctantly get them moving again, but we're going so slowly we might as well be standing still. Neither of them is in any condition to continue. I call for a stop, but have to repeat their names twice to get their attention.

"Okay, that's it. Let's head back to that SUV and crash for the night. Deal?"

It takes a few seconds for my words to penetrate the fog of their exhaustion, but eventually they mumble something in agreement. We turn around and go back the way we came, and within a few minutes we're at the SUV. Simon climbs wearily into the back, and Google flops out on the bench seat in the middle. I recline the driver's seat back as far as it can go. Before we close our eyes for the night, I lock all the doors, more out of habit than anything else. The Gray squats down against a tire. In seconds, the three of us are out cold.

I'm the first to stir. The dim light slanting in the windows glows faintly behind my eyelids, and I ease one eye open. My neck is stiff from sleeping in a seat made for driving upright, but experience tells me that this pain will soon pass. I lift my head and peek out the windows, and jump so hard my head cracks on the roof when I spot the Gray with its black eyes staring at me.

"Jesus! Don't do that!" I bark at it, reflexively shying away from the dirty glass. The stupid creature doesn't flinch, but inspects me like I'm a new and intriguing organism it's never seen before. The two in the back wake up in a hurry at the commotion. I swear I hear Simon giggle.

"You okay up there, Scout?" he asks innocently, smiling.

I rub my head. "Yeah, I'm fine. Stupid Gray startled me, that's all."

Google yawns, covering his open mouth with the back of his hand. "You know, Scout, you should be used to Susan by now. Besides that, she's already saved our lives several times. That should count for something."

Ugh. He's still calling it by name. That just seems so very wrong to me. Ignoring him, I open the door and step out, pushing the Gray out of the way with the door. Outside, the morning rain settling on everything in a fine mist reminds me of baby powder, turning the red of the SUV into a shimmering pink, but otherwise the air is very still today. The calm after the storm, I guess.

"Grab a bite to eat," I tell them. "Then let's get going. We can't afford to waste any time."

We each select something from our diminished supplies, wolf it down, then start walking again. The two of them are stiff from the previous day's efforts, but besides an occasional groan or stretch neither of them complains much. The pain in my neck vanishes, as I knew it would, a benefit of my healing abilities. The road before us reaches out to infinity in the fine mist that falls gently from above.

We walk for a while in silence, our scuffing footsteps on the damp asphalt the only noise for miles around us. The devastation caused by last night's tornado is everywhere: toppled and uprooted trees, telephone poles snapped at the ground, weeds and dead grass smashed flat by the incredible winds. Wires from the phone poles are draped over the roads, but without electricity they are no more dangerous than wet rope. A semi-truck is on its side a hundred yards away, its empty trailer ripped nearly in half and smashed flat like a stomped-on beer can. Holy crap, I hope we never come face to face with another storm like that again. I can't help but think we somehow royally pissed off Mother Nature, and She was bent on erasing every last shred of mankind's trivial and waning existence.

Once in a while, Google bends over and picks up a small rock. I watch him as he inspects each one, pocketing some, and tossing others back on the road. I can't figure out what he's doing, but before I can ask, he slows enough to sidle up next to me. "Scout, now that we have a few minutes of peace, I'd like to talk about something."

"What's on your mind?"

"It's your slo-mo ability, and how inconsistent it's been lately. Without that, while you're still quite skilled at protecting us and yourself, I'm afraid we no longer have the upper hand in some of these...engagements."

I want to say, "No shit, Sherlock," but I don't. He actually seems to be sincere, so I clamp my lips down on my snarky reply and answer him honestly.

"Yeah, I know. I don't get it either."

"The first time it failed to manifest, was that at the grocery store where Max was killed?"

You mean, where poor Max was killed for no reason? Where you hatched that stupid plot about catching a Gray without telling me? Where BamBam had his windpipe crushed and almost died? Where the Gray would have killed me if Simon hadn't stepped up and saved my ass? But again, I keep all those sarcastic and angry retorts bottled up, and answer him as calmly as I can because I can see he's trying to be helpful.

"Yes, that was the first time."

"But eventually it kicked in, right? When exactly did that happen?"

It's hard to remember precisely, but I think back. "Um, when I saw that Gray trying to get at Simon. I had locked him in the car."

"Okay. And the next time? When was that?"

"Really, Google? Do we have to do this? What are you going for here?"

He bends down and picks up another rock, a smooth one about the size of a marble. He slides it in his pocket. "Humor me, Scout. The next time?"

I sigh and think back, rewinding events until I'm back at the Mound, when I encountered Hunter. That time it seemed to engage as soon as we ran into each other, and was working until I cracked my head after he catapulted me into Ted's car. I tell him that.

"Very good. And after that? Did it turn on when you saw your brother?"

This one's easy. "No, it never did, but to be honest I never thought about it. The Grays were running toward me, but then yours attacked them and Lord stopped the fight."

"So, you never felt threatened?"

I shake my head. "No, not really. I was pretty calm, actually. And you guys were already out in the boats and safe, so I wasn't worried about you."

He nods quickly, his head bobbing up and down in excitement, as if I just said something very important. His eyes are alight behind the thick lenses. "Excellent! And when we were attacked back there in the town. Did it come on right away? We were hidden under the boat and didn't see what happened."

Okay, he's got me hooked, now. "No, it didn't. Not right away. Not until more of them showed up, and you guys were in danger."

He rubs his hands together. "Yes, that's what I thought."

I stare down at him. "Thought what?"

"I suspect your slo-mo abilities have become, for lack of a better term, situational. Think about it; each time it's turned on you've been under extreme stress, like when you encountered Hunter, or when one of us has been in danger. For the most part, if it's just you and you remain calm and in control, nothing happens. But when the threat level increases, your body reacts and your enhanced abilities engage. Perhaps it's tied to adrenaline, or some sort of extreme maternal instinct to protect those important to you. You need that extra jolt for it to work."

"Wait. Are you saying I've become so used to killing Grays that under normal circumstances my slo-mo won't work?"

"Maybe, maybe not. What I'm saying is that, perhaps you don't care enough about yourself for it to manifest. Only when you're extremely distraught, or someone dear to you is in danger, only then will it come to your aid."

I open my mouth to argue, but no words come out. Could he be right? Could I care so little about myself that my mind doesn't give a rat's ass if I live or die? I think back to the grocery store parking lot when it happened the first time, when those three Grays were charging at me. I remember thinking about how much I had changed in the last few years, and how different I had become since the Storm.

"I've become a killer," I mumble, quoting myself. "And I take no pride in saying so, but I'm very good at it."

"And your mind is struggling to come to terms with that," Google replies, thinking I'm talking to him, even though I'm not. "I would bet that in your mind you're still Jean Louise, brother of Lord, and loving daughter to your parents. You're not a killer. You can't see yourself as one, even though that's what you've become."

"But I still go into slo-mo, eventually," I counter. "Most of the time, at least."

He tilts his head and shrugs. "I'd have to guess that no matter what your conscious mind believes, at times your subconscious takes over because the survival instinct trumps everything. That, and your maternal instinct to protect others you care for. It's a classic Freudian Id versus Superego conflict, if that helps at all."

No, it doesn't, since I have zero idea what he's talking about. He could be making up words for all I know. Regardless, as much as I'd like to, I don't know if I can dispute him. He's sort of making sense.

"That's all well and good, I suppose," I finally say. "But what the hell am I supposed to do about it? If this Superego thing is keeping me from going into slo-mo?"

He shrugs again. "I don't know. This is something you have to reconcile in your mind, I suppose. You have to get over this inability to care what happens to you, unless the threat is extreme or someone else is in danger. Maybe," he concludes, "you just need to Hulk-out."

I stutter to a stop, and after a second, he does, too. Ahead of us, Simon, who's been keeping one ear on the conversation, does the same.

"Hulk-out? What the hell does that mean? You mean the big green superhero guy?"

"Precisely. The Hulk's alter ego Bruce Banner can't typically change into the Hulk unless he's threatened, injured, or gets really mad. Somehow you have to take control of your slo-mo on your own terms by doing one of those things, preferably by getting mad. That's probably the best scenario and the one least likely to cause you harm."

"I just need to get mad."

"Hulk-out. Yes."

I start walking again, the two of them a step behind me as we go. We keep moving down the deserted highway, not talking now, the pair keeping an eye on me with sideways glances. I don't know why I feel like I should disagree with Google and what he's saying, but for some reason I do. I've never considered myself to be all that gullible, and I'm actually more cynical than I should be. Maybe it's just that I'm uncomfortable being analyzed like this, but I keep conjuring up reasons why I think he's wrong, only to dig deeper inside my head and find he's making way too much sense. It's true. I don't like what I've become. But is it true my conscious mind would stand by and watch while Grays took me out? Do I really hate what I've become that much?

"This Hulking-out thing," I eventually say. "So, I would just need to get mad?"

"Perhaps. I can't say for sure. That, or always have someone you care about nearby who would be in terrible danger if you stood by and did nothing. That would likely do it as well, although I hope I'm not that person. That doesn't sound very enjoyable."

We take another few dozen steps. "Okay, I can work on that. The 'mad' thing, that is."

He perks up and claps his hands again, pleased I seem to be on board with his theory. I stare down at his smiling face. His glasses are so thick that anything seen behind the twin lenses is tremendously distorted, his thoughtful eyes huge. I've thought a lot about my sketchy slo-mo lately, and I haven't been able to determine the problem. And here this little mad genius may have solved it, just like that. I don't know whether to be angry at him for figuring this out so quickly, or pissed at myself for not being able to.

"You're really smart, you know that?" I tell him.

He nods sagely. "Yes, I know."

CHAPTER
TWENTY-TWO

We can be thankful that last night's tornado was as severe as it was. For the rest of the day, there's not a threat to be seen. There are certainly no Grays around, or none that are still alive, that is. I've said before that under normal circumstances the damn things are almost impossible to kill, but yesterday's storm was anything but normal. For now, at least, I'd say we have a free pass.

Next to me, Google bends down and picks up another few rocks. He runs them through his fingers like a Vegas craps player looking to hit seven or eleven. I've been watching him do this all day, and up till now I've resisted asking him what he's up to. But my curiosity finally trumps my reluctance to give him yet another chance to display his intelligence, so I nudge him.

"Okay, I give. What are the rocks for? You've been collecting them all day. You gotta have a whole pocket of them by now."

Google's not one to get in your face to prove he's been victorious. That's not his style. But from the way his one eyebrow raises and the corners of his mouth twitch up the tiniest bit, I can tell he's been waiting for me to ask. He holds out a hand filled with roughly equal sized rocks. They're all smooth and round, each no larger than a dime.

"You don't carry a gun, I've noticed," he states. "Why is that?"

I sigh, wondering what prompted this. "Haven't we had this conversation before? I don't like guns. Plus, I'm a terrible shot. I've tried before and I'm no good at it."

"You don't think you could get better with practice?" he asks.

"No, I don't. I've always been pretty athletic, but my aim with one of those things is terrible. Anyway, I don't like them. I prefer Chuck." I tap my thigh where my trusty friend resides.

"Hmm. It's funny you named your knife."

I scowl down at him. "No funnier than you naming that damn Gray."

He ignores that. "But your knife is only good for close-up work."

"Yes," I agree. "He's been very effective so far, thanks. I think that's been proven again and again."

Google nods. "True enough. But back in the town there were more attackers than you could handle at one time. Am I right?"

He knows he is. I don't say anything, and after a few moments he holds out his hand, gesturing for me to do the same. He pours twenty or more into my palm. I heft them, feeling their weight.

"Take these," he says, and then explains what he wants me to try. I look down at the rocks in my hand, then slide them into my pocket. There's a small bulge there, and I can feel the slight weight of them pulling down my pocket. I really can't believe I didn't think of this before. I stare down at him, my lips compressed. I'm not going to give him the satisfaction of telling him again how smart he is. Turns out he doesn't need me to.

"I know," he says smugly, as if reading my mind.

Yep. Sometimes the little snot annoys the hell out of me.

We continue down the featureless highway, stopping only long enough to eat or drink. I spot a sign telling us what country highway we're on, and I dig in my backpack for the map to check our location. What I pull out is more pulp than paper.

"Was that the map?" Simon asks.

I nod at him. "Yeah, it was in the outside pocket of my backpack and got soaked. It's useless now."

I ball up the worthless lump and stick it back in my pack. We start out again. I'm mad at myself for not protecting it better, but it's too late to do anything about it. At one point we come across a derelict motorhome, one of those huge ones as big as a bus. How it didn't get blown to bits in the storm is a mystery to me, but after I check it out and find nothing horrible inside, we all go in for a break. The interior is in remarkably good condition, but I almost laugh when I see how everything is so small and compact, like a full-sized house was grazed with a shrink ray. There isn't any food, of course, but the water tanks still have some in them. We take turns drinking from a spigot outside, and then fill up our plastic bottles. Back inside, I sit in the driver's seat while the two of them crash on the couches.

"This is nice," Simon mumbles, careful not to put his muddy boots on the cushions. His parents must have trained him well. "It's good to be out of the rain for once. I'm sick and tired of being soaked all the time."

"It is, isn't it?" Google answers after a long pause. "I underestimated how uncomfortable being wet all the time would be. I miss Rumpke Mountain."

Simon spies a small TV built into the wall and pushes a few buttons hopefully. The black screen remains dead, and I hate to tell him it's likely to stay that way forever. But seeing him messing with the TV reminds me to check the radio. When I turn it on, nothing but static hisses from the small speaker. The last time we tried it I could make out some fragments of words here or there, but not any more. I slide it back into my pack, let down that Ted has been lost to us.

"You know what I miss most?" Simon asks, the question directed at the ceiling. "I miss watching TV with my dad and my brother. Movies, mainly, but a lot of old comedies, too. My dad loved comedies. The older, the better. The black and white ones were the best."

Google doesn't move, except to maybe wiggle his slight body deeper into the couch cushions. "You talk about your brother and dad a lot," he says. "What about your mom? What happened to her, if you don't mind my asking?"

"No, that's okay," Simon answers, not bothered in the least. "They got divorced when I was little. I don't ever remember mom and dad living together. She lived a few hours away from us. My brother was staying with her when the Storm hit. We never saw either of them again. You?"

"Me?" Google asks. "My mom was a teacher, and my dad was a researcher for P&G in Blue Ash, down near Cincinnati. I don't have any siblings. My mom and dad were with me until…until they changed. They both left when it started. They knew what would happen if they stayed."

Despite how much he annoys me, my heart goes out to Google. Well, to both of them. Their stories are so similar to everyone else's, but each one is so sad in its own way. My own parents couldn't bring themselves to do what Google's did, not really. Mom started to change first, and when dad figured out what was happening, he took her and they both left. They had seen others change already, and he knew that if he didn't, if they took the easy way out and stayed, that Lord and I wouldn't survive. There was no time to plan, and nothing else they could do. Mom insisted he tie her up completely, arms and legs bound with scraps of towels and sheets. She even instructed him how to do it through her tears. She was almost completely Gray when he carried her out of the building, and out of our lives. I was screaming for them as they left, and I tried to chase after them as they floated away on some construction debris, but my brother held me back. We never saw either of them again. My throat clenches up when I think of them, my mom thrashing in silence, and my dad crying as they drifted away and out of sight.

"That's awful," Simon eventually says to Google.

"It was."

We go back to resting in silence, deep in the rabbit holes of our own memories. Rain patters on the roof of the RV, a quiet hissing no louder than a gas burner on a stove. I reach into my backpack and pull out my pride and joy, the candy bar that Ted gave me. It's a little mangled from being squished in my pack, but otherwise it's no worse for wear. I tear open the wrapper and divide it into thirds, handing each of them a section. Neither of them accuses me of hoarding food, or keeping a secret stash, which I appreciate. Simon stuffs the entire piece into his mouth and chews fast, rolling his eyes and working his tongue around the amazing and novel taste. Google is more clinical with his section, nibbling it slowly as if he's performing an experiment, until it's gone and he's licking his fingers. I try to emulate his technique, but in the end I find that I can't, and I stuff it in my mouth. The sugary, creamy sweetness fills my mouth and courses throughout my body, jangling all of the pleasure centers of my brain like multiple balls banging around a pinball machine. The caramel sticks to my teeth in that particular and wonderful way that caramel does.

"Oh my god that was awesome!" Simon moans. "I forgot how awesome chocolate was!"

Google doesn't answer, but sits there with his eyes closed, savoring the last traces before they vanish. Eventually, he opens his eyes and nods at me.

"Thank you. That was wonderful."

"You're welcome," I answer, happy to be still toying with the last bits of caramel stuck to my molars. "I just thought we could use a pick me up, you know?"

"You don't have any more of that, do you?" Simon asks, leaning forward.

"Sadly, no. That was the only one."

He flops back against the cushion with a soft thud. "Damn. That's too bad."

Our silence returns, only this time it's less about the horrors of the past than the recent memory of the explosions of flavor we experienced together. Eventually, however, I have to be the bearer of bad news and tell them that break time is over. But our emotional states have improved, and we're all in better moods as we exit the RV, a little more spring in our steps. Never underestimate the healing power of chocolate.

We walk the rest of the day and into the early evening. I have no idea how far we've gone. Besides the random car or SUV on the side of the road, the lack of a map and any landmarks makes our progress difficult to judge. Who knew that this slice of Ohio was like this? I sure didn't. Of course, the tornado didn't do us any favors when it comes to figuring out where we are. I still can't believe how huge that thing must have been to cause so much widespread damage. Not a single phone pole remains standing, and every tree has been toppled over or reduced to kindling. I mention this to Google.

"There's no way this was a single tornadic event," he tells us, waving at the damage all around us. "Whatever that was, it must have been multiple tornados. Perhaps a series of satellite tornados. I can't imagine the weather imbalance necessary to spawn so many at one time. I doubt we've seen the last of them."

"Well, that's cheery as hell," I tell him, suddenly very conscious of possible changes to the slate sky overhead. "I was hoping that was just a one-off."

"Hmm. Doubtful. We will have to stay vigilant

and prepared in case of another round."

This talk about the possibility of more bad weather makes me a little edgy, but it's even worse for Simon. He's been pretty quiet ever since the storm cellar. As I watch him, he spins around in a circle, his eyes to the heavens. I can't say I blame him. He's walking backwards and scouring the skies, when he stops and peers behind us. He squints and juts his chin out a little.

"Scout," he says, drawing my name out. "I can't be one hundred percent sure, but I think I see someone behind us. Well, two people. Can you see them?"

Startled, I turn my gaze back the way we came. As hard as I try, I can't see anything but endless road and fields.

"No, I can't."

"Well, I don't know what to tell you, but I'm pretty sure they're there. Two people on the road behind us. You sure you can't see them?"

I try again, but my abilities apparently don't include enhanced vision. I see nothing but the wet road vanishing into a distant point in the mist. But I don't dismiss Simon, since I've noticed in the last few days his eyesight seems to be better than mine, and certainly better than Google's.

"Are you sure?" I ask him. I glance at our Gray, but it's not twitching or reacting at all. That's a plus, at least.

He's still staring behind us. "Yeah, pretty sure. They've stopped now that we've stopped, and they're just standing there. I can't tell if they're people or Grays."

"Could it be the two from your brother?" Google asks me.

"I don't know. It's possible. Simon, keep your eyes on them and let me know if they get any closer. Maybe they're the same two that saved us in town, or maybe not. Either way, let's keep going until we find someplace to hole up for the night. I don't like being out here in the open like this with those two things behind us."

But we don't find anywhere safe. There's nothing around us but open fields, and no standing structures where we could hide. Not that I relish the thought of hiding in a house or barn that's not protected by water, even if we found one. Right now, I'd be thrilled with a lake or a large pond, assuming we had something to float on. The grey sky is beginning to dim, the first sign that night is approaching. My already raw nerves start jangling.

"Are they still back there?" I ask Simon.

He glances over his shoulder. "Yeah, they are. They haven't gotten any closer, though. They're still hanging back."

Damn. I'm not sure if that's good or bad. If they are the two from before, then maybe we don't have anything to worry about, although I still can't wrap my head around the fact that we've got a couple of supercharged bodyguards shadowing us. Just the thought of it is creeping me out. Without a word between us, we pick up the pace a little, moving faster than we have for several days.

A little farther up the road we come across an abandoned car. I check it out wistfully, wishing one of these things still worked. Imagine how great it would be to hop in, turn the key, and zoom away from whatever is tailing us. It's a Mustang, dark purple with a black top. It's an old one, although I have no idea what year it might be. My dad would have called it a classic muscle car. The vinyl top is shredded from the storm, and water is puddled in the floor. Just for fun I reach in and turn the key that's still dangling in the ignition, but nothing happens. Bummer. If we could just fire this thing up, we could leave our shadows in the dust behind us.

Wait. Fire this thing up...?

I pull my head out and peer down the driver's side, toward the back. Not finding what I'm looking for, I scamper around to the other side. Google and Simon stare at me like I've lost my mind. I don't see what I'm looking for on the passenger side, either. Damnit, where is it?

"What are you doing?" Simon asks.

I run around to the back of the car and pop the small trunk. Inside are some tire tools, an old blanket in some sort of black and white Mexican motif, and a few unopened quarts of oil. Perfect! The yellow Ohio license plate below the bumper says 72STANG, with the word "Historical" across the bottom. There's a big silver disk with a prancing pony emblazoned just above it. A-ha! I twist the disk, and it comes off in my hand. The strong smell of gasoline wafts up.

"Google. Give me your lighter."

"Wait. What for?"

"Just do it!" I snap at him.

He fumbles in his pocket and holds the red Bic out to me in a shaking hand. I take it, then rip off a long piece of the blanket. I douse the strip of cloth with the oil, slopping it all over the place in my haste. The thick golden fluid has the consistency and look of honey, but is slick between my fingers, not sticky. I quickly stuff one end of the oil-soaked cloth down into the gas tank.

"Get back," I shout at them. "Way back. I don't know what's going to happen."

"Scout, no!" Google yells. "If you set this thing on fire Susan will panic. There's no telling what she'll do!"

I don't have the time or inclination to argue with him. They see that I'm not stopping, and together they stumble back thirty feet or so in alarm. I flick the Bic and light the strip of cloth, and Google's Gray hustles away from the open flame. The oil-soaked fabric catches easily, a long blue flame that travels the length of it. I sprint away from the car with my head down, not sure what to expect.

I reach them and spin around, and just when I do a column of flame as thick as my arm bursts from the filler nozzle with a roar. The flame shooting out of the back of the thing makes it look like a rocket taking off.

"Holy crap. It's the Batmobile!" Simon shouts.

I'm beginning to wonder if this is going to work at all, when the rear end of the Mustang goes from classic muscle car to a mass of flames, and the car itself is blown into the air. The explosion is so fierce the shockwave knocks us backwards on our asses, and the stench of burnt hair mixes with the sudden and unfamiliar reek of melting plastic, burning paint, and gasoline. A ferocious ball of flame boils into the sky like a vengeful genie released from a bottle. The car seems to float several feet in the air for a moment, hanging there in complete defiance of gravity, and then it crashes back to earth. The two back tires blow out with twin booms, then they catch on fire, too. The entire back half of the Mustang is engulfed in flames that dance into the darkening sky. Snaps and pops come from the trunk as other parts of the ruined car begin to catch fire.

"Come on!" I yell at them. "Find other stuff we can burn. Anything will do."

I run off toward a fallen tree not far away. I grab the trunk above the root ball and pull, and after refusing to budge for a split second, the tap root snaps and the thing slides across the ground. The heat is so intense I'm afraid my poncho will melt, but I drag the whole tree towards the flaming car, and with a heave I toss it on. Then I pick up the end of a fallen phone pole and throw it on, wires and all. The fire is so hot the tree and the pole quickly catch, chemicals in the telephone pole popping louder than bubble wrap squeezed in a vice. Simon adds some branches, shielding his face from the raging heat. Google is running around, but he's not helping. What the hell is he doing?

"Let's go, Google!" I scream at him. "Find stuff to burn!"

He either can't hear me or isn't listening, but I don't have time to mess with him. Out in the nearby field is another toppled tree, a big one this time. It's too much for even my strength to manhandle, but several of the larger branches snapped off when it fell. I grab those and run back and hurl them into the blaze. The fire is now licking up twenty or more feet into the sky. I stop and catch my breath, satisfied for now that we're safe. There's more around us we can burn if we need to. His face blackened with soot, Simon steps up next to me, panting hard.

"You think we're okay now?" he asks.

I nod. "As long as we keep this fire going, no Gray is going to come near us. So yes, we're safe for now."

Google walks slowly up to us, his head down.

The planes of his face flicker in the firelight, but his eyes are shadowed and dark. He sighs heavily, hands jammed into his pockets. When he looks up I can see he's crying, the tears mixing with the dirt smeared across his young face.

"Yes, you're right," he says softly. "No Gray is going to come near us. Susan is gone."

TWENTY-THREE

I'm so used to Google being cool and analytical I sometimes forget he's really just a little kid. A brilliant, weird little kid, but a kid nonetheless. He's sitting on the road, cross-legged, and staring into the fire. He hasn't spoken for a long time. His tears stopped a while ago, but every so often he sniffs and wipes his eyes. The loss of his Gray hit him way harder than I thought it ever would. I wasn't thinking about that when I set the car on fire.

Simon, sitting close to me, leans over. "You think he's going to be okay?"

People have lost so much since all this began. Friends, family, pets, their very way of life. I think back to how I felt when I lost Lord, and I try to put myself in Google's shoes. I can't believe that damn creature meant so much to him, but maybe I'm wrong. Maybe it did, and I just can't understand it. A friend of mine's grandparents had a dog. I don't remember its name, but it was a yappy little thing they kept outside all the time. To them it was an animal, the same as a pig or a cow, and they would never consider letting it in the house, much less on any of their plastic-covered furniture. Fast-forward to our house and our dog Larry, and he was an integral part of the family. Hell, he slept on my bed with me, his big head drooling on the pillow next to mine. The point is, I consider Grays to be monsters that need to be killed before they kill me. Google, on the other hand, may think of them differently, at least this one. He may have held some real affection for the damn thing.

"I don't know," I finally answer Simon. "I'm sure he'll be fine. He just needs some time, I guess."

Simon looks back at our companion, the fire flashing across the thick lenses shielding his eyes. Eventually he nods at me, taking me at my word.

"I hope so," he says.

Google doesn't turn our way, but he says, "I told you not to set it on fire. I told you it would freak Susan out."

I sigh. "Yes, I know you did. But we couldn't take that chance. I'm sorry."

"There was no immediate threat," he goes on. "Those two Grays were keeping their distance from us. They weren't doing anything. We weren't in any danger. And now Susan is gone."

I run my hands through my damp hair. The ever-present rain is very light now, and I can hear extended sizzles when it strikes the remains of the burning car. I threw more branches on it a while ago, just to be safe. The acrid stench of melting rubber and plastic tickles the inside of my nose in a very unpleasant way.

"We don't know that for sure," I tell him, my voice soft but firm. "These things are unpredictable, you know that. Look what we've seen in just the last few days. I couldn't take that chance."

He uncrosses his legs and leans back, never taking his eyes from the burning wreck. "This is your fault, and if she's gone for good I'll never forgive you."

I'm half-tempted to tell him I can live with that, that I would do it again in order to ensure our safety. But I don't. I take a deep breath instead, in through my nose and out through pursed lips.

"I'm sorry," I say. "I really am. Maybe we'll run across her again. I doubt she went far."

He doesn't answer me, but instead lays down and covers himself with his poncho. His eyes are closed, even though I doubt he's asleep. Either way, I follow his lead and settle down, my backpack as a pillow. The warmth of the fire is almost too much in the still night, but our natural human inclination is to be close to the flames, and I don't fight that. Next to me, Simon hunkers down for the night as well. In minutes his breathing is steady and low, while I'm wide awake next to him, stewing in my guilt at what I've done but would do again in a heartbeat.

I wake up a few times in the night and toss more fuel on the fire. In the morning, there's not much left of the car, just a blackened steel skeleton. The hood is still in one piece, but the rest of it hasn't fared nearly as well. It's nearly indistinguishable as a car. Underneath each wheel well is a smoking puddle of blackened rubber that used to be the tires. The acrid and very unpleasant stench of the melted rubber overwhelms all other smells, making me queasy.

In the morning, Google is already up and wandering around, apparently searching for his missing Gray. There's nothing around us where it could be hiding, no houses or other structures, not even a standing tree. The open fields march into the horizon in all directions, the full extent of their size limited by the misting rain. I wake Simon and ask if he can spot anything.

"No, nothing," he finally says, after spinning a full three hundred and sixty degrees, his eyes squinting with effort. "Not even the two from last night. We're all alone out here."

That's both good and bad, but mainly good. I don't like having anything or anyone trailing us. I've become more suspicious these days, and I rarely trust anyone I don't know. I certainly didn't know who was behind us. I still feel a pang of guilt for running Google's Gray off, but it was worth it in the long run. No good can come from having those two unknowns back there.

To try to make amends with Google, I strap on the harness containing the shortwave radio. He doesn't acknowledge this, but I have to think he noticed. The weight of the bulky thing isn't bad, but that means I have to carry my backpack. Shortly after that we're at it again. Soon the remains of the smoldering Mustang disappear behind us. Even so, it takes a while for the reek of the burnt tires to vanish, but eventually it fades to nothingness. After walking for half an hour, I look back and even the faint column of smoke is out of sight, now one with the mist. There is nothing but empty road behind and in front of us.

Simon notices Google is still in a funk, and apparently my blond companion is uncomfortable with awkward and extended silences. To break up the pregnant quiet he chats me up, even though I'm really not in the mood for it. He talks about his brother, things they did together, places they went, and so on. I play along, mainly just to keep him happy, but it does help to pass the time.

"Was he older or younger than you?" I ask.

"Older," he answers with a smile. "By a few years. But we were very close, you know? With mom and dad broken up, we stuck together a lot. We did everything together."

Everything, he tells me, included hunting and fishing with their dad in southern Ohio at a cabin, and summer camp for a week or two each year north of Columbus.

"It was a church camp called camp Sequoia," he continues. "We had a blast. We learned how to canoe, shoot bows and arrows, and all kinds of stuff. It was great."

I glance down at him. "You know how to shoot a bow and arrow? I didn't know that."

He scrunches his face up. "Me? No, not really. He was great at it, but I never got the hang of it. He won contests every week. He had ribbons all over our bedroom walls."

It goes on like that for several hours, until I've pretty much tuned him out as he chatters on and on. But he's happy, and that's a nice balance against Google, who still hasn't said a word. I check out the little genius once in a while, walking with his head down and his hands deep in his pockets. I hope I haven't completely alienated him. He's a crafty one, for sure, and I would much rather have him with me than against me. I recall BamBam's warning about him, that I shouldn't trust him, and I'm suddenly concerned that I may have turned him permanently against me – which is not something I want.

Later that afternoon Simon touches my arm, and I stop.

"There's something up ahead," he says.

I squint and try as hard as I can, but I can't see anything, just the road and fields, like always.

"What is it?" I ask.

"It's a building, I think. Maybe a few buildings. It's hard to tell from here."

I take him at his word and call a halt. "I don't know where we are, exactly," I tell them. "But we have to be getting close to Cedar Ridge by now. There's something up ahead, a town or something. I know we've been cautious out here, but we'll have to be even more careful from here on out."

Even Google nods, understanding that where there's a town, Grays are much more likely. History has shown that to be the case, at least so far, since they do seem to congregate in cities of any size. After all, there's nothing for them to eat out here in the boonies.

"Let's hope it's Cedar Ridge," I say. "If it is, we'll just have to find a boat or some way across the channel to Church Island. Once we get closer, we'll move fast and quiet, okay?"

I shift the weight of the radio on my back, and we head out, walking slower now, even though we're still miles away from whatever's up ahead. Ten minutes pass, and I start to make out shapes. There aren't many, just a few low buildings, one and two stories tall, from what I can tell. When we're close enough to start counting the structures themselves, we see a green sign that says *Welcome to Pittsville* on the side of the road. I tap each one of them on the shoulder and hold my finger to my lips. *Quiet.* They both nod, Simon with blue eyes as big as quarters.

The huge storm that wiped out so much of the territory behind us made it here, too. Any building not made of brick or cinder blocks has been flattened, some of them down to the foundation. We edge closer. There's the remains of a gas station with its

awning and roof ripped off with only the concrete islands and a few toppled over gas pumps remaining.
On the opposite corner is the burned out remains of a
small restaurant, the husky smell of wood smoke still
lingering around the rubble. A few hardy craft shops
and a boarded-up stone house turned office are on the
other two corners. There are several other shredded
buildings, the roofs gone and the walls cut down like a
scythe swept across the entire town. As far as a downtown goes, Pittsville probably wasn't much before, and
it's even less of a draw now. We quietly walk through
the intersection, the only sound around us is the occasional scrape of our feet on the damp road.

"Not much of a town, is it?" Simon whispers.

I shake my head. We pass the rubble of the
restaurant and keep going, until we see a large brick
building on our left a little farther down the street that
somehow survived the insane winds intact. The sign
outside proclaims it's *Pittsville Elementary*, and I motion
for the others to follow me. We creep up to open front
doors, cautiously go up the concrete steps, and step
inside.

"What are we doing?" Google asks in a hushed
voice.

I look up and down the dark hallways, and spot
a sign hanging above a door that says *Library*. I motion
them to follow me, and together we tip-toe towards
the door. Leaves and random papers are scattered on
the floor at our feet, and the two of them can't seem

to grasp the concept of stepping over the noisy debris instead of kicking through it. I wince at every crunch. We enter the library.

The far wall is all windows, and I have no idea how, but they are completely intact. They let in a decent amount of light, too, enough that we can easily scope the place out. There's a checkout desk on the right, and all around me are thousands of books neatly lined up in tall shelves, all in seemingly pristine condition. The harsh and unforgiving elements that have been doing battle outside have not been able to breach these walls. The entire room looks much like it did before the Storm. It's so unspoiled and wonderful my breath almost catches in my chest, and I have to reach out an unsteady hand to the checkout desk for support. If I had a choice, I could spend the rest of my life here in this amazing place. Damn how I've missed libraries.

Google and Simon don't share my bliss. In fact, they're both so jumpy I'm afraid any errant sound would send them bolting from the room. They don't like being inside, especially not in a place as different and unprotected as this. But I have to admit, if I weren't so smitten, I'm sure I'd be acting the same way. This place holds so much more reverence for me than it ever will for them, and that's a shame. People all over the world had their favorite holy sites, but this one is mine.

I walk up to the nearest shelf and tenderly run

my fingers along a dozen spines, feeling the bumps and ridges of their titles, then pull one out at random. It's a smallish hardback, a novel by Robert Heinlein called *Rocket Ship Galileo*. Okay, so it's science fiction, which is not my favorite, to be honest, but I would be thrilled to just sit in the windowsill and read it anyway. Somewhere along the line I've heard of the author before, although I don't know why or where. But I don't care. I flip to the back, and see it was last checked out almost seven years ago. The due date is stamped on the card in red ink with one of those hand-held gadgets that *ka-chunks* when the librarian would push down on it. I sigh and replace it on the shelf with all the respect it deserves. As much as I desperately want to stay forever and browse every row of every shelf, that's not why I'm here.

I quietly move to a section with the word *Reference* hanging from the ceiling above it. Looking up and down, there are books of all shapes and sizes here, uniformity clearly not followed as closely as in the fiction sections. The light from the windows is too distant to be very useful here, which makes it hard to read the writing on the spines. With a little more searching, I utter a whispered "Ah-ha!" finally finding what I'm looking for. I carry the oversized, thin reference manual over to the checkout desk. Simon taps me on the arm.

"What is it?" he asks, his voice low.

I point to the cover, a bright and beautiful picture of some rock formations from out west jumping off the cover at us, the words *USA Atlas* in bold print above it.

"Maps," I reply, in a voice equally as low as his.

I flip it open and leaf page by page until I spot the familiar shape of the state of Ohio. It's almost impossible to make out any of the tiny text in the low light. I finally locate Dayton in the lower left, then travel north until my fingertip stops at a small yellow square, tiny compared to the others all around it. *Pittsville.* Just a little to the left of that is a larger irregularly shaped yellow shape, with the words *Cedar Ridge* above it. I tap on the map.

"We're here," I tell them, then slide my finger left. "We need to get here. It can't be far. It's the next town over. Let's go."

I roll up and stuff the atlas into the harness with the radio, where it juts up like an empty quiver. We backtrack to the front doors and down the steps to the street with all the stealth of burglars wrapping up a heist. With the two of them close behind me, we make our way to the intersection and go west now, past the devastated restaurant and the remains of several wiped-out houses, until we've left the city limits. I have to admit, Pittsville wasn't much, but I won't forget that library any time soon. Someday I'll be back, and I may spend the rest of my life there.

TWENTY-FOUR

Now that I know we're closing in on Cedar Ridge, I'm starting to get very excited, and, if I have to admit it, a little scared. I haven't been there in over a year, and I didn't exactly leave under the best of circumstances. In fact, the smell of fuel oil from the furnace room still haunts my dreams, and I'll never be as fond of small spaces as I used to be. On the other hand, the thought of being with Singer again is causing me all kinds of emotions I haven't felt for a long time. I don't realize it, but I'm so amped up by all this emotional whirlwind I'm almost sprinting. The possibility he didn't survive his injuries is pushed way back to a corner of my mind where other dark thoughts are locked away, ones that only pick the lock and escape when I'm drifting off to sleep, or when I'm in a really foul mood.

"Scout, can you slow down a little?" Simon asks a little breathlessly. "Why are we running?"

We're not, but to be fair we're probably closer to running than walking. But they don't understand! Singer is close! And so is Carly! Some of the people I love most in the world are only an inch away, at least in map distance, that is. I force myself to ease up on my power walking, and the two of them catch up, one on either side of me. A tiny flame of resentment they're slowing me down flickers inside me, but I do my best to douse it. It's impossible for either of these two to understand what all this means to me.

"I'd like to stop and eat now," Google says, and the mention of food wakes my stomach up, getting my attention with a loud growl. I should be starving, but my enthusiasm is driving me on like someone stranded in the desert with an oasis in sight. But he's usually right, and this time is no exception. I call a halt.

"Here," I tell them, holding out a can of beef stew. "We've only got one left."

We divvy that up between us, each one taking a bite in turn, until the can is empty. I toss it to Simon, who wipes it out with his finger, licking it until it's as clean as the day it was made.

"We're going to have to find more food soon," Google says, telling us all what we already know. "We won't make it long without more supplies."

"Don't worry," I explain. "Church Island has a huge storeroom of food. Plus, there's a warehouse in Cedar Ridge packed to the rafters with more. We just have to get there."

I doubt either of them can envision a warehouse full of food and supplies, but hopefully they'll be able to witness it firsthand soon. Pittsville slowly recedes from view behind us, and before we know it we're back in the desolate farmland again. All of the telephone poles and trees around us have been knocked flat here as well, but facing west, the same direction we're going. I still can't get over the size and scope of a tornado able to do so much damage. Google mentioned something about weather patterns changing, and that we might expect more storms like this in the future. I don't know if the little genius is right this time or not, but I shudder to think this sort of weather event, as he calls it, might happen again.

As we trudge along, always aimed west, we begin to notice slight changes starting to take place around us. Where there used to be nothing but open fields and little else, there are more and more foundations of demolished houses sprouting up. Where we would only spot one or two every mile not too long ago, now there are five or six, sometimes more, clustered together. Up ahead I spot a large pond, debris of all kinds floating on the surface, with more than ten destroyed homes circling its outer rim. The number of vehicles scattered on and off the road has increased, too, to the point where several times we have to detour out into the muddy ditch just to get around them.

"I am guessing that we're getting close to Cedar Ridge," Google whispers next to me. It's one of the first times he's said anything without being prompted, and I don't know if that's good or bad.

"I'd say you're right," I reply. "We can't be too far away now. Let's be prepared, okay?"

The two of them get my meaning and fumble out their pistols and hold them at the ready, or at least as ready as they can. Simon is growing into the use of his, but Google couldn't look more uncomfortable if he were holding onto an angry snapping turtle. I sigh and we start walking again. I'm trying to figure out the fastest way out of the harness holding the radio equipment, just in case I need to move fast. Chuck almost seems to give me a nudge, and I slide him out of his sheath.

In less than an hour, the fields on either side of us have thinned out to nearly nothing, replaced with small neighborhoods of houses, little bungalows of brick that survived the winds fairly well. Most have lost all or most of their roofs, but the walls are still intact. This must be the older, original part of town. I recall passing through areas like this the last time I was in Cedar Ridge, although I don't think I came down this exact street. Ahead on the side of the road is a sign that's been blown flat on the ground, and I walk over to it, kicking some debris away so we can read it. Simon is standing next to me, looking down.

"So we're here? This is Cedar Ridge?" he asks.

I nod. "Yeah."

"We keep going straight?"

I nod again. "We should go through more houses like this, and then we'll be downtown. Once we get there, we'll be able to find the channel. Then we'll just have to find a boat to get over to Church

Island."

"Easy as pie, right?"

"Yes," I say. "Easy as pie. Both of you, I know this place usually has Grays. If all else fails and we can't find a boat, you're going to have to run like hell for the water."

Google looks at me. "But how will we get across if there's no boat?"

"You're just going to have to swim for it."

Simon makes a face. "Swim for it? In that stuff? Are you crazy?"

"Maybe, but it may be our only hope. And for god's sake, keep your heads above water and don't get any of that stuff in your mouths."

Simon's face scrunches up even more. "Okay, but that sounds terrible."

Google looks around for a moment. "I can't swim."

Damn, I never considered that. "Oh. Well, we'll help you if we need to. I'm a good swimmer, and my strength should help. Simon, how about you?"

"Thank you, Camp Sequoia. Yes, I can swim."

I take a deep breath. "Let's hope it doesn't come to that. But remember, Grays can't swim at all, so even if you go out a little bit, it might keep you safe."

Google doesn't look in the least bit convinced, but he nods his head, accepting the facts. I force a smile that hopefully comes across more genuine than it feels.

"We'll be fine. That's a last resort, okay?"

We start moving again. Google's face is a mask of worry, more concerned about the prospect of swimming than of attacking Grays. I have no desire to put a toe in that disgusting stuff either, but it's not because I'm worried about drowning.

The blocks of houses go on and on, until the tiny bungalows are gone, morphing into bigger homes on more expansive lots set farther off the road. The ones on either side of us are larger and more ornate, huge brick structures of all different shapes and styles. Sidewalks start up where there weren't any before, here in the ritzy side of town. The street is filling up with cars, too, SUVs and some pickup trucks, all pointing in odd angles, up on lawns, smashed into each other, with one sedan half in and half out of the picture window of a house. At some point several of the homes caught fire and only portions of brick walls are still standing. All of the roofs are either gone or damaged beyond repair.

"This place is creeping me out," whispers Simon. "I keep thinking people are watching me from the houses."

I put my finger to my lips for quiet, and in response he sidles up close to me. I reach out a hand and put it on his far shoulder, pulling him even closer.

The road ahead curves to the left, obscuring what lies beyond. We carefully dodge around a multicar pileup in front of us, and I can't help but notice the remains of several horribly decayed bodies in the cab of a smashed pickup truck. I gently steer us away from the sight, around the crash, and quickly put it behind us before either of my companions can see it. We don't need to be reminded of death any more than we already are.

Once we're clear of the wrecks, downtown Cedar Ridge opens up before us. The first thing I see that I recognize is the marquee of the State Theater, or at least what's left of it. The winds that tore through here ripped it clean off the wall, and only the brackets that held it in place are left. The small craft shops I remember have been leveled as well, just a few brick or stone walls left to mark their previous existence. Metal streetlights march down the street in defiance of the wind, too thin and strong to be knocked over. The storm that swept through here seems to have aged the place by decades in a matter of minutes, and my mental images of it are no longer accurate. Still, the roads haven't changed, so finding the channel to Church Island shouldn't be a problem. I'm about to whisper to them to follow me, when I spot movement in front of us. Simon sees it too, and grasps my arm with his free hand.

"What was that?" he hisses through his teeth.

I pat his shoulder with my free hand, but make sure Chuck is secure in my other. Without a word, as a group we backtrack to the wrecked cars and ease behind them, ducking down low.

"What did you see?" I ask Simon, making certain my voice is low enough it won't travel much past his ears.

He shakes his head. "I don't know. Movement. Something. Someone. Near one of the buildings."

I peek my head out and squint, scouring the area. I don't see anything now, although I do notice a street sign up ahead. Maple Street. Wasn't the warehouse down Maple? I'm pretty sure it was only a few blocks from downtown.

Simon grabs at my arm again. "There!"

I follow his gaze and see it. Well, not it, but them. It's people, regular people, not Grays, thankfully. They're creeping along the sidewalks in front of the businesses. At first there's only one, but then more follow. Ten, twenty or more of them, all armed. I'm too far away to see details, but I'm pretty sure I spot a blond head in the lead. Jacob? Single file, they move quickly and quietly, hugging the front of the buildings like soldiers in battle, then turn down Maple Street. I put my head down low and gather my two companions close.

"It's people from Church Island," I whisper. "It looks like they're on a raid, heading toward the warehouse, although it's a bigger group than usual. We're going to meet up with them. But be careful and don't startle them. They're all armed and I don't want anyone shot, okay?"

They both nod at me, two bobble-heads on a car dashboard. I motion them behind me, and together we step out from behind the wrecks. We quietly scoot over to the nearest building, and begin to ease forward, stepping over and around trash and debris. I'm as nervous as the first time I came here on that raid with Singer. My palms are sweaty, but I don't have any way to dry them.

We creep up to the intersection at Maple, and I cautiously lean forward and peer around the corner. The raiding party is well ahead of us, halfway to the warehouse already. But something's different. Oh hell, the warehouse is gone. Well, mostly gone. The storm must have leveled it, too. Where the three-story structure once stood, now all that's left are girders and mangled sections of walls. There's a massive pile of debris in the middle, the remains of toppled over shelves and whatever they held. The raiding party has fanned out around the site and are frantically filling canvas bags with supplies. A few hearty souls are inside the debris field, picking their way through the wreckage. Some are climbing onto the piles themselves.

"Come on," I tell them, waving us forward.

We move out at a jog toward them, me in the lead. When we're still more than a block away, I spot two guards keeping watch. I start waving my hands above my head. One of the guards sees us and lifts his rifle, and I'm about to throw all three of us to the ground when the one next to him pushes the weapon down. I breathe a deep sigh of relief, and we continue on. In seconds, we're standing in front of them, Google and Simon partially hidden behind me.

The guard who stopped the other from shooting us is standing there, staring at me. I recognize him. He was on the boat with me and Singer on our raid. I don't know the other guard with him.

"Joseph, right?" I ask. I tap my chest. "I'm Scout. Remember me?"

After a second. "Scout? Sure, I remember you. Long time no see. You're back?"

Ah, yes. Joseph, man of few words. Now it's all coming back to me. He told us about living in Cedar Ridge before the storm. His house wasn't far from here.

"Yeah. Is Jacob still in charge? I need to talk to him right away."

He looks over his shoulder. "Yeah, he is. He's inside."

I smile at him. "Thanks. Oh, and what are you guys doing? Why so many on this raid? There has to be two dozen of you out there."

"Storm took out the warehouse the other day. We're getting what we can before it all goes bad. This is our second raid in two days. Strength in numbers, you know?"

"Oh, okay. I get it. Thanks."

We start to go by him, and he reaches out his hand. "Good to see you again, Scout."

I smile at him. "You too, Joseph."

"And be careful. Lots of Grays around these days." He hefts his rifle to emphasize the point. "Two quick shots, and we all take off. You know the drill."

I give him another smile of thanks, and we move out toward the wreckage. Simon tugs at my sleeve.

"Who was that?"

"Joseph. I met him last time."

His eyes look beyond me, toward the people rummaging through the warehouse. "Who did you say is in charge here? What's his name?"

"Jacob. He took over after Eve went Gray."

He obviously wants to say more, but we don't have time now. I urge them on, and the three of us quickly arrive at what's left of the warehouse. A slight breeze blows scraps of paper and other trash around fitfully, some spinning around like miniature dust devils. Random stuff is scattered everywhere from cardboard boxes that have been smashed and torn open. Some of the contents are certainly worth saving, but so much of it is worthless crap that was important to someone sometime, but not to us. Napkins, plastic silverware, stuffed animals, other stuff that I can't even recognize. I'm convinced one box is bleeding, until I realize it's full of plastic bottles of ketchup leaking all over the ground. At one point I stop and pick up a dirty cellophane bag that contains a toothbrush and tiny tube of toothpaste. With a silent cheer I stuff it in my pocket. It crinkles pleasantly as I jam it down deep, so I don't lose it.

Some of the people scrounging have noticed us, and one by one, I can feel their eyes on me. I hear my name a few times, not in anger or fear, but maybe just tinged with awe. Work stops as I walk by. They all know how I left Church Island, the place they call Home. I have no doubt the events have been embellished over time. Maybe they've also heard stories of what I've been doing since I left. Whatever they have heard, or know, or think they know, it would appear I may have earned some level of celebrity status. I walk up to a skinny kid I haven't seen before, his face filthy from the digging around in the mud and debris.

"Where's Jacob?"

The kid doesn't say anything, but points farther back into the warehouse. I thank him and keep going, my two companions following so close to me they're nearly tripping over my feet.

Just around the next heap of trash and debris, I spy Jacob. He's gotten taller, which I should have suspected, and he's busy directing a few other young kids around, showing them something. He's too busy to notice us, but when we're about twenty feet away he glances up and sees us. He spots me first, and after a moment's apparent shock, he starts to smile and lift his hand in greeting. But then his gaze slips to my side, and I look down to see what grabbed his attention. Simon is standing there, and the two of them have locked onto each other. Suddenly Simon breaks away from me and sprints toward Jacob, and at the same time Jacob drops whatever was in his hand and runs at us. The two of them meet halfway and nearly collide, then embrace each other. They stand there in silence while the rest of us look on in confusion.

"What's that all about?" Google asks quietly.

I shake my head. "I have no idea."

The two finally break their extended hug, and together they walk over to where we're standing. The smiles on their faces are huge, reaching nearly ear to ear, and Jacob has an arm draped over Simon's shoulder. Their faces are wet, not with rain, but with tears.

"Scout," Jacob says when we're close. "Good to see you again."

"Good to see you, too."

"I want to thank you," he tells me, his voice catching in his throat, "for finding my brother."

TWENTY-FIVE

When you look at the two of them together, you can see it. The resemblance is there in the general shape of the face, the blue eyes, and certainly the blond hair. Jacob's eyebrows are even fairer than Simon's. But that's the superficial stuff. I've spent a lot more time with Simon than I ever did with his older brother, but knowing the two as I do, I can also see the similarities in personality and their overall "goodness", for lack of a better word. They are both good people, and in hindsight it's no surprise I found Simon so likeable. He's just like his older brother.

"How in the world did you find him, Scout?" Jacob asks, wiping at his eyes and hugging his brother so hard he might break him. "I never thought I'd see him again. Figured he was gone from my life forever."

Simon is happier than I've ever seen him; his face almost lit from within. He's holding onto his brother's arm like he'll never let go, and I don't blame him. I know very well what an older brother can mean to a person, the loving bond two siblings can have, especially when they've lost their parents. As sad as

I am that I've lost Lord forever, I'm so happy to have been able to bring these two together, even if it was by accident. I place a hand on each of their shoulders.

"Jacob, I have no idea. It was just luck. Just pure, good luck."

Google clears his throat next to me. "Serendipity," he says.

We all turn to him. "What?" I ask.

"Serendipity. The occurrence and development of events by chance in a happy or beneficial way. Serendipity."

Jacob stares at Google as if seeing him standing there for the first time. Simon grins at all three of us.

"Jacob, this is Google. Google, my brother Jacob." He looks at his brother, a smile still plastered on his face. I haven't seen him smile this much in a year. "Google is really smart," he adds. "He helped save me, too. He knows even bigger words than Scout does."

Jacob holds out a hand, which Google takes.

"Thank you for helping save my brother."

Google nods, eyes a little downcast, certainly aware that he only had Simon in his lair at Rumpke Mountain because I ordered him to take care of him. Without those orders, he might have died along with all the others. Still, he should take some credit. He's helped in other ways since then. I'll give him that much.

"Why don't I tell you all about it when we're safely back on Church Island?" I recommend.

Jacob chuckles. "Church Island? I'd forgotten you guys call it that. But yes, let's wait and you can fill me in from the beginning. I'm sure it's quite a story."

"Hold on a second. Before we do anything else. Carly? Annie? Eve? And, um, Singer? How are they?"

"Carly and Annie are fine. They're on Home. Eve, well, I'm sorry to say, she didn't make it. She went Gray after you left, and…" He shrugs, for a moment not able to meet my eyes. But then they light up again, and he sticks a thumb over his shoulder. "Singer? He had a rough time for a while, but he pulled through. He's waiting back at the boats for us."

My heart leaps and involuntarily my hands go to my face. My fingers start trembling, and for a moment I can't catch my breath. A few seconds pass before I can talk again.

"Singer is here? In Cedar Ridge?"

Jacob can't hide his amusement, and laughs out loud. Workers around us stop and stare at their leader before getting back to hurried scrounging.

"Yes, he's here. And I'm sure he'll be as surprised to see you as I was." He hands each of us a spare canvas bag. "In the meantime, load up. The more the merrier. Then we need to get out of here as soon as we can."

I'm so excited I can't even properly scrounge.

Singer is alive, and he's here! Emotions I haven't felt since our time together on Church Island are hammering away at me. In the course of several seconds, I'm overwhelmed with desire, anxiety, and longing like I've never felt before. I'm suddenly like any teenage girl with her first real crush, and the waterfall of emotions crashing over me is almost more than I can withstand, so strong I can barely breathe. Questions roar through my head, some stupid, others more expected:. Will he still like me? Can we pick up where we left off? Does he hate me for leaving him here? Am I still the person he fell in love with? So many questions!

Before I know it, Jacob taps me on the shoulder and motions with a jerk of his head that it's time to go. I open my canvas bag and realize I haven't put a single thing of value in there. Slightly ashamed, I throw in a few random items to make it look less empty and fall into step behind him. My head is spinning so fast I'm surprised I don't spin and topple over from vertigo. I'm hardly paying attention when all of us gather as a group by what used to be the main front door of the warehouse.

"Everyone ready?" Jacob asks the group. "Okay, you know the drill. Slow is smooth and smooth is fast, okay? We made a good haul. Let's not screw it up now."

I can tell right away this isn't their first raid. This group is well organized, and they handle themselves like pros, quiet and disciplined, with no unnecessary noise or confusion. They are nothing at all like the ragtag bunch Singer and I were with last time. All twenty or more of us heft our bags over our shoulders and silently move out. What was it that my dad used to say? Quiet as a church mouse? Yeah, I don't understand that one, but that's what he would say if he were here. We're all in single file again, except for Google, who is huddled close to me, and Simon, who is ahead of us and latched onto his brother like he'll never let go. Which, you know, he might not. We march away from the warehouse.

In no time we round the corner and turn off of Maple. After a few more blocks, I can finally see open water, with Church Island in the distance. I can't believe I'm back here after being gone so long. And while I couldn't leave fast enough after what happened to me last time, my opinion of the place has changed. Instead of terrifying me, the sight of the steeple rising into the sky gives me hope and a sense of safety that's been missing for so long. As we walk, Jacob drifts back until he's next to me.

"Scout, I'm sorry about Eve. Please understand we made her as comfortable as we could, until the end."

I shiver involuntarily, remembering the time Eve and I were locked in the furnace room together. Another breeze flutters my hair as the memory of that horrible place revisits me, never truly far away. I've thought about this a lot since then, and to be honest, my opinion of their solution has subtly changed over the past year. They lock people down there until they've fully changed, and then they're killed. It's a terrible solution to an equally terrible problem. But is it any better than ours? Really, ours might have been worse. We kicked people out of our group, our family, and sent them away at gunpoint if needed. We left them all alone in their final days. I can't imagine that happening to me, made to take a hike, then left by myself, scared, knowing what was to come, but having to do it all without help. I'm not sure which way is worse. There is no truly compassionate solution, only solutions with varying degrees of awful.

"I understand, Jacob. I really do. There's not a good answer here. They're all bad."

His small smile is tight, one not meant for humor but to show compassionate understanding. We walk on in silence, the distant shape of Church Island firming up in front of us as we go. I look for the red doors, but the building is facing the wrong way, and I can't see them from here.

"At least I haven't had to do that again," he finally says with a sigh.

I look at him as we walk. I used to have to look down when we talked, but he's my height now. "What do you mean, you haven't had to do it again?"

"The whole furnace room thing. We haven't had to use it for that since you left. It's been a blessing, really, and a huge weight off of my shoulders. Eve hated locking people down there. Now I've gotten off easy."

I grab his arm and we stop. Those behind us detour around and keep going.

"Are you telling me you haven't had a single person go Gray since I left?"

He shakes his head and smiles, a genuine one this time. "Nope. No one. And we have plenty of people who are old enough to change, too. And if you're going to ask me for an explanation, don't bother. I don't have one. No one does."

"Not one person has changed?"

"Not a one."

"Are you saying you've all been cured somehow? Do you mean I've been searching for over a year for a cure, and it was right here all the time?"

"Again, I don't know. But no one besides you and Eve have changed since you and your group showed up. That has to mean something, wouldn't you say? That can't be a coincidence."

We start walking again, but I'm blown away by this revelation. What's going on around me barely registers. Nobody has gone Gray since we showed up? What does that mean? Was it something we did or brought with us? Or was it one of us? Perhaps it was all of the above? My mission since I left was to find a cure and locate Lord. I succeeded in one, even though that didn't work out. Could I somehow be responsible for the other and didn't even know it? I rub my arm where Lord bit me so long ago. While there's no scar, I can pinpoint the exact place. Did it have something to do with this?

But as stunned and shocked as I am at all this, and maybe just a little resentful that I've been scouring most of Ohio for a cure, and damn if it wasn't found right here, Jacob's news is more than anyone could have hoped for. Something in or on Church Island is a cure for going Gray. Or maybe not a cure, but perhaps an antidote? Or a barrier of some kind? Whatever it might be, I'm reminded of that word Google used back there: Serendipity, the occurrence and development of events by chance in a happy or beneficial way. This fantastic news even makes Lord's rejection of me easier to take.

I'm still rolling this information around my brain when I hear a shout from in front of us, near the water's edge. I pull myself out of my head and look around for the source of the noise. The first thing I see are at least a dozen boats pulled ashore where the road aiming at Church Island meets the foul brown water. Several of them are tied up to flat rafts, which are already heaped high with cedar trees, the wood they use for fuel in the kitchen. The smell of the freshly cut cedar cuts through the putrid reek of the water, reminding me of a chest my parents had at the foot of their bed. It's a wonderful, earthy aroma I could live with forever.

But standing next to one of the boats is a figure, one with long black hair tied back. He's thin, and taller than I remember, but there's no mistaking him. I would know him anywhere. Singer is here.

He sees me at the same time, and without hesitation he drops the oar in his hand and sprints towards me. I drop my bag and backpack. I don't have time to rip off the harness containing the radio, when we basically run into each other.

I feel like the force of our crashing together had to be felt by anyone standing around us, like when the Mustang exploded and knocked us flat. His long arms are wrapped around me, and my face is buried in the crook of his neck. His hair covers my face, and I realize it has a certain smell I had forgotten, a musky, heady smell. While I'm momentarily sad that it had slipped my mind, I'm so happy to be inhaling this essence again that I don't care. Then I realize I'm crying, big stupid sobs that I might find embarrassing sometimes, but not now. These are tears of joy, and I don't care if everyone knows it. Finally, he pushes me away and holds me at arm's length, staring at me. His deep brown eyes look me up and down, as if he can't believe I'm here. Hell, I can't believe he's here, either.

"You're alive," he says, half question, half statement.

I sniff, my smile huge. "You are, too. I wasn't sure. You were so hurt, and I couldn't do anything…"

He tenderly brushes some hair out of my eyes,

tucking it behind my ear. "I know. Jacob told me."

I sob again, but this time the happiness is over-run with despair and the total helplessness I felt back then. "I didn't know what else to do. I couldn't stay, and I thought you were dying."

He places a hand on my cheek. "You did the right thing. I might have died without Martin and Annie. Even with their help, I was in a bad way for a long time. But that's behind us. Now, you're here. I can't believe you're actually here."

I nod, and try to wipe the tears from my cheeks, suddenly aware how filthy and disgusting I must look. I'm covered in grime and mud and who knows what else. I'm also soaked to the bone from the constant rain. How can he look so damn good and I look like something that's been living under a rock?

He responds to my unease in the best way possible, with another embrace that seems to swallow me whole. We stand there together for what seems like hours, like forever, and I never want it to end. But of course it does when Jacob clears his throat.

"Come on, you two," he says kindly. "We'll have a full reunion tonight. Right now we need to load the boats and get out of here."

We slowly pull apart from each other, smiling in that goofy way people in love do, kind of awkward yet kind of sweet at the same time. We stand there holding hands and not saying anything. We're just looking at each other like a pair of idiots, oblivious to what's going on around us.

"Hey, lovebirds," Jacob says, a little firmer now. "Let's get going!"

We grin at each other and nod. Singer lets go of one hand and we move towards the boats. I look down and see the outline of his harmonica in his back pocket, and I smile again. Hopefully, we really can have a reunion tonight, like Jacob said. Maybe I can talk Singer into playing something. Perhaps even *American Pie*.

For the next ten minutes, we help load the boats. The haul from this raid is huge, like nothing I've ever seen before, and the boats are filling up fast. Singer and I keep catching ourselves looking at each other. Every time it happens we lock eyes and smile like the giddy teenagers we are. When we're about done, I realize my backpack is still where I left it when I first saw him.

"You still have the book?" he asks me, his voice so soft and melodic that anything he says could be put to music.

I nudge him playfully. "Of course I do. I'll keep that forever. It's in my pack. I'll be right back."

Our fingers linger for a second before I pull away, the two of us leery of being separated for even a moment. I trot back up where my pack is on the ground, passing a few of Jacob's guards along the way. When I reach down to pick my pack up, I hear something. Someone talking? A muffled voice?

"What the hell?" I ask myself, inspecting my

backpack.

And then I realize what it is, and I tear into one of the pockets and pull out the radio. Ted's voice is shouting through the tiny speaker. I must have forgotten to turn it off the last time I had it out.

"Scout, do you read me? Scout, come in. Scout, this is urgent. Come in."

I have to wait for a pause before I can interrupt him. Finally, there's a break.

"Ted! Ted, this is Scout. Come in. Ted?"

Then, "Scout, oh thank god! Are you still on the mainland, or are you on Church Island?"

"We're getting ready to leave now. Ted, how do you know where we are?"

"Never mind that now," he says, almost yelling. "You've got a small army of Grays heading your way. They'll be on you in minutes. Get out of there!"

I depress the button again. "Ted, how can you know this? Your drones can't go this far."

And then it hits me, and I know what he did.

"Oh my god, Ted, did you leave the Mound? Are you outside? You can't do that! You'll start to change!"

A pause, then, "Yes, I left. I couldn't stand it there any longer. I found some handheld controls for Larry and Curly, and I left days ago. But that doesn't matter now. Larry died a little bit ago and crashed somewhere, but not before I saw those Grays coming your way. Get out now!"

"Damnit, Ted, that was stupid, but thank you. I'll check back in when I can. Keep this line open."

I stuff the radio back in the pocket and rush to find Jacob. I finally locate him down by the boats, talking to Singer and a few others.

"We've got a problem and have to go. Now!" I yell at him. I quickly explain what I know, and how I know it. His blue eyes go wide, so like Simon's, when he learns what's coming our way.

"Come on, people," he shouts. "We're leaving now!"

Then we hear a gunshot, followed by several more in quick succession. Several dozen Grays round the corner at Maple Street and head our way at a full gallop. Twenty or thirty more descend on us from the other direction. The guards have just enough time to start shooting, but there are too many and they're quickly overrun. Their shouts are cut off short. In seconds, there are at least thirty Grays standing in front of us in a ragged line. I keep waiting for them to attack, but they stand there staring at us, hands at their sides. Then the line parts, and a solitary figure steps out from behind them.

"Hey, y'all," Hunter says in his southern drawl. "Fancy seeing you all here. Nice of everyone to wait for us."

CHAPTER
TWENTY-SIX

Hunter takes another few steps towards us, a big grin on his face that doesn't match the cold glare in his eyes. His red hair is pulled back like it was on the Mound, the white streaks easily visible in the low daylight. Somewhere he found another shotgun, and he's holding it in front of him in a casual, relaxed way I know can change in an instant.

I feel a hand touch my shoulder and I nearly jump out of my skin, until I realize it's Singer. He's so much taller than I am now he can see over my head without any problem.

"What can we do for you, Hunter?" he asks, his voice as casual as if he's asking directions at a gas station. "We're just finishing up here."

Hunter laughs out loud, his head thrown back. "Singer? I can't believe my eyes! I thought for sure you were dead, son."

"Afraid not. The reports of my death have been greatly exaggerated," he replies, his hand still on my shoulder.

Was that a quote from Mark Twain? I think it

was. Where did he come up with that?

"I guess so, seeing as you're standing here in front of me," Hunter says to him. "That does complicate things a little, I'm afraid."

I tense up, and Singer's grip on my shoulder increases, like he's trying to tell me not to do anything. I don't like where Hunter is going with this.

"You see," he continues, "I have a score to settle with a young lady here on Church Island. And besides that, I'm here to claim what is mine."

Jacob steps up. "If you're talking about Eve, you're too late. She's already dead. She went Gray down in the furnace room. You know what that means."

The rest of the people from Church Island have slowly gathered behind us, now standing in-between us and the water's edge. Their guns are drawn, and several of them are whispering among themselves, anxious voices full of fear and anger. Feet shuffle nervously, and I hear the muffled click of safeties being turned off. I'm trying to figure out how many of us are left, versus how many Grays there are and the likelihood we can come out of this alive. I don't like our chances.

"Well, shit," Hunter says, his round face turned down in a frown. A gust of wind blows his ponytail around in front of his face, and he flicks it out of the way with a twitch of his head. "That is disappointing. I had a score to settle with her, for sure. Well, I'll just have to get even with the rest of you instead. It won't be the same, but that's life."

Singer steps forward and pushes me behind him protectively, using his body as a shield between me and Hunter.

"You don't have to do this, Hunter," he says, his soft voice somehow sounding louder than it is. "This won't end well, no matter what you think."

Hunter levels his shotgun at him, suddenly all pretense of humor gone. In its place is the feral anger I've seen on his face before, that blank yet horrible look of bland indifference to any life but his own.

"Oh, I think I do. And when this is all over, she's coming with me," he states flatly, his dark eyes boring straight into me.

I'm about to scream at him in protest, when out of the corner of my eye I sense some movement. Behind the mass of Hunter's minions, I see a pair of Grays walking towards us. One of them is bald, and the other is still wearing that ridiculous dicky around its neck. I can't believe I'm thinking this, really I can't believe I would ever be anxious to see any Gray at all, but I've never been happier than I am right now to see these two. With that pair on our side, the odds just shifted to our favor and I'm pretty sure we can win any fight. I smile and point to my two guardian angels, so thankful Lord sent them to watch over us.

"Careful, Hunter," I tell him, feeling a little cocky all of a sudden. I motion behind him. "Those two are fast Grays sent by my brother to protect me. Not only that, I've seen them fight and take out seven Grays in a matter of seconds. With the two of them and all of us, I'd say we have the upper hand."

Hunter glances over his shoulder, then looks back at me. I'm a little shocked at how unconcerned he is. In fact, his face gets red, and suddenly he starts laughing. Not just a chuckle, either, but a big belly laugh. He tosses his head back, his laughter rolling across the channel behind us.

"Those guys? You mean Thing One and Thing Two?" He turns and waves towards them, and the pair comes and stands by his side. "You think your brother sent them? That's a good one, Scout. No, I'm afraid these two belong to me."

I feel my mouth drop open. My cockiness is banished as quickly as it came, blown away in the increasing breeze.

"But...but they protected me. They wiped out all those Grays."

Hunter's exaggerated humor winds down fast, proof it was fake to begin with.

"Oh, Scout. I sent them to keep an eye on you. After all, you and I belong together, and I couldn't have anything happen to you, could I? These two work for me." He lifts his shotgun and aims it directly at Singer. "But first things first." He chambers a round with a loud click-clack. "I've been looking forward to this for a long time. Time to clean up some unfinished business."

Explosive anger detonates within me, fury like I've never felt before. It's all focused on Hunter and what he's done, who he is, and what he's about to do. I've never experienced rage like this before, a primal thing that bursts from my gut and blasts from deep within my core. The back of my mind slaps a palm to its forehead, and thinks, "Oh, so this is what it's like to Hulk-out," as my slo-mo kicks into gear faster than ever before. There's no tickle behind my neck, no bees buzzing back there, it's just on before I know it, BAM, and the world in front of me stops cold.

Before I do anything else, I give Singer's shoulder a gentle push, just enough to make sure he's in no immediate danger from Hunter and his shotgun. Then I reach into my pocket and pull out a handful of the rocks Google gave me. As hard as I can in this wet concrete, I throw all of them at the assembled Grays using a sort of side arm motion that scatters them in a flat plane, like I'm throwing a Frisbee. The rocks fly straight and true, no arc to them at all. To me they move no faster than a feather in a stiff breeze, but when they start to connect with Hunter's minions, they're like oversized bullets shot from a cannon. Huge bloody holes erupt across their bodies like distant volcanoes exploding. But instead of spewing lava, skin and bone are shattered and blown outward in blooms of red and white. Limbs are sheared off, heads explode, and at least twenty of them are thrown backwards in falls that seem to take forever. I'll never be able to figure out my totals now. Two hundred and fifty? Sixty?

But I don't wait and watch. I can't.

Before Hunter and his two fast Grays can mobilize, I fling my last few stones at them, while charging towards them at the same time. The rocks get there before I can, and I notice in satisfaction as Dicky takes one right through the heart, punching out the other side in what I can only imagine is a massive, gaping hole. Baldy is on the receiving end of my last two, one that rips open his shoulder, shards of bone protruding, and the other that skips off the side of his head but isn't fatal. Hunter is just starting to react when the stock of his shotgun explodes from an impact, splinters radiating outward like it was detonated from within.

I reach for Chuck, knowing I don't have much time. I launch myself at Hunter, but dammit he's gone into slo-mo now, too. He flings the ruined shotgun in my direction, and I have to dodge to the side while it spins past me. A quick learner, he slowly reaches down to his feet and scoops up a handful of dirt and gravel. Using the same sideways throwing motion that I did, he heaves it all in my direction, and I have to duck under the incoming barrage. I jump up just in time to see Baldy lunging toward me, its fingers curled into claws. I spin with Chuck in front of me and slice it across its exposed neck. Its cold eyes close in a slow, almost thoughtful blink as its head begins a serene separation from the rest of its body, tilting sideways until the creature starts to topple over, the body going one direction, its head drifting in the other. I start to turn when something smashes into me from behind, and I go flying. I spin, tumble, and crash into a light pole. Then without warning my slo-mo turns off.

I'm lying on the wet road, my body one huge ache, feeling like I've broken every bone on my right side. I try to sit up, and then Hunter is standing over me, breathing heavily. He's got a long piece of steel rebar in his hand, and he's smacking the end into his open palm methodically like a batter approaching the plate. There's blood across his front where the splintered shotgun stock wounded him. He peers down at me.

"Scout, I'm beginning to think you are more trouble than you're worth," he growls. He reaches down and grabs my hair, and starts to pick me up. I open my mouth to scream for help, when I see a blur. Hunter is no longer standing in front of me. He's on the ground thirty feet away, where he moans in agony, his rebar weapon lost. Where he stood is now Singer, smiling and looking down at me. He reaches out a hand and effortlessly pulls me to my feet. I stare at him with what has to be a truly epic and stupid expression.

"What just happened?" I ask, glancing between him and Hunter.

Singer glances down and to the side sheepishly, in that adorable way he has. He smiles and pulls me close, and I melt in that embrace.

"Scout," he whispers, his mouth close to my ear. "Did you think you were the only one who could do that kind of stuff?"

I laugh, stunned, my face pressed against his shoulder. I want to stay that way for at least a few hours, or maybe a few days, but he gently pushes me away. His long black hair is right there in front of me, and out here in the dim light I can see it now, the white speckles throughout, like he walked through the smoke of a campfire and tiny bits of ash got stuck in it.

"Come on," he says. "We still have a problem."

Over a dozen of Hunter's minions are left, and they're moving on Jacob and his team. I nod at Singer, and the two of us face off against the remains of his small army. I'm about to try and go into slo-mo again, when a huge gust of wind smacks against my face. It registers then that I've been feeling smaller gusts like this for a while now. The last time I felt anything like this was when Simon, Google, and I were almost caught outside at the farmhouse, before the tornado. I grab at Singer's shirt.

"We've got to find cover. There's a storm coming, and we can't be caught out in it."

He shakes his head. "What? We can't leave now. The rest of the group will get slaughtered by these things!" To punctuate his distress, gunshots start ringing around us as Hunter's minions redouble their attack on Jacob and his group. Several screams rip through the increasing wind as some of them are overwhelmed by the charging Grays.

I glance over his head and behind him, to the east. Above the horizon I see the same boiling black clouds I saw before, back at the farmhouse. Lightning arcs down in a dozen spots, and a long rumble of thunder vibrates the air around us. But he's right. We can't leave them like this.

Chuck is still in my hand, and I launch myself into the fight, Singer at my side. Without slo-mo, I'm not nearly as effective as I could be, but that doesn't stop either of us. I take out a Gray that has Jacob hoisted up by the neck. Singer doesn't have a weapon that I can see, but he's at least as strong as I am and is a whirlwind of destruction, tossing Grays into the toxic water as easily as if they were stuffed animals. A dozen or more guns go off while people yell all around us, that panicky kind of yelling filled with both terror and adrenaline, a sound anyone intimate with battle would recognize.

The wind kicks up another notch, to the point where it's going to be hard to talk soon. I take out what I think is the final Gray, then mirror Singer's move and grab it by the leg and heave it into the near-by water. With quick head jerks all around me, I look for more attackers, but I don't see any. Of the twenty or more of Jacob's men that started the raid, only a handful are left standing.

"Come on!" I yell at both of them. "We've got to find cover!"

I run around in mounting panic, until I finally locate Google and Simon hiding behind one of the boats. Simon has his pistol out and appears ready to defend his companion, but I sweep him up into my arms and hug him tightly, not willing to let him go. The wind is whipping his hair around like his head out the window of a speeding car.

I grab Google and toss him to Singer, who tucks him under an arm. Together we dash around and find any survivors and tell them the same thing. Find cover, and find it now. Jacob sees us, and together all of us fight against the increasing gale that threatens to knock us flat.

"Where?" Singer shouts, and while I can't hear him, I can make out what he's asking. Rain is pelting me so hard it stings any exposed flesh. I point toward town.

"Movie theater!" I scream, but he shakes his head that he doesn't understand.

Instead of trying again, I break into a run, Simon still under one arm. The others all follow in my wake. We fight against the storm that is trying its best to toss us backwards, into the water far behind us. Everyone grabs onto the person in front of them to keep from being ripped away, and together, we struggle towards the theater. I don't know where else to go, but that building survived the last tornado, so hopefully it can make it through this one, too.

We hug the walls of the buildings and finally leap into the lobby of the ravaged theater. Gasping, Singer and I gather everyone up as we dive deeper into the dark building, the ominous sound of a freight train approaching fast. We stagger into the actual theater itself, the floor slanting down before us, as we throw ourselves between the seats. Simon is under me, and Singer is on top of me with Google. We're wedged in so tightly the jaws of life couldn't yank us out.

Then the roof above us is torn off, and I'm screaming. The freight train passes overhead as the world goes black.

CHAPTER
TWENTY-SIX

The silence, when it comes, is startling.

The four of us are piled on top of each other, and below me Simon is crying. I push myself off of him, and the rest of us try to stand up. We're soaking wet and covered in all kinds of dirt and debris, but it would seem that we survived. Around us, I hear other people moaning or sobbing.

"Is everyone okay?" I ask, immediately thinking that was a dumb thing to say.

"I...I think so," Simon says quietly.

Google stands. His glasses are gone, and his face looks very different without them. He pats his head and around his body in mounting panic, then breathes a heavy sigh of relief when Singer hands them to him. He shoves them onto his face.

"Yeah, I think so too," he says.

Other people are getting to their feet and brushing trash and dust from themselves. Jacob is in the next row over, and Simon clambers over the seats. The two of them hug. I look up at the roof, or where the roof used to be, and I see bright sunlight slanting down into the devastated theater. Bright sunlight?

I grab Singer's arm, and we head out the doors and into the street. Whatever the first storm didn't destroy, this one most certainly did. The entire downtown area is nearly unrecognizable now. The few buildings that were standing have been flattened, and besides the State Theater and a few others, nothing much remains. The streets are almost impassable with rubble. I can only hope Church Island fared better.

But that's not all. In fact, the destroyed downtown barely registers right now.

The sky above us is a clear, pristine blue. Not a cloud remains, and the sun is an unfamiliar and almost foreign yellow ball overhead that is so bright we're all squinting like moles. The slate grey sky that has been our constant companion ever since the Storm has been blown away. Not a trace remains.

"It's beautiful," I whisper to no one and everyone, shielding my eyes.

We all stand out in the street in a daze. I remember walking out of an afternoon matinee with Lord and my mom one time, and for some reason I expected it to be dark outside, even though it wasn't even dinnertime yet. That's how I feel now, only magnified a thousand times.

"Come on," Singer says to me, taking my hand. "I want to see something."

All of us head back to the water's edge. The boats are gone, blown away, along with all of our supplies. But that's not what he's searching for. He tears through the rubble, hoisting up a sheet of drywall here, a piece of roofing there. He does this for a few minutes while I watch in confusion. Finally, he comes back to me.

"He's gone."

"Who?"

His lips compress into a frown. "Hunter. I can't find his body anywhere."

Oh. "Maybe he got blown out into the water."

"Yeah. Maybe. I'd just feel better if I could find his body."

On the plus side, there are no Grays around, none, not even any bodies. Anything that wasn't anchored to the ground has been blasted out into the channel. I look out into the water itself, and I'm devastated to see several bodies floating there amidst all the wreckage. I don't see the bodies of any Grays, since they sink like stones. Good riddance.

I stand next to Singer and lean my head on his shoulder. He places his arm around me, but he's strangely quiet. I want to ask what's wrong, but there's so much wrong now that asking something like that wouldn't make sense.

"The sun and sky are beautiful," I finally say, feeling the warmth of its rays on my skin for the first time in years. He doesn't respond, so I finally ask what's bothering him.

"The rain. It's gone," he says softly.

"Yeah. Finally."

"If it doesn't rain anymore, then all this will eventually dry up."

I nod against his shoulder. "Yeah. So? That's a good thing, right?"

He stares out over the water. "If this channel dries up, then there won't be anything protecting Church Island. Grays will be able to attack whenever they want."

Suddenly the sun on my skin feels hot and uncomfortable. I never thought of that. I've been so used to the constant rain and flooding I never imagined what would happen if it stopped. And he's right. If the channel dries up, then the entire island is defenseless. Somewhere on that island is the cure to going Gray, and soon it's going to be vulnerable. I can envision the water in front of me evaporating, and the road to Church Island once more intact and in place, with hundreds of Grays charging across it towards the church. I shudder. I've said from the beginning it was up to me to save the world. If Church Island falls, and its unknown cure is lost, I may never get my chance.

"Oh, shit," I whisper.

"Yeah, oh shit is right," he says softly, watching the sun sparkle on the brown water, the spire of the church finally clear and sharp in the bright light.

I grab onto his arm. "Oh my god. This changes everything…"

"Yes, it does."

We stay there for just a moment while the survivors move around us. Then I stand on my toes and give him a brief kiss on the lips. Nothing long, sloppy or overly romantic, just a quick peck that lets him know how much I missed him, and that we'll have more time together later. Later, being the operative word here.

My name is Scout, and I'm a killer. But that simple, two-dimensional description is not enough to define who I am any longer. I realize now I'm so much more than that. The relationships I've forged with people since the Storm began are so dear to me, and I know that I'll go to the ends of the Earth and back to insure their well-being. Lord is my brother, yes, but Carly, Tiny, Simon, and the others are like my siblings, too. And Singer. What can I say about Singer? He's here with me now, and that makes this lousy world a much better place. Whoever is left alive and un-changed now, wherever they are, they've become my responsibility. Whatever happened to me that makes me who I am, I now have a duty, one greater than I ever thought possible. After all, I'm the Firebrand. The survival of the world rests on my shoulders, but I'm confident I can carry that load. Singer sees me smiling at him, and grins back at me. No, correction, we can carry that load together.

"Come on," I tell him, scouring the immediate area for a serviceable boat. We need to get everybody back to Church Island and to safety. "I don't know what it is, but the cure is over there."

"Yeah. And?"

My smile widens, touching my entire face. "And, we're going to find it."

CPSIA information can be obtained
at www.ICGtesting.com
Printed in the USA
BVHW041914241021
619768BV00015B/678

9 781737 841111